Radha
and Jai's
Recipe
for
Ra

To Dr. R. K. Sharma, who always put
the dreams of his children before his own.
Love you, Daddy.
This one's for you.

STRIPES PUBLISHING LIMITED
An imprint of the Little Tiger Group
1 Coda Studios, 189 Munster Road,
London SW6 6AW

www.littletiger.co.uk

Imported into the EEA by Penguin Random House Ireland,
Morrison Chambers, 32 Nassau Street, Dublin D02 YH68

First published in Great Britain by Stripes Publishing Limited in 2021
Text copyright © Nisha Sharma, 2021
Cover images © Maria Qamar, 2021

ISBN: 978-1-78895-213-2

The right of Nisha Sharma to be identified as the author of this work has been
asserted by her in accordance with the Copyright, Designs and Patents Act, 1988.

A CIP catalogue record for this book is available from the British Library.

Printed and bound in the UK.

MIX
Paper from
responsible sources
FSC® C020471

The Forest Stewardship Council® (FSC®) is a global, not-for-profit organization dedicated to the
promotion of responsible forest management worldwide. FSC® defines standards based on agreed
principles for responsible forest stewardship that are supported by environmental, social, and
economic stakeholders. To learn more, visit www.fsc.org

2 4 6 8 10 9 7 5 3 1

NISHA SHARMA

Radha and Jai's Recipe for Romance

LITTLE TIGER

LONDON

An Indian classical-dance competition shouldn't have hype music. It was a serious occasion, and random Bollywood movie songs cheapened such a prestigious event.

Holy Vishnu, I'm starting to think like my mother.

The basement walls vibrated with the sound, which drowned out her footsteps until Radha reached the dressing room.

She stepped through the doorway, and over the faded bass from the DJ upstairs she heard the sound of conversation coming from the other side of the lockers.

"Yeah, my mom sent me an SMS and said she did amazing," Diya said in her screechy voice. She was the oldest of the semifinalists – twelve years Radha's senior – and had trained with her when they were in Rajasthan, India, a few years ago.

"She could dance like a gorilla and she'd still win," Rippi said. "Haven't you heard about her mother?"

"Sujata Roy Chopra? The famous kathak dancer, right? Then she just stopped. People forgot about her until Radha showed up, but from what it looks like, Sujata controls Radha like a puppet." Trish, a Canadian dancer, snorted. "It's like her mother says do a chakkar, and Radha turns without question."

3

Oh my God, Radha thought. They were talking about her. She froze, hoping that her ghungroos hadn't given her away. All thoughts of bathroom visits disappeared.

"A few people from the committee told me that Sujata Chopra was seen with a principal judge after the celebratory cocktail party," Rippi said. "Apparently Radha's mom and this judge were very, very friendly, if you know what I mean."

"I don't think I'm following," Trish said. "Was it just flirting or … more?"

"Well, from what I was told, they left together. I believe it too. Sujata Chopra has a reputation in the industry. She'd lie, cheat, and steal to make sure her daughter won."

No. No way. Radha felt bile burning in the back of her throat. Her mother was a little pushy, but she would never betray her and her father like that.

Would she? The idea of her mother cheating… *Oh my God.*

"Gross," Diya said. "It makes sense why we've all lost to her so many times, though. Remember the Singapore competition in May? Radha choreographed her own number, and it was awful. She still won, which confused everybody there."

"I can definitely see her mother cheating for her to win in Singapore," Trish said. "I wonder if Radha knows. Like, is she the kind of person who is okay with that? She must have an idea of what Sujata is doing. Or *who* she's doing."

"Even if she didn't know about her mom," Diya replied, "she probably wouldn't react if someone told her. She has no personality at all unless she's on a stage. If you ask her a question, it's like you're asking a piece of cardboard. She's nothing, nobody, outside of dance."

"The fact that she's boring and a mommy's girl doesn't make me feel bad for her," Rippi said. "What does make me angry is that I spent years working for this moment, to get to the International Kathak Classics, just like you two have, and Radha gets to the finals because her mother is having an affair? That's dirty, and it cheapens our art form."

Radha felt the radiating sting of Rippi's words like a punch. Dancers could be mean to each other. She wasn't completely clueless. But Radha had considered these dancers her peers. Instead they were picking her apart and slut-shaming her *mother*.

What was worse, they weren't just talking about her mother cheating, but about her mother doing so to help

Radha win a competition that Radha didn't even care about.

They had to be wrong. Her mother was pushy and demanding, but she would never jeopardize their family and Radha's career like that.

Even as she vehemently denied it in her heart, puzzle pieces from the last few months started to pop into place. Her mother had been acting stranger than usual. Then, last night, she'd said she had to go attend some business meetings. Radha hadn't thought anything of it before putting on a sleep mask and going to bed.

She hadn't asked any questions. She never asked questions.

Radha wanted to yell, to scream at Diya, Rippi, and Trish. To show them the cuts and bruises on her feet from her hours of practice. To pull out her training calendar and prove to them that she'd worked just as hard as everybody to get to where she was, maybe even harder. Four a.m. wake-up calls for early-morning practice followed by another three to five hours after school every day. No breaks, no vacations, no friends. Her father owned an Indian restaurant in Chicago, for God's sake, but she drank protein shakes and ate steamed veggies every day of her life just to stay in shape.

That only proved Diya's point, though: that she had no life outside of kathak. When she was a kid, she used to say that kathak gave her "dance joy" and made her feel complete. But where did that leave her? No personality, and a slew of competitive wins that were now questionable.

She rocked on her heels, and her ghungroos made the faintest ringing sound. Her breath came short and fast now as her lungs tried to pull in enough air.

Oh my God. Was she having a panic attack? She could tell because it felt familiar, even though she hadn't experienced one in a long time. She'd been managing her performance anxiety just fine. Especially when she focused on her love for dance, and not the onstage part. But there wasn't a stage in sight.

Her hand trembled as she pressed her fingertips to her lips. She breathed in deep through her nose, hoping to stop the dizziness, the urge to gasp for air. The hype music began to fade, and the three girls moved in a flurry of ruffling costumes and bells.

"Let's go," Rippi said. "We don't want to be late."

Radha was still standing in the doorway when they appeared from behind the lockers. Their faces were a study of shock and horror when they saw her.

She didn't care. Radha watched them for a moment, feeling a sickening sense of satisfaction at their discomfort, before tilting her chin up. Like hell would she let the competition see her trembling, struggling to take deep breaths.

She walked past them, hands fisted, toward the back of the dressing room. Radha focused on putting one foot in front of the other until she reached the table that had been assigned to her.

The surface was covered in tubes, color palettes, hairpins, and safety pins. She picked up her empty bag from the floor and, with one quick jerk of her arm, swept everything into the duffel.

She then went to her locker to put on her coat and shoes. In less than a minute she had all her things together and was ready to go.

Her three competitors were still rooted in the spot where she'd left them.

Radha strode forward until she was nose to nose with Rippi. The twenty-six-year-old looked fake in her stage makeup, with rosy red cheeks and eyeliner that covered most of her lids.

Radha's voice was as sharp as a blade. "Slut-shaming is a reflection on you more than anyone else. Don't ever talk about my mother like that again."

Rippi jumped and visibly swallowed. She didn't say another word as Radha walked around her and left the dressing room.

She passed familiar faces, people who touched her arm, as she made her way into the lobby. She was going to keep walking until the sounds of the DJ's horrible music went away and she could find silence at the hotel.

Her pulse raced as she grew closer and closer to the exit doors. This place was no longer for her.

"Radha! Radha, where are you going?"

The familiar sound of her mother's voice didn't slow her down.

"Radha Chopra, stop this instant!"

Long, slender fingers grabbed her arm and whirled her around. Her mother, radiating anger, looked more out of place in the lobby than Radha did. Sujata's white pencil heels and white pantsuit were what Radha always thought of as her mother's pharmaceutical-company-executive attire. Now she realized that the woman was trying to stand out in a sea of South Asian clothes. She wanted the spotlight more than Radha ever did.

"Where do you think you're going?" Radha's mother hissed. "They're about to announce the finalists! I went downstairs to get you, and those *girls* told me you left with your bags. Do you know how embarrassing that was for me? What's gotten into you, causing a scene like this? You're lucky this competition allowed so few people backstage; otherwise, you would never have been able to leave my side for one second!"

"Did you sleep with one of the judges, Mom?"

The question should've warranted a slap across the face. It was crude, and disrespectful, and delivered with all the bubbling hostility Radha felt inside her body. Some Indian parents wouldn't have hesitated to deliver a swift punishment.

Instead Sujata's grip slackened, and her jaw dropped. "Where did you – where did you hear that?"

"It's true, isn't it? It's true that you... How could you? I think I'm going to be sick."

"This is not a place to talk about family. Come on, stop the dramatics. Let's go."

Radha stepped back, out of her mother's reach. "No. You swore you'd never lie to me. That you'd always be honest.

And you are! Just this morning. My makeup needs work. My feet are slow. I start slacking at the two-minute mark. Now I'm asking you for the truth again. Did you cheat on Daddy? Did you do it with a judge? For what, because you wanted me to win?"

Radha's mother straightened. "Don't you dare talk to me like that, Radha. I don't know why you've decided to misbehave now, but we have been working for this moment for your entire career. You will not lose sight of what is important."

"You can't even deny it," Radha said. She felt revulsion, like she was on the verge of vomiting, and the idea of dancing only made the feeling worse. The tremors that had started in her hands were now quaking through her whole body. "It's all over your face. How c-could you? How could you d-do this?"

"Radha, it's not … it's so much more complicated than you think, sweetheart." Her mother's voice softened almost to a whisper. "Your father and I have a lot of pressure on our shoulders, and this has nothing to do with you, or with the competition. For years I—"

"This has been going on for *years*?"

"No! Yes. I mean – just come backstage." She tugged on

Radha's coat sleeve. "Finish the competition, and we'll talk."

Radha pulled away even as her vision blurred and her muscles tightened. She was going to vomit all over the lobby floor. "No. I'm not going anywhere with you."

"Radha, you have nowhere else to go! Look where you are!" She waved her hands in a windmill motion.

"To Dad. I'm going to Dad," she said with a wheeze.

"And then what?" She clapped inches from Radha's face. "I'm the one who travels with you, who comes to every practice, to every performance. I'm the one who has always had your future, your *life* as my best interest."

"Dad has always loved me!"

"You and your father don't even speak to each other!"

Radha felt the air get sucked from her lungs. People were watching now, and she wasn't going to fall apart in front of them. Not like this.

"At least he would never betray me," she whispered. She backed away, and for the second time in the span of minutes, in moments, she was satisfied at seeing the shock on someone else's face.

"Radha, Radha, don't go." This time, her mother's voice cracked. "You've fought so hard to be here! Please. Please don't do this."

"I can't, Mom." Her voice hiccupped with the sob she could no longer control. "All I'll ever be able to think about now is whether I'm dancing for me or dancing for you. Or, worse, if you didn't think I could win on my own, so you went behind my back, behind Daddy's back, because you wanted to win more than me, because you stopped dancing before you could win this competition yourself."

"Don't say that, Radha. Will you please just – please calm down for a second? You love to dance. Your dance joy, right? The moment when you're so happy? You'll never lose that."

"I think I already have," Radha sobbed. "And you're the one who took it away from me."

She spun, racing for the door. Her heart was being shredded into a thousand tiny particles as she rushed toward her hotel. The sound of her ghungroos rang like an alarm signaling the end of everything that had made her feel safe.

Chapter Two

Radha

Radha,

I'm sorry we haven't had our phone calls the last two weeks. I know this move from Chicago to New Jersey hasn't been easy for you, and I hoped that I could clear my schedule at the restaurant a bit more than I have so we could talk about it.

Your mother texted yesterday and told me that you're not willing to "dedicate yourself to your dance career" at your new arts school.

If dance is no longer your passion, then I think you need to find a new one. You know, to keep your mind occupied. Why don't you try cooking? Hopefully, you now have the time to learn more *about my side of the family.*

I'm sending you a recipe notebook I got when your dadaji died. It was my rule book when I opened my restaurant here in Chicago. Dadaji used it when he opened his dhaba in India.

Cooking is an art form, just like dance. It may never replace kathak in your life, but maybe you'll learn something new about yourself in the process.

Love you, chutki,

Papa

P.S. Sorry about the chicken scratch. This was the only piece of paper I could find to write on before packing up this box. Don't worry about the chicken, though. I'm making a nice chicken curry with it later. Get it? Chicken scratch? Chicken curry? I know you're laughing!

The ghungroos Radha tied around her ankles didn't feel comfortable anymore. She hadn't put them on in months, and they pinched now. She shifted, hearing the subtle ring of bells echo through the empty dance studio as she stood for inspection in front of the three judges.

The woman who sat in the center, Director Japera Muza, held a tablet in one hand and arched a brow until it almost touched her brightly colored dhuku. When she spoke, Radha felt instantly soothed by the lyrical sound of her accent.

"So, you want to be a new student this year."

"Yes, ma'am."

"Radha Chopra. Am I pronouncing that correctly?"

"Yes, ma'am."

She nodded as she scrolled through her tablet. The action was so regal, Radha was fascinated.

"It looks like from February through the end of this past school year, your grades plummeted. Care to explain?"

"I, uh, transferred to a public high school in the second half of my junior year. March through June. In that time, I was in a … transition period with my family."

"Ahh," the director said. She tapped the edge of her tablet screen. "Well, you'll have to keep your grades up for both your academic curriculum and your dance classes at the Princeton Academy for the Arts and Sciences. In the dance department, and in the school as a whole, we take education very seriously."

"That won't be a problem."

The woman turned to the teachers sitting on either side of her before she spoke again. "Normally, we host auditions for incoming freshmen only. Students find it hard to keep up if they join the curriculum in a later year. However, your mother was ... persuasive about your skill. Tell me, why do you want to come to our school?"

The truth was on the tip of Radha's tongue.

Holy Vishnu, why do you think *I'm here?*

Because I can't stay in Chicago, since my entire dance community hates me for giving up at the International Kathak Classics.

Because I have nothing in common with my father, and I feel like dance had something to do with why he's so sad.

Because this is supposed to be my new beginning, and I'll never have to dance again if I finish this one year at this new school.

Radha glanced at the door and saw her mother's face through the glass pane. She'd become more frantic, more demanding since the Kathak Classics. When her eyes narrowed and she looked like she was about to barge in, Radha answered the director.

"Kathak is a form of North Indian classical dance that

is about stories. The name kathak is a derivative of katha, which means 'story,' so it's an art form that meshes music, dance, and drama. My gharana, or house style, is Jaipuri and focuses on a combination of complex footwork and hand movements. These were the building blocks of my storytelling. When I … when I danced and everything came together just the way I wanted it to – the feet, the hands, the expressions on my face – I used to call it my dance joy."

All three audition judges nodded at her.

"Things have changed for me since the beginning of the year. Princeton Academy for the Arts and Sciences is my second chance." A second chance for what, she didn't know. The one thing she was completely sure of, though, was that she'd never experience the same dance joy that she used to when she performed. It wasn't possible. The panic attacks consumed her anytime she tried.

But she had to tell these guys something.

"Is kathak the only style you know?" the judge to the right of the director asked.

Radha shook her head. "I have familiarity with regional folk dancing, and I've also been exposed to contemporary, funk, and hip-hop, the last to help with my muscle isolation."

Director Muza looked her up and down. "With your mix of styles, you must have done some Bollywood dancing, then."

The observation made her pause. Radha had been through a ton of programs, and she always knew the good ones from the bad. A good program had educated performers who became teachers. A bad program had teachers who couldn't tell Bollywood from a two-step.

"I'm familiar with the styles individually," she said carefully, "and, yes, the fusion of the styles that create Bollywood dancing too. I've even taken Bollywood as an elective during summer courses in India. Most people wouldn't have been able to recognize that as part of my skill set."

"I'm not most people," the director said with a smile. "Okay, Ms. Chopra. We believe in second chances here, too. Why don't you perform for us? We'll take your seven-month hiatus into account."

Radha's heart began to pound. Here it was. That clenching in her stomach that made her queasy and light-headed. *Keep it together, Chopra*, she told herself. She couldn't break now. She had freedom to secure, and she only had to fake it for forty-five seconds. A slight tremor in her fingertips shot up her arms and into her chest.

Adrenaline. Stress. Performance anxiety. She'd had it all her life, but since her return from London, her body and brain would go on the fritz anytime she tried to perform. That was part of the reason she'd had to transfer out of her dance school: there were performances every Friday night. Thankfully, Princeton didn't have that same curriculum requirement, according to her mother.

She patted her crown of French braids to make sure nothing would come loose and walked with wobbly knees to the left side of the studio to take her starting position.

You can do this, you can do this, you can do this. Just breathe. Your future happiness depends on holding it together, Radha.

Her feet were sluggish. Her skin felt clammy. Her vision began to blur. Were her ghungroos always this heavy? Why was it so hot?

The music started, and she missed the first three beats be.fore, thank God, her body took over and the routine came to her like muscle memory. As hard as she tried, her facial expressions felt off, her feet too sluggish, but she remembered the steps for the most part. It was the piece she'd prepared for the semifinals of the International Kathak Classics. A fitting choice, to pick up where she'd left off in her performance career. It had been a time of beautiful ignorance.

Radha spun across the floor, and then it happened.

The click. That magic that she hadn't felt in so long, that she'd been sure didn't exist anymore.

Dance joy.

It burst through her and left her weightless.

Oh my God.

She tried to hold on to it, but it was gone between one second and the next.

The magic ended, the music stopped, and she held the last pose, gasping for air, before returning to stand in front of the judges in the center of the room. She ruthlessly fisted her hands until her fingernails dug crescents into her palms, the clamminess coming back in a slow rush. Her legs were going to fold under her any minute.

The judges, ignorant of her panic, continued writing notes on their tablets for a few more moments before Director Muza looked up. "Can I ask you something, Radha?"

"Yes, ma'am."

"Do you want that second chance for yourself? Or for your mother?"

If Radha hadn't trained for years to keep a controlled expression, her jaw would've been on the floor. How had this woman seen through her that quickly?

"A-a little bit of both, ma'am."

"Mm-hmm." Director Muza pursed her lips. "I guess that's as close to an honest answer as I'm getting. You did well. I can tell that you're out of practice, but you have skills."

"Thank you, ma'am."

Director Muza consulted with the other judges, who pointed to their tablets and deliberated among themselves. Radha felt an itch in her throat while the silence mounted.

"Congratulations," Director Muza finally said. "Welcome to the academy's dance program. Start working on your endurance and your muscle tone over the next couple of weeks. You're weak. When you come in for your first day, we'll plan your schedule with you. For your kathak focus, you'll complete an independent study. On top of that, you're going to have to work hard to catch up, not only with your dance classes but with your general classes as well. But we're not going to give up on you."

"Yes, ma'am."

"And, Radha? Director is fine."

"Yes, Director. Thank you for the opportunity."

Radha put one foot in front of the other and walked toward the door, where she retrieved her phone from the student manning the speaker. She shoved it in her duffel bag and exited the studio. Her mother nearly jumped her the minute she walked into the hallway.

"That wasn't your best. You should've practiced. What did they say? Are you in?"

"Yes, but by the skin of my teeth."

Sujata's eyebrows furrowed. "Do you want me to talk to them?"

"No, definitely not. I start in two weeks. I'll get my schedule then."

"Oh, good," her mother said. She clasped her hands. "I start my new job at the same time. We can go to the gym together in the mornings. That's the quickest way to get you in shape. It'll be just like old times. Wouldn't that be fun?"

"No, we aren't going back to old times, Mom. Nothing like it used to be."

Her mother recoiled. "You should be grateful for what

I'm doing. I've changed my life too."

"Sorry," Radha said. She cleared her throat and tried again so that the hurt on her mother's face would go away. "Sorry. But I just want this year to be over so I can move on."

"You came with me to New Jersey because you promised you'd give this opportunity an honest try. If you're not going to dance like you said you would, then you need to be in Chicago. That's what the therapists all said."

"Well, the therapists are wrong," she said evenly. "I came to New Jersey because everyone I know in Chicago hates me for failing the entire American kathak community in January." That was the truth that she couldn't tell the judges during her audition. "Mom, you promised that if I do this for a year, then I'm free. None of my reasons have anything to do with wanting to get on a stage again."

Her mother huffed. She looked up and down the hallway before leaning in. "Yes, but for you to stay, you have to put in the effort to see if you can be competition level again in one year. But the key word is *effort*. I need to see you try, Radha; otherwise, our deal is off and I send you back."

"The more you repeat your promise, the more I think you're just trying to convince yourself that this is the best thing for me. You know what? Maybe Chicago is the lesser of two evils here."

She turned to walk down the hall, but her mother stopped her with a hand on her shoulder. "Okay, what if I make you another deal?"

Radha rolled her eyes. Did non-Indian dancers have to put up with the same kind of crap from their dance parents? "What more could you promise me other than leaving me alone?"

"College. Your father's contribution in the settlement will barely cover living expenses."

"What in the world? Mom, what are you—"

"Radha, the amount is so little that even if I match it, you still wouldn't be able to afford state school without student loans."

Radha crossed her arms over her chest. "What's wrong with student loans?"

Her mother mimicked her pose. "Do you really want me to go into a lecture about interest rates?"

"No, I want to avoid this conversation altogether," Radha said.

"How about this. I can pay for whatever your tuition will be at whatever school you decide to go to." She steepled her fingers together, her expression eager. "You can even study whatever you want. Dance, storytelling, cooking like your father. Whatever. I'll be so supportive I'll become the mom that sends you care packages. But only if you give me everything you can for this one year to prove to me that you never want to dance again."

"What if I don't want to go to college?"

"Then I really will turn into your Indian mother from hell," she said in Hindi. "Not dancing is one thing, but don't test my limits."

Radha had to hide her smile. "Fine. Why would you make this promise? It's not like you get anything out of this."

Her mother squeezed her shoulders. "Because I love you. Because I want you to get your dance joy back. Because I know how it feels to stop dancing and regret it years later. And because you've worked too hard, and you're too talented, to let all this go. You need to be in the spotlight, Radha. I'm so sorry I had any part in taking your dance joy away, but together we can do this."

There was a catch. There had to be a catch. Her mother was promising her complete freedom if Radha got back into competitive shape with her Kathak training.

Yes, she thought. *That's what I want.*

"I don't have to perform?"

Something flickered in her mother's eyes, even as she looked away. "I won't force a performance on you, but you'll have to meet whatever your class requirements are and pass with flying colors."

Well, *that* was something at least, Radha thought. As long as she didn't have to perform … it didn't sound like too bad a deal. "I want it in writing."

"For God's sake, Radha—"

Radha held up her hands. "You're the one who always tells me that verbal promises are broken promises."

Sujata rolled her eyes. "Fine. I'll put it in writing."

"Okay, then," Radha said slowly. "Offer accepted. You pay for whatever school I want to go to, and I'll commit to dance."

"Good. Great! Now. We have so much to do to get your muscle tone back. I'm going to order some weights for the house. Come on, sweetheart. Let's go to the car." She reached for the duffel bag, but Radha jerked it away. She'd tucked her grandfather's notebook inside at the last minute. She wasn't ready to share it with her mother.

"I'll meet you there. I want to take my ghungroos off and stop at the bathroom."

"I can wait."

"I just need a moment, Mom."

"You sure?"

I wouldn't have suggested it if I weren't, Radha thought. But she'd used up all her snark for one day. "Positive. Go ahead."

Her mother's skinny heels clipped against the tiled floor as she went back to the parking lot. Radha took a few deep breaths and then walked on wobbly legs to the classroom next door. She peeked through the window before she opened it.

That was when she saw someone standing in the far corner. He had been facing the music system, so she hadn't spotted him at first glance.

"Oh, I'm sorry."

She turned to go, but he waved a hand to stop her. "No, it's all right. I'm leaving in a few minutes, so feel free to use the space."

That was when Radha *really* noticed him. If her legs hadn't been shaking already, they would've started. She wasn't someone who'd spent a lot of time around guys, since she'd always been so busy training for the next performance, but – hai bhagwan – this one put

Ranveer Singh to shame … if Ranveer Singh were a toned seventeen-year-old.

"Hi," he said slowly. He approached her with an unhurried swagger that made her want to giggle. His hair was just a little too long and perfectly tousled.

Ooh, and he moved with grace and a complete awareness of what his body could do. Praise the gods.

"I'm Jai. You're … Radha, right? Radha Chopra?"

When he said her name, her distraction turned into confusion. "How did you know— Whoa. Shit."

Her knees gave out as if they'd been waiting for this perfect, inopportune moment to fold on her. She fell against Jai's chest and was immediately consumed by his incredible scent while simultaneously feeling horrified. How cliché could she be?

"Oh my God." She pushed back. "I'm so sorry."

"It's okay," Jai said with a laugh. "Have to admit, it's the first time someone's fallen in my arms by accident. I thought that was only in the movies. It's pretty nice. I mean, not that you fell. I'm just saying—"

"My name," Radha interrupted. "How do you know my name?" It was best to get some distance, so she sat down against the wall and started tugging at the nylon strings that kept her ghungroos together. She had to concentrate to get her fingers working.

"Right. Your name. Well, one of my best friends is Winnie Mehta. She said you were probably going to join the dance track. Since I know every other Indian dancer…"

"Oh." Winnie Mehta. Radha hadn't seen her in years, but they'd kept in touch since they were old enough to talk. If Radha didn't hear from Winnie after a couple of months or vice versa, their mothers would give an update. Radha was pretty sure that Winnie's mom was one of the reasons her mother had chosen to move to New Jersey.

And Winnie, being kind and considerate as she'd always been, had told the young, hot Ranveer Singh about her.

And Radha had fallen right into his arms. So embarrassing.

"Here, let me help," Jai said. He crouched and brushed her fingers gently aside.

"Oh. Uh, it's okay." Her embarrassment grew when she realized how close he was to her feet. Despite how long it had been, her feet were still dancer feet. Callused and scarred.

He quickly undid the first set.

That was way easier than Radha had expected. Well, if he was going to be blasé about her feet, so would she.

"Thanks," she said.

"Don't mention it. Just had your audition, huh?"

"Yeah."

"Was the director tough on you?"

"I-I don't know. I guess. She called my bullshit."

Jai chuckled, and the sound had Radha's fingers fumbling.

"She's one of the toughest teachers here, but she's changed my life. If you let her, she can change yours, too."

"Who says mine needs changing?"

Jai shrugged. "Transferring for your senior year? Sounds like it already has."

Radha finished untying the second set and tucked the ghungroos away. She took the first set from Jai and packed her duffel.

"Hey," Jai said. He was still sitting cross-legged in front of her, his elbows braced on his knees. "I make a pretty great friend. Just ask Winnie."

"I'm sure. And thanks. I appreciate the help." Radha stood. She felt grounded again. "Uh, see you in class, I guess."

She'd turned the doorknob when Jai said her name. "I'm head of the Bollywood dance team here at the school. If you're interested, you should join."

"Oh, no thanks. I don't perform anymore."

"Wait." He scrambled to his feet and rushed passed her so he could hold open the door. "You don't perform like at all? But you're taking the dance track."

Radha nodded. She probably had to get used to people asking her that. "It's not by choice. Well, it is, but the whole situation is a bit complicated."

"Well, if you change your mind."

"I won't."

She waved and tried to moderate her strides as she walked down the halls toward the exit. No matter what, Radha was never going to change her mind about performing.

Her kathak performance career was dead. After this one year, she'd have time to find out what else she could do with her life.

Chapter Three

Jai

To: JMuza@PAAS.edu
From: JPBollywoodBeats@gmail.com
Subject: Career Questionnaire

Masi,

Attached is the career questionnaire you asked for.

Based on this, I don't think college is in the works
for me right now.

I doubt I'll even bother with the Common App.

Jai watched Radha stride away with her head high and
her shoulders pushed back.

"Wow," he whispered. Talk about impact. The way
she held herself had Jai wondering what she was trying

to prove to the world. He'd have to ask Winnie for more intel. When his old film-club friend had texted him and asked if he could keep an eye out for the new girl, Jai hadn't thought he'd be floored after one look.

A door opened, and three judges filtered out of the audition room. It wasn't until Director Muza and Jai were alone in the hallway that she gave him a knowing smile.

"How was she?" Jai asked.

"I haven't seen talent like that in God knows how many years. You can learn a few things about form from her."

"Hey, now. I'll have you know, I've gotten compliments on my form as a dancer."

Director Muza scoffed. "Not from me. Or if they were from me, not since you were ten. Help me to my office."

Jai presented his elbow. She smiled and let him lead her down the empty corridor. When Jai had first met the director, he'd discovered that her old knee injury bothered her on long days. It wasn't until he started at the academy that he realized auditions were always the longest days for her during the school year. Maybe he'd ask one of his brothers to swing by her house tonight to drop off some of the store's ice packs in case she needed them.

"Oh, I'm seeing Nana Veeru later. We're working the

same shift at the store tonight."

Director Muza shook her head. "My father loves that place. I just don't understand it."

"Masi," Jai said, calling her the familiar endearment for "aunt," which he often used when they were alone. "You're talking about a guy who worked in hospitals most of his life. He likes being busy."

"And he's an eighty-year-old stroke survivor, Jai. He has more than enough money to keep him healthy and happy. He could go fishing or watch movies. Instead he's imposing on your family."

"Think of it as his version of a hobby. You know, Nana needs to feel like his time is occupied." Jai's earliest memories of the man were doing memory exercises by reading biology textbooks out loud and trying to draw diagrams on a whiteboard. Word recitations just wouldn't cut it for him. The fact that Nana was working part-time behind a cash register four days a week now was a vacation compared to when he was a physician.

They turned in to the corner office at the end of the dance wing. Jai let go of the director and collapsed in one of the guest chairs facing the wide oak desk. He looked around at the familiar space, which he'd visited countless times over the last three years. There were a few more additions of framed photos from past students who'd become principal dancers, but for the most part it remained unchanged.

When the director finally took her place behind the desk, he saw the strain in her eyes.

"What's wrong?"

"A lot of things," she said. "I asked you to come speak with me because I had dinner with your mother last week."

"Oh? She didn't tell me that."

"Because she wanted to talk about you," the director said.

"Great." He slumped in the chair. "What did I do now?"

"It's more like what you *didn't* do." She pulled a folder from a drawer and dropped it in front of him. Jai flipped it open and saw the printout of his career questionnaire and cover email, along with a copy of his transcript and his near-perfect SAT scores.

"I don't understand. This is the stuff you asked me to send you."

"Yes. Jai ... your mother said that you didn't visit a single college this summer. That your brothers offered to drive

36

you, but you refused to leave the store. What happened?"

She pointed to one of his answers on the questionnaire.

Interests: None

It was a lie. Masi knew it, he knew it, and anyone who spent time with him knew it.

He was interested in dance, and biology, physiology, and math. But, most important, he was interested in supporting his family.

"Masi, you know I can't afford college," Jai said quietly.

She knocked on the desk loud enough for Jai to bolt out of his seat. "I know you beyond the walls of this school, and you know me better than that too. I did not immigrate to this country yesterday. What is really stopping you?"

He began to pace the small area of exposed carpet. "You promise to keep this to yourself? Please don't tell Mom."

"Tell me first, and then I'll promise."

"Really? You won't just trust me?"

"No," the director said. She crossed her arms over her chest and arched one brow.

"Uh, fine." He shoved his fingers through his hair once, then a second time. "Okay. Well, you know how my family has struggled since the day that Dad had his accident, right? The medical bills, the store, the house almost being foreclosed on."

"Yes. Both our families changed at the same time."

"Then you know my brothers didn't get to finish college. They had to quit to keep the store going so we could pay for everything. Anything extra went into the family fund."

"What does this have to do with you?"

He swallowed. "I give up a percentage of my paycheck too. If I went to college, then I wouldn't have the money for my share anymore. How unfair would it be if my family, my brothers, had to make sacrifices to the family store while I pursued my dreams?"

"Oh, sweet boy." Director Muza shook her head. "This is what your mother and father want for you."

"Most Indian parents wants their kid to be a doctor."

"Except not every Indian kid wants to *be* a doctor too. You love it! You have ever since you would sit with our fathers gobbling up medical abnormality stories like some people read those *Twilight* books."

"You know, I was just thinking about rereading those, too—"

"You have ranked highest as a dual-track student in the

history of this school. You are destined for greatness. How could you not be?"

"If I'm peaking in high school, might as well go all the way, right?"

"*Jai.*"

"Yes, ma'am," Jai said. He couldn't look her in the eyes. "Masi, you know more than anyone else that my family is a team. I'm sorry, but medical school is out. I'll take part-time classes, and maybe work my way up to an undergraduate degree, but it'll be a slow process. Something I'll do in the future."

"Your mother agrees that it's your responsibility to fulfill your potential."

Responsibility.

If his mother and brothers were honest, they'd admit that Jai needed to continue taking the evening shifts. Nana couldn't do it on his own anymore. Plus, Jai was in charge of the accounting system, because he was better at it than anyone else in the family. He'd watched his family share responsibility and work together while he'd had to sit and do nothing for years. Now it was his turn to help grow the business. To take what his father had started, what his brothers grew, and build from it.

Jai sat down again, leaned over the desk, and took the director's hand. She was like a second mother to him, and he knew that she was only trying to save him, like she always had.

"I came to this school because I got a full academic scholarship, and because you vouched for me. I danced because, truthfully, I wanted to make you happy. Then because I loved dance. But I'm still able to work and help at the store while I'm doing those things. If I got a scholarship and left, I'd never forgive myself for leaving my family in the lurch by only thinking of myself."

To Jai's horror, Director Muza's eyes filled with tears. She squeezed his hand, and held on even when he tried to pull away.

"Jai, what happened to your spirit? That little boy I met in the waiting room of the rehab unit was so angry."

"Masi, please don't—"

"He had fighting spirit," she said. "It's as if you gave up. Help me understand how we can get some of your ambition back. There has to be something that will convince you to rethink college. I'm sure you have one dream school you'd love to go to."

Columbia.

The name was in his mind before he could stop himself from dreaming.

Nana Veeru always talked about how when he first came over from Zimbabwe at age forty-five, he'd had to do a US residency at Columbia. Then he'd worked for the University Medical Center for years. Jai wished he could follow in Nana Veeru's footsteps more than anything, but there was no way he'd ever be able to attend Columbia.

He gave Masi his brightest smile. "Don't worry about me. I'll be fine."

They sat in silence, hands clasped, as if they were experiencing a moment of mourning. Whether it was Jai's future or the director's hope of changing his mind, Jai wasn't sure. He slowly pulled away and stood.

"I promise you that even if I'm not going to college, I'll still make you proud this year."

Director Muza's smile didn't reach her eyes. "You always do. No matter what you decide, you always will. And this year you'll have it especially tough. Classes aside, you have a team depending on you. As captain, you should've started auditions for your empty spot by now. More importantly, Bollywood Beats hasn't submitted a concept for the Winter Showcase for the group dance category.

That's due the end of the first week of school, you know."

"I know. Don't worry, Bollywood Beats will get you something." He had a few ideas that he was running by the senior members of the team, but he really needed input from their choreographer. Payal wasn't returning his calls, texts, or emails. If she was still AWOL when classes started, Jai would have to ask Director Muza for more time.

She rarely gave extensions, especially to him.

"I'll see you later, Masi," he said. He pointed at her and winked. "I'll say hi to your dad for you." He left the room, and kept his smile plastered on his face until he left the building.

When he was sitting in the driver's seat of his car, he leaned against the headrest and closed his eyes. He hated that conversation. He knew that he'd upset the director, and that he was letting her down. There had to be something he could do to lessen her disappointment.

He'd get his A's this year. That was the easy part. The only other thing he could think of was the Winter Showcase. Bollywood Beats always did well, but they hadn't won the whole showcase since long before he started at the academy. If they took home first place, they'd get the coveted spot at regionals, and he'd leave the academy and Masi on a high note. But first he needed a choreographer.

Phone in hand, he decided to swallow his pride and call in some reinforcements to help him get in touch with Payal.

Tara picked up on the second ring.

"Hey, Jai," she said.

"Hey, Tara. What's up? How was your summer?"

"Good," she replied slowly. "You didn't come to the shore like you promised."

"Sorry. Work. You know how it is."

"Yeah, but you're always working. Did you get any break?"

"Uh, you know … a little." He winced. How lame did that sound? "Listen, Tara, I wanted to ask … I know you're friends with Payal. Have you heard from her?"

"Yeah, a couple weeks ago. Why?"

"Well, I need to get in touch with her about Princeton's group dance. Do you know where she is? She's not answering any of my messages."

Tara gasped. "Oh no. She didn't tell you?"

"Tell me what?"

"Payal isn't here anymore. She left for India."

"She's in *India?* Okay, well, do you know when she'll be back?"

"Jai ... she's not coming back. She got her lucky break – she's doing the choreography for an upcoming Bollywood movie. She'll be gone for at least six months, if not more."

"She's gone for *how* long?"

"Six months. Please tell me that she wasn't your only option for group choreographer."

Jai dropped his forehead against the steering wheel. "Uh, yup. Yeah, she was."

"Shit."

"Yeah," he said, and echoed his ex-girlfriend's word with feeling. "Shit."

Chapter Four

Radha

Translation of Bimalpreet Chopra's Recipe Book

Masala Dabba

The classic Indian spice tin

To begin, prepare the cooking station and stock appropriate spices. In addition to ghee, fresh herbs, ginger, garlic, and onions, also include in your masala dabba:

Dried mango powder
Turmeric
Green and black cardamom pods

Red chili powder
Cumin seeds
Salt
Coriander seeds
Mustard seeds
Whole cloves
Carom seeds
Fennel seeds
Pomegranate seeds

Place each spice in one of the individual silver cups inside the masala dabba, with turmeric on the outside to avoid contamination. Whole cloves are best placed in the center. Additional spices may include black peppercorn, black salt, bishop's weed, fenugreek, asafetida powder, saffron, and curry leaves.

Sent August 22 2:46 PM

RADHA: Thanks for Dada's notebook. Mom is on my case and wants me to start therapy again, but I want to try something else first. Maybe cooking can help.

Sent August 23 1:43 AM

DAD: Sorry it's taken me so long to reply, chutki. You're welcome! Your dada's recipe book that I sent you was how I learned to cook. He wrote it like a manual, so it's the perfect starting point for you. Knowing your mom, you don't have all the kitchen essentials to get started. I'll mail some.

Radha tried to catch her breath. Who knew that hauling half a dozen boxes from the front porch to the kitchen could be such sweaty business?

She surveyed the deliveries that she'd placed on the counter and next to the kitchen island. Most of them looked like they came from a restaurant-supply warehouse for professionals. When her father had said that he was going to hook her up with some essentials, she hadn't thought he'd go to this extreme.

Her therapists in Chicago had both said that there was a chance her father would try to overcompensate for not being physically present in her life anymore, especially since he wasn't big on verbalizing feelings. Radha hadn't believed it at the time. Even though they all used to live in the same house, she'd rarely seen her father for long anyway. Their schedules were completely different.

But now, looking at all the gifts he'd sent, Radha couldn't help but think there might be some truth to what her therapists had said.

She picked up her grandfather's recipe book and traced her fingertips over the etched lettering on the cover. In Punjabi it read: PROPERTY OF BIMALPREET CHOPRA. He'd written tons of recipes and instructions inside. The words were often in different-color inks, with some sections scratched out and others with added text in the margins. The tattered, uneven pages, the musky scent, and the rough torn binding made her feel connected to both Dada and her father.

She wished she'd had time with Dadaji, but he'd died before she was born. As Radha flipped through the book, she remembered the stories her father would share about how Dadaji started cooking after he lost his crops one bad harvest and had to make money to feed his family. He'd opened a small counter-service dhaba, and it was so successful that it became his family business.

A few years ago, she'd wanted to travel to Punjab so she could visit her father's family and the dhaba in Chandigarh, but her mother wouldn't let her miss dance lessons.

Radha opened one of the boxes and pulled out a shiny silver spice tin. Her very own masala dabba. It was just about big enough to hold all her regrets, she thought.

"What in the world is going on here?"

Radha looked up to see her mother's shocked expression. She stood in the kitchen doorway with her phone in hand. Radha must've been loud enough that Sujata had left her home office to investigate.

"Dad sent me some stuff." She held up the spice tin. "We had one of these at the Chicago house, right?"

"You don't need that here," Sujata said. She stepped forward and poked one of the boxes. "You don't need any of this."

"Then where will I put all the spices and stuff for when I learn how to cook?"

"There is no need for you to cook. I pay for a gourmet meal kit twice a week. It's calorie controlled. Just like Dad's kitchen used to prep food for you while you were competing."

"It's not the same thing."

"No, but it can be." Her mother went over to the freezer and pulled out a bag of fruit. "Look, you can smoothie with me in the morning. Just like we used to. We'll try new smoothie recipes if you want to be adventurous. Quick and easy ones filled with nutrition. Cooking your own food is a waste of time."

"Mom, do you hear yourself when you say things like that? You're two posts short of being a fitspo account. No, I don't want to 'smoothie' with you. Please tell me you didn't join a workout circle and they're giving you horrible advice."

Sujata frowned. "It's my new spin instructor, actually."

"Just shoot me now."

Her mother laughed. "Radha, there are so many other things for you to do, like practicing and keeping your grades up. Academics never come easy to you."

"Seriously, is that all you want to talk about with me? Dance and school?" It stung that her mother's priorities never included her feelings.

"Well, of course."

"At least you're honest. After all, I am just a dancer and a student. Did you know that I have no other things I'm into?"

Sujata genuinely looked confused. "Well, what more do you need?"

Talking to her mother sometimes was like trying to

have a conversation with a robot. "Mom, I don't want to be a cardboard box." Radha pointed to the packages. The words of her competitors at the International Kathak Classics competition were burned in her brain. "I think this cooking thing is a good way for me to … I don't know, stay in touch with Dad. It's also a coping strategy or whatever the therapists call it. You're always quoting them – you should know."

"Don't be sassy. I think the therapists were talking about you continuing sessions here in New Jersey and starting dance again."

"I'm not ready for either option yet."

"And I won't stop bringing it up. But do you really think this will help you connect with your father?"

Radha shrugged. "Why not? It's like I'm speaking his language, right?"

"Yes, food is definitely his language." She sighed and pulled out a stool at the counter to sit. "If it'll help you two connect, then fine. If it's just to deal with your anxiety, you know how I feel about that. Either way, I want you in bed early tonight. You have your first day of school tomorrow, and an early workout to regain strength and stamina."

Radha knew where the conversation was headed. She had more pressing things to think about ... like if the stuff her father had sent her was dishwasher safe. "Mom, why don't you go see Aunty tonight? Winnie said she's home weeknights."

"Oh? You've been keeping in touch with Winnie since we got here?"

There was no way Radha was going to tell her mother that she'd texted Winnie to find out more about Jai, the mystery dancer she'd met at her audition. "I, uh, just wanted to know how film school was going and when she'd be back for a visit."

"I'm glad you're keeping in touch. As much as I'd like to go visit my friend, I'll stay in, though. You're going to need help putting things away."

"Oh, no way. No, I'm fine. Once I finish, I'll get my lunch packed for tomorrow and get my gym bag ready."

Sujata pulled her phone from her pocket and checked the screen. "Fine. If you're sure, and as long as you also use the exercise bike downstairs, I'll see if Aunty is free."

Radha walked around the counter and kissed her mother on the cheek. "Go. Stay out past curfew. Maybe even smoke a joint."

"Radha!"

"Kidding. Dad's humor. Please stop mothering and leave the house for a bit."

With one last scan of the room, and a kiss on Radha's forehead, Sujata left the kitchen.

Radha waited until she could no longer hear her mother's footsteps before she made quick work of unloading the rest of the boxes and lining up the contents on the counter. Bowls, spatulas, spoons, measuring cups, a mixer, a blender, an immersion blender, a food processor, a Crock-Pot, an Instant Pot, whisks, pots, pans, woks, sifters, sheet pans, a mortar and pestle, and a rolling pin. Her father had even sent a box of Indian spices, teas, and dry-noodle packets.

She picked up one of the noodle packets and inspected the yellow wrapping. Radha used to love noodles. The only problem was that she had no idea how to make them on her own.

But, like with dance, she had to begin somewhere. In kathak, Radha started with the basic steps. The footwork. What were the basics in the kitchen? The masala dabba? That sounded right in her head, but all the spices her father had sent were labeled differently from her grandfather's notebook.

She glanced at her phone, and, ignoring the twisting nerves in her gut, dialed her father's restaurant. What was the point in having an award-winning chef for a father if he couldn't give advice on following instructions to set up a spice tin?

"Tandoor Kitchen, this is Kriti, how can I help you?"

"Hi, this is Radha Chopra. I'm sure he's really busy, but I was hoping to speak with my father—"

"Oh yes! One second. I'll transfer you to the kitchen."

The sound cut off, and Radha waited. A few moments later a deep baritone voice answered. "Radha?"

"Hi, Dad."

"Did I miss one of your calls? I'm so sorry, chutki. I promise I'll try to do better. The restaurant has been so busy, and I—"

"I'm calling to say thank you," Radha interrupted. "I don't want to keep you too long. I got all the stuff you sent me. It's a lot."

"Oh. You're welcome. I don't know what you already have to work with. This way, you have a little bit of everything—"

"Dad, the problem is I have no idea where to start."

Her father laughed. "What do you mean you don't

know where to start? With one of the recipes in the book. Starting is the easy part of cooking."

"Dad," Radha said. She shifted, and the twisting in her stomach tightened. "I don't think I've ever boiled my own water. I probably need a bit more guidance before I grill a chicken, crack an egg, or whatever people do in the kitchen."

"Chutki, what do you fix yourself at home?"

"Oh, I don't do anything. Mom bought this fancy meal subscription. It's fresh, organic, calorie-controlled, blah, blah, blah. I just nuke it in the microwave. It even comes with utensils."

"You *nuke* it? That's absolutely unacceptable! How can she— I'm going to have a word with your mother, I swear."

"Uh, no you're not. It's fine. Seriously." She toyed with the edges of the noodle package. "Remember when you used to make me Maggi with peas and onions?"

Her father chuckled. "Yes, that's all you wanted to eat for almost a year."

"Well, I know there are a ton of spices you added to it, and I guess, I don't know, I should figure out what those are first before making the noodles. Should I google it? This is dumb. I could look it up online. I'm capable enough to do this. I'm sorry I bothered you. Forget I called. We can talk next week when you're free."

"No, wait," her father said. "I have an idea. Can you give me a second?"

"Uh, sure?"

Radha didn't know why he wanted her to hold, but she waited on mute. Maybe he was going to email her translations of the spices or something. Technically, she could've done that on her own. She hadn't talked to her father on the phone in so long, and so she'd chosen to ramble about noodles as her conversation starter.

Maybe it was too late for them to try to connect.

Her phone vibrated in her hand, and a request popped up indicating that her father was switching to a video chat. Her finger hovered over the green button for a second before she accepted.

A scruffy older man's face appeared on the screen. He wore a white chef's coat and sat in front of a large set of windows Radha recognized as Tandoor Kitchen's business office. She'd only gone once or twice to either drop something off or pick up takeout.

"Hey, chutki. Sorry, I had to tell the kitchen staff to work for the next half hour without me. Okay, let's

56

see what you've got."

"What do you mean?"

He motioned with large, scarred hands. "Your kitchen! Let's see your setup."

"Uh … okay?" Radha rotated the camera and scanned the room.

"Wow, nice space. If there is one good thing I can say about your mother, it's that she knows her real estate. Do you have designated cabinets for the stuff I sent you?"

"I guess. Almost all the cabinets are empty."

"Excellent. I'll tell you the best way to store your things, but for now, unwrap the spices I sent you, the recipe book, and the spice tin. Then we'll need a saucepan and a packet of Maggi for later."

Radha rotated the camera so it faced her. "Dad? What are you doing?"

He shrugged. "There wasn't much I could do to help you when you danced, but I can be there for you with this. What do you say we have a mini lesson? Something simple. Some kitchen-organization basics, and Maggi, just the way you liked it. We can even have you make enough for lunch tomorrow."

"And you want to do this on video chat?"

"Pretty good idea, huh?"

Radha thought about spending the next half hour with her father this way, and some of the tension in her stomach began to ease. "Yeah. Yeah, I guess I could give it a try."

"Good! Now, let's start with the haldi and amchur."

"Yes, Chef," she said, trying to hide her smile. "But first, what are those in English?"

Chapter Five

Jai

To: JMuza@PAAS.edu
From: JPBollywoodBeats@gmail.com
Subject: Choreographer

Hey, Masi,

Sorry I missed you this week.

We may have a bit of a problem with the Bollywood Beats routine.

In addition to filling the last dancer spot, we can't find a replacement for Payal who is willing to work with us on such short notice. This means we won't have a finished piece for the Winter Showcase. I don't want my team to lose this opportunity. Can we talk about options?

Also, Dr. O'Hare wants to meet with me one-on-one about my college essay. Even though the essay is assigned to the entire English class, he thinks that as a candidate for valedictorian, I need the special attention. You wouldn't know anything about that, would you?

Jai stood at the entrance of the cafeteria with eight of his dance-team members. It was the last lunch period on the first day of school. His plan was to gently let the team know about their choreographer dilemma. Unfortunately, while they were waiting for their cue, the truth bursts out of his mouth.

"We can't start our choreography yet, because we can't find a choreographer."

Nice job, Jai.

His team members stared at him in various degrees of shock.

"What are we going to do?" Shakti asked. She tugged on the end of her braid with its rainbow scrunchie. Her neon-pink shirt read DECOLONIZE YOUR MIND. "I need to be in the Winter Showcase. How else are we going to get in front of scouts?"

"Forget scouts," Hari said. "We need to perform in the showcase as part of our senior-year dance *grade*. Is the director going to make us write a paper instead? I don't have time for another paper."

Jai held his hands up for attention. "We are going to figure this out. Let me talk to Director Muza first, and I'll report back. Right now, the only thing we have control over is finding another person to complete our team. That is why we're here, and that's what we're going to do. I need you all to focus on one thing at a time."

"Are you sure this will work?" Shakti asked. She peered over his shoulder into the cafeteria. "It's a bit risky. If the other dance teams are in there, they may try to challenge us. I think we'd be fine against the pointe or tap dancers, but the ballroom dancers are fierce. We may be booed."

Jai followed Shakti's line of sight. There was a long aisle dividing the cafeteria in half. Round tables and colorful chairs were occupied by students from all four grade levels. He scanned some familiar faces, and then he saw Radha sitting at a table by herself. She was reading a textbook and eating what looked like yellow Maggi noodles from a glass container. A bag of carrots sat at her elbow.

"Yeah," he said, and faced his team. "Yeah, this is going to work. I mean, it works in the movies, right?"

Jai's phone buzzed.

SU-JIN: Starting the music!!!

"It's go time," he said, and moved into formation. Shakti took the lead, and the surround-sound speakers began to thump out a bass line. The song was a remixed Hindi-Punjabi number with an English chorus.

Shakti stepped into the cafeteria, cupped her hands around her mouth, and shouted, "Down the middle!"

It was just enough warning for people to rush out of the way. She took a running leap and did a front handspring step-out, a roundoff, and then a back handspring, followed by another roundoff and a full twisting layout.

"Show-off," Jai said with a grin, and glided into the cafeteria on his cue. He was met with cheers, and people moved their trays as his dancers jumped up on tables. The chaperones were already having a cow, but their protests were muffled by cheering and music.

When he'd told Masi that he needed to meet prospective team members, Jai had neglected to mention that he planned on doing it via flash mob.

He led the routine, laughing when one of his friends did an aerial cartwheel in front of him and mimed rolling out the red carpet.

Jai didn't mean to, but he slid across the floor until he was sprawled on the round-table bench seat next to Radha. "Hello there, new girl."

She arched a brow, as if waiting for him to make the next move. He always believed in keeping the crowd happy, so he motioned for her to give him her hand.

She looked like she wasn't going to take it, so Jai dropped to one knee. People around them started chanting his name. Radha laughed and, to his relief, swung her legs around so she could face him and place her palm against his.

He spun her in a circle and pulled her in until she sat on his knee.

"Happy first day of school," he said.

"Thanks," she replied. "What are you doing?"

He spun her again into his arms.

"Recruiting," he replied, and grinned when she stepped up onto the bench seat.

"For your dance team?"

She turned and fell back into his arms. He spun her in

a circle, loving the sound of her delighted laugh, before setting her in her seat.

"Yes. Want in?"

"I'm okay, thanks." He sat as well, hip to hip with her. She scooted over one seat, and he did the same so they remained side by side. They moved one seat after another, to the rhythm of the music, until they'd circled the table.

The bass vibrations began to fade. In one last effort to be close to her, Jai reached around Radha and grabbed one of her carrot sticks.

"Let me know if you change your mind," he said. "About Bollywood Beats."

Her eyes widened a fraction as he popped the carrot in his mouth, winked at her, and slid away to join the rest of his team.

They exited the cafeteria to sounds of cheers and applause.

When the doors swung shut behind them, Hari draped an arm around his shoulder. He stroked a hand over his barely-there beard. "What was that?"

"What was what?"

"The *girl*, Jai. The little flirting dance with the girl. She new?"

Jai nodded. "She's new."

"Do you think she'll want on the dance team? She kept up with you back there."

With one last look over his shoulder, Jai shook his head. "No, man. She's not interested. We're stuck finding someone else for the spot."

Hari nodded. "That sucks." He raced ahead to catch up with the team.

"Yeah," Jai said to himself. He combed his fingers through his hair. "That really sucks."

*

Jai was still thinking about Radha and his Bollywood Beats flash-mob routine later that night at work. He was pretending to study his physiology-orientation homework when he heard the chiming bells of someone entering the empty convenience store. Dr. Vimbai Muza – Nana Veeru – walked in, followed by a bearded man wearing scuffed work boots and torn jeans and a button-down shirt.

"It's my favorite honorary grandfather," Jai called out.

"I am here for my shift!" Nana replied. He pointed to the man behind him. "Your brother brought me."

"Oh, that's who it is? I would've never guessed under

the beard." Jai nodded toward Gopal, who was looking more and more like their dad every day, except with thick Punjabi hair from their mom's side.

"It is him all right," Nana said.

Nana's speech wasn't sluggish, which meant it was a good day for him. His stroke had caused aphasia, and years later, after regular speech therapy, he was able to regain some of his vocal abilities. There were still some moments, especially when he was tired, that he required extra focus, but the man worked hard and earned all the progress he made.

Not that it mattered to Jai. Nana and he had telepathy most of the time.

"Where is Neil?" Gopal asked.

"In the back, finishing inventory."

"Did someone say my name?" Neil pushed through the back door, wearing an almost identical outfit to Gopal's. "What's up, my favorite honorary grandfather?" he said, and tapped his fist against Nana's.

"I'm here to work."

"That he is," Gopal added. "Jai, did you do the register?"

Jai rolled his eyes at him.

"I saw that," he said.

"You may be ten years older than me, bhai—"

"And your boss."

"And my boss, but that doesn't mean ... fine, I guess it does. As always, money bag is on the counter. Slip is inside. Nana, are you ready?"

"I was born ready." The old man straightened the knot of the tie that peeked above the V-neck of his sweater vest.

Jai rounded the counter and enveloped Nana's frail, slender body in a gentle hug. Like always, he smelled of talcum powder and cologne.

Seven years. He'd hugged his nana the same way for seven years. Not only because the doctors told him that repetition and consistency were important for Nana's memory, but it had also become a way for Jai to sleep better at night. He liked knowing that his honorary grandfather was feeling comfortable.

"Did you get a chance to take a look at the expense report before we send it to the accountant?" Neil asked. He grabbed a piece of parchment and pulled out a stale muffin from the pastry case. "I feel like I turned twenty-five, and my body no longer wants to process this delicious sugar."

"Then why do you eat it? I emailed you about the

expense report a little while ago. There was an error."

"An error?" Neil said. His brow furrowed. "Really? I thought it was clean."

"No, you were off by fifteen hundred bucks. I fixed it. Cell is marked in red."

"Thanks, kid." He cuffed Jai on the neck before biting into his muffin.

"Jai is the smart one," Nana said with a toothy grin. "You two are the clowns."

"Hey!" Gopal said, even though he was laughing. "Who stopped at McDonald's to buy you a milkshake?"

Nana shrugged.

"This is the thanks we get," Neil said with a grin. "But, unfortunately, you're right. Jai, Mom was telling us you were being a butt."

"Because I balanced an expense report, or because I'm the smart one?"

"No, you're a butt because you won't go to college full-time and then to medical school." Neil snorted and fist-bumped Gopal.

"Ha-ha. You both really *are* clowns." He did not want to have this conversation again. Someone was always trying to convince him that the impossible could happen.

"No, seriously. We'll be completely fine if you decide to go," Gopal said.

"No you won't."

"We will."

"Not if you want to open up that second store." Jai reached around the counter for his bag and took out a piece of paper. "Here," he said. He didn't want to see the numbers again. He already knew what they said. It was time for his family to understand how important his shifts were too.

"I don't understand," Neil said.

"The right column is how much money I contribute to the family fund. That's how much money you'd be losing. If you replace me with someone full-time, you'll be paying more in benefits. But if I work full-time, you save a lot. I highlighted that amount in green."

"Shit," Gopal hissed as he scanned the report.

Neil peered over Gopal's shoulder, then whistled. "That moves our timeline to open a new store up by a few years."

"Yup. Even if I go to school part-time and work the same hours I'm working now, it'll affect your chances of growing the business." The door chimed, and a woman walked in with her hair piled on top of her head, and a single credit card in hand. She paused, giving Gopal and Neil a second look, before she stumbled over her own two feet.

"Hey," Neil said with a toothy grin.

The woman blushed and rushed down the first aisle.

"I say we stay on the same timeline," Neil continued without missing a beat. "We don't have to expand sooner. Besides. If you go to school, you can contribute a hell of a lot more money as a doctor than you can contribute without a college education. In the long run, school is the best option for all of us."

"Or you can win the money," Nana said.

The old man had poured a cup of coffee from one of the dispensers and was settling his creaking bones into the chair they'd set up behind the register for him.

"What do you mean?" Jai asked.

Nana's eyebrows rose nearly to his hairline. His mouth opened and closed a few times as he took a moment to form the words. "The dance competition."

"We're not following, Nana," Neil said.

"My Jammie told me today about the dance show scholarship. It's a lot of money."

"Are you talking about the regional competition?" Jai asked.

Nana nodded.

"I have to win the Winter Showcase first to go to regionals. Yes?"

"Yes."

"Wait, which performance of yours is the Winter Showcase?" Gopal asked.

"It's in January. You guys all came last year. The dance-school and music-school scouts show up. The winner of each category goes on to the high school association's regional dance or music competition. I didn't think there would be money involved at regionals, though. Maybe a dinky trophy."

"Well, Nana says there is," Neil said after swallowing his last mouthful of muffin. "That's your ticket, Jai. Win regionals, apply to a school that will give you a full ride, give us the money from the competition to fill the family-fund gap for the first year, and you're golden. You'll spend the summer working full-time, and then when you start your second year, we'll all be ahead of the game. Everyone is on top at the end."

Jai rubbed his hands against his eyeball sockets. "Yeah,

that's never going to happen."

"Why not?" Nana Veeru asked.

"You mean other than the fact that our team hasn't won since before I started at the academy?"

"Yeah, other than that," Gopal said.

"Well, we also lost our choreographer, Payal. She didn't tell us that she was leaving for India, and now we don't have anyone to help us with our routine. How about that as a reason?"

There was a chorus of swearing that made Jai feel marginally better.

"What are you going to do?" Neil asked.

Jai shrugged. He'd spent the last two weeks and weekends trying to find a replacement through the Bollywood group dance network. He called in all of his friends from other schools and asked every teacher for input. Unfortunately, Tara was right. There was absolutely no one available on such short notice. "We may have to join other dance groups if we can't pull something together on our own."

"What does my daughter say?" Nana asked.

"I haven't gotten a chance to talk to her yet. I emailed her about the situation, though."

"You *emailed* that kind of news to Masi?" Gopal asked.

He took the paper Jai had given him and tossed it back on the counter. "You better be prepared for tomorrow, kid. You know she's going to hunt you down."

"I know." Jai slung his backpack over one shoulder and fist-bumped Nana. "I have to finish some reading. I wrote up the schedule, by the way. It's in the office. Let me know if you need me for more than those hours."

He was halfway to the door when Gopal called his name.

"Yeah?"

"I still think you should apply. We'll make it work."

There was complete faith in his brother's eyes. Jai had no idea what he'd done to earn that kind of trust, but he wasn't going to break it by deserting his family when they needed him. It was time for him to carry more responsibility, and that meant forgetting Columbia.

Chapter Six

Radha

Translation of Bimalpreet Chopra's Recipe Book

Punjabi Garam Masala

This is one of the basic flavor profiles of
Punjabi cooking.

*First, dry-roast all spices until fragrant, then finely grind
cumin seeds, coriander seeds, green cardamom pods,
black peppercorns, nutmeg, fennel seeds, cinnamon,
and whole cloves into powder form.*

Store in a sealed container for up to three months.

RADHA: Dad, why do none of these recipes have measurements???

DAD: Why waste time? Measurements differ by how much you want to make, the type of ingredients you have, and the freshness of your ingredients.

RADHA: ... I have no idea how much to put into the Vitamix to make garam masala.

DAD: Start with one teaspoon or piece at a time until it tastes just right.

RADHA: Seriously? No measurements at all??

DAD: Radha, you won't know if something is right for you until you try it. Just don't put too many cloves in there. Those are strong.

Radha learned that on a nice day, some science classes took place in the rooftop arboretum.

An arboretum. It was so much easier to pay attention to basic biology when there was a light breeze and the smell of local flora.

"Dr. Chen?" Radha approached her teacher after the bell rang.

"Yes, Radha. Nice job answering the questions today. I threw a couple tough ones at you. I know it's only the third week of classes, but you're doing great."

"Oh, uh. Thanks. I was wondering, is there another class up here next?"

Dr. Chen looked at his watch. "I don't think so. Why do you ask?"

"Well, I have lunch now, and I was wondering if there was any way I could take my lunch in the arboretum?"

Dr. Chen, with his kind eyes and soft smile, nodded at her. He gave her a yellow slip.

"Don't let the other kids know," he whispered.

Radha was pretty sure Dr. Chen would say yes if anyone asked.

"I promise," she said with a smile.

After he left, Radha grabbed her bag, left the rows of benches at the entrance of the arboretum, and walked down the gravel path until she found another clearing. This one was covered with a cedar pergola wrapped in vines. Slivers of light pierced the green canopy, shining onto a grassy surface.

Radha dropped her bag and took a few tentative steps into the center of the clearing. She looked down at her arms as she moved through shadows and light. *What an amazing place to dance*, she thought as she walked in a circle.

She remembered the short routine Ms. Olga had tried to drill into her during her contemporary-dance class yesterday. The music was a quick jazz number, and it was so much harder than Radha had thought it would be.

She rolled her shoulders back, tilted her chin up, straightened her spine, and then lifted one leg to the side to make a ninety-degree angle. Then she focused on her core muscles and used momentum and strength to spin on the ball of her foot. She stumbled and almost fell on her backside but managed to catch herself in time.

"You're leaning too far to the left."

The intrusive voice had her screaming.

"Holy Vishnu!"

Jai stood hands up, palms out. "Whoa, Radha. I didn't mean to scare you."

"Well, you did," she said, pressing a hand to her chest. She'd practically jumped out of her skin. It took her another moment before she spotted his lunch bag in one hand and his backpack slung over one shoulder. "Is there another class up here, or are you also eating lunch in the arboretum?"

"No class," Jai said. He held up a yellow slip he produced from his pocket. "I asked Dr. Chen if I could come up for my lunch period too. I have some homework to do since I'm working tonight. He said you were here, but I told him we were friends."

"Did you?" She backed up when he dropped his things and took long strides toward her.

"A friend of Winnie's is a friend of mine. Contemp with Ms. Olga?"

"Yeah." God, she must've looked like a novice.

"Stand heels together, shoulders back."

"What? Why—"

"I'm trying to help. Give it a shot."

Radha hesitated, but she moved into position. Her shoulders lifted and relaxed into place.

"Good. Now one arm up, one to the side."

When Radha obliged, Jai stepped in front of her, inches away, and wrapped his hands around the curve of her waist. Her breath caught, and she looked up at him; her heart began to pound like a drum. She felt each individual finger press against her spine. They were so close like this, and when he touched her, it was different from anything she'd experienced in a dance class.

"You need to open your hips more so you're centered. Lift your right leg up to the side."

She swallowed, but pointed her toe and did as he asked. He gripped her hand and lifted it over their heads, and they shared the same air.

Jai pressed against her lower back again, and when she felt balanced, he stepped away.

"Turn."

She used her leg to get momentum, and completed one graceful spin, smiling as her heels met again. "Wow. Thanks."

"Don't mention it." He rubbed his hand along the back of his neck. "Want to take a break? Eat some lunch. With me, I mean. Want to eat with me?"

"I thought you had homework to do before work."

Jai shrugged. "It's my family's store. If my brothers get pissed that I'm doing AP Calculus at the register, then I'll just tell Mom they're picking on me."

Radha laughed. When was the last time she'd done that? "Well, if you're sure, we can go to the picnic table near the stairs."

"Yeah, sounds good." He stepped aside for her to lead the way. "Tell me, new girl. Are you liking the place?"

"Yeah. So far so good. My kathak independent study is honestly the only easy class I have, though. I used to sail through studio classes as well, but they're difficult for me now too. The core-curriculum subjects are probably the worst."

They reached an empty picnic table and sat facing each other. Radha unpacked her pink glass tiffin with matching hot pink silverware while Jai removed a Tupperware container from his bag. When he lifted the lid, a vaguely familiar spice scent hit her. She remembered it from when she used to visit her father's kitchen as a child. Jai's lunch looked like chicken, rice, and masala. It had to be biryani. At least, she thought it was biryani. She looked down at her lunch. After a week, she was tired of making noodles.

"Is that Maggi?" Jai asked, peering into her bowl.

"It is. The stir-fry kind with the Maggi sweet-and-sour sauce."

"I used to love Maggi when I was a kid. Mom would make the noodles in the broth, though, not with stir fry. Did your mom make yours for you?"

"My mom only heats food; she doesn't cook it. I made this myself."

"Oh yeah? Do you like to cook?"

Radha laughed. "Oh, Jai. If you only knew the can of worms you're about to open."

"I don't mind worms. Tell me more, new girl."

"I feel like you know enough about me."

"And I doubt I'd ever feel like I know enough about you." His smile had Radha blushing again. Was that flirting? She wasn't an expert, but she was pretty sure he'd just flirted with her.

"Why don't you tell me when you started dancing," she said. "Then maybe I'll tell you about how I learned to make Maggi noodles."

"I was about ten." His smile slipped a little as he folded creases in his napkin. "Dancing was a coping mechanism for me. My father had invested in a convenience store that year. He was working long hours, and after he closed the store one night, he was hit by a car on his walk home. Someone saw him and called 911. Unfortunately, he had traumatic brain and spinal-cord injuries."

"Oh my God, Jai."

"Yeah, it was bad." Jai spoke as if he were reading her the news. "He was in the ICU when another patient was admitted that same night. A doctor. His stroke was bad enough that he was hospitalized for as long as my father; then they ended up in rehab on the same schedule. Nana Veeru's daughter is Director Muza."

Radha's jaw dropped along with her fork. "You met the director in a hospital?"

Jai smiled again. "I did. And while we waited, she taught me how to dance so I could channel my nervous, angry energy. I think it helped the director feel better too. We just … clicked. I mean, she clicked with my entire family, really, but me first. Then I started taking classes with her at the local rec center. When I turned fourteen, I aced the entrance exam here, which meant a full ride for dual-track science and dance."

"*Dual*-track?" Intelligence instantly made him so much more intimidating. Sure, she could dance, but school had always been really hard for her.

Jai didn't seem to notice her shock. He scooped up some of his biryani. "I like to dance, but I'm obsessed with biology. I'm the kid who not only wants to know how a person can get a dance injury but also wants to learn how to fix it."

"Is that what you're going to study in college? I can sort of see you in sports medicine."

The smile on his face faded, and he busied himself with his food. "I'm actually not going to college."

"Really? Why not?"

"I can't afford it. At least not right away. My brothers need me to start working full-time at the store. My family is a team. Even though my dad started the store, we all work together."

She wanted to reach out, to touch his arm and tell him that he looked so sad, but she didn't really know him, and the last thing she wanted to do was offend the first person who'd treated her with respect at her new school. "I ... well, I'm privileged. But, my mother says the only way that I'll get to go to college is if I take out student loans or if I 'put in the effort' and do my best in the dance track in school. I doubt that anything I do will be enough to make her happy. At least you have family, right?"

"Yeah. I always have family." Jai forked some noodles from her tiffin. She watched in fascination as he took a bite of her food, not minding the smell or the fact that she'd brought something so desi with her for lunch. When the tines of the fork slipped through his lips and he chewed, Radha looked away.

"Wow," he said as his eyes rolled back. "This is amazing. You did something to it, though. There is no way this is straight from the yellow package."

"I seasoned it, and added onions, carrots, spinach, and

peas. Not bad, right? It took me a week to get comfortable cutting onions and sautéing the noodles after boiling."

"This is next-level, Radha. I'm stealing some more."

"Sure." She grinned like she'd just won *Iron Chef.* So she wasn't imagining things. Her cooking wasn't that bad. True, she'd had to go through a few burnt batches, but she was getting the hang of it now.

"From someone who has eaten their fair share of Indian food, being in Jersey and all, I have to say this is incredible. What else can you make?"

"Not much. I just started learning how to cook. My father is teaching me. He's a chef in Chicago. Has a restaurant and everything."

Jai scooped up some more Maggi and shoved his biryani container to the center of the table. "Wait, you have a dad who is a chef, and you are just now learning to cook … after you moved away from him?"

Radha hunched her shoulders. "I used to be really busy with dance. Now that it's no longer a time suck, I decided to kill two birds with one stone: talk to my dad and learn how to cook. Funny enough, I talk to Dad more now than I ever used to when we were living together. It's nice. And cooking is, I don't know. I feel like I'm discovering a new passion. It feels right."

"Well, this Maggi," Jai said, taking another forkful, "feels pretty right too. You have natural talent. It makes sense that food is a passion for you."

She moved her container forward so that it sat next to his biryani. "It took me a week to learn how to cook an onion, Jai. Let's not get ahead of ourselves." She took a bite of his biryani and stifled a moan. *Holy cow,* she thought. Now *that* was awesome cooking. "Do you think your mom will share this recipe?"

"Sure. I'll ask her. If you tell me why you stopped dancing."

She looked up at his amused expression and narrowed her eyes. "That's bribery."

"Sorry. The biryani is worth it, though."

She sat back and thought about his question, about her decision to stop dancing. She missed the pure joy of it. The dance joy. Her mother and all the performances never used to matter if she got to put on her ghungroos and get lost in the music. But now she hated that every time she thought about kathak, it was mixed with the truth of her mother's cheating and the shame of not knowing whether she'd ever won a competition on her own merit.

Then those thoughts would spiral out of control and include things like wondering whether dance had made her father unhappy and driven him away. She'd shared some of her beliefs with the multiple therapists she visited in Chicago, but they just wanted to talk about the reason, not a solution for how she could get her dance joy back.

Radha spooned up more biryani and said, "I choked. At the International Kathak Classics in London. It's the biggest kathak competition in the world, and I made it to the semifinals. Then I couldn't go through with it. And since then, I swore I'd never perform again. My mom thinks I'll get over it. She used to be a dancer too, so she thinks if I stop, I'll regret it like her."

"Yikes. Hopefully you'll be okay for the Winter Showcase in four months," Jai said.

Radha froze. "Wait, what do you mean?"

"About what? The Winter Showcase? For a dance-track senior, performing in the January Winter Showcase is part of your graduation requirement. It's a huge event."

Radha knew words were coming out of his mouth, but she couldn't comprehend them over the roaring in her ears. "There has to be an exception to the rule."

"Not really," he said. "You have to have a family

emergency or injury to replace the performance by writing a paper."

"Can I elect to write a paper? What if someone has, like, stage fright?"

Jai shook his head. "Dance track is not for people who like it as a hobby. Well, maybe except for me, since I'm not going to dance school after graduation. You're groomed at the academy to perform. A dancer's whole high school career revolves around this showcase."

"And there is nothing I can do? I have no choice?"

"Unless you have an injury or family emergency, or you drop out, no." He used the fork to point at himself. "Or you're on a Bollywood dance team and you— Hey, what's wrong?"

The muscle tightness and trembling in her fingers came first.

Oh no.

She grabbed the lid of her tiffin and struggled to close the glass food container and shove it in her bag. "I'm sorry, I have to go. I didn't realize ... thanks. Thanks for everything."

"Wait, is there anything I can do?"

She waved over her shoulder as she rushed to the

exit and down the stairs. She couldn't perform. No, she wouldn't. She swallowed a few shallow breaths to suppress the nausea as she struggled to remember how to get to the director's office. She had to ask Director Muza if there was a way out. There had to be a way out. Performing had taken everything away from her. Her family. Her career that was more her mother's career.

No, she couldn't think of her mother right now. She wove through the empty hallways, praying that no one would stop her. This was a misunderstanding. She wasn't supposed to perform at all. The director had to know that.

Radha's head began to pound when she reached her destination. The door was closed, and a schedule taped to the glass pane showed that the director wouldn't be available until after school. She gasped for air, and had to close her eyes because of the floaters.

Just as she felt like her panic attack would swallow her whole, she heard her name from down the hall.

"Radha!" Jai jogged down the empty hallway until he reached her side. "I just want to make sure that you're okay. For a brown person, you are very pale right now."

"I-I have to go home," she said. She had to talk to her mother about this *now*.

But the thought of confronting anyone about this sent a sharp pain piercing through her chest. Then her brain went fuzzy and she started hyperventilating.

"Hey," Jai said. His voice was hard, and she looked up at him. He grabbed her hands and pressed her palms against his chest. "It's going to be okay. Can you still hear me?"

Radha nodded.

"Okay, now keep looking at me. Breathe in and out with me. We'll do it together. Ready?"

Radha nodded again.

"Okay, in … and out. One more time. In … and out." His chest expanded and contracted under her hands, and she followed the rhythm, focusing on that simple movement until she could think again.

She didn't know how many times they stood and did the exercise. On the last big push of air, her head emptied, and she swayed once, twice, and then steadied herself. Some of the pain in her chest eased too. She took a step back, losing the warmth of his body. Embarrassment swamped her.

"That looked like the start of one really bad panic attack. My older brother Neil used to get them. Want to go to the nurse's office or to your house?"

"Home," she croaked, then repeated herself so the word was stronger. "Home, please."

Jai hooked an arm around her waist and led her out of the building. "Come on."

He held on to her as he walked her to the parking lot and ushered her into a faded red sedan with a scratched bumper and bent license plate. The fabric seats were clean, but the vehicle had to be at least fifteen years old, if not more. Radha hugged her backpack to her chest and dropped her head back against the headrest. She told Jai her address, and he plugged it into his phone. They drove with only the sound of the GPS guiding them.

When they pulled up in the wide stone driveway behind the white Audi, Jai gaped. Radha knew the size of the house was obscene for two people, but her mother was big on making a statement.

Radha turned to Jai and tried to smile. "Thanks," she said. "I'm sorry for falling apart like that. I, uh, don't make it a habit to trip, or have panic attacks in front of people. It makes me feel like I'm..."

Jai grinned. "In a Bollywood movie?"

"Yes. And my inner Shah Rukh Khan is shuddering in embarrassment."

"There is nothing to be ashamed of or embarrassed about. People have panic attacks. I'm just happy I could help."

"Yeah. Thanks."

"Now, tripping and falling straight into my arms…"

She laughed, but the sound was watery to her ears. Before she could fall apart again, she opened the car door. "Thanks. Really."

Jai touched her arm again. "Wait, can I have your phone?"

"Why?"

"So I can give you my number."

Radha pulled out her cell from her backpack and handed it over. He punched in his digits and then handed it back to her. "I called myself, so I have your number too. Let me know if you need anything. I'm sorry if I said anything—"

"No," she said, cutting him off. "No. You were so … great. Thanks for the ride. One more thing. You were right. You make a pretty great friend."

With one last smile in Jai's direction, Radha slipped from his car and into her house. She had a few hours to think before her mother came home.

Sujata Roy had to have lied to her. She knew about

the Winter Showcase when they made their deal. She betrayed Radha again, just like she betrayed Radha at the International Kathak Classics by keeping secrets.

And if she had, that meant only one thing: Radha would have to do something to get out of dancing in the Winter Showcase. She knew that if she was forced to perform in front of an audience that was going to judge her, she'd break, and no amount of cooking, or therapy, or friendship could ever help her recover again.

Chapter Seven

Jai

JAI: Hey. You doing okay?

RADHA: Yeah. Thank you again for driving me home yesterday.

JAI: Happy to help. I'm here if you ever want to talk.

RADHA: 🙂 You have been nothing but a hero since we met. Are you like this with everyone?

JAI: I try to be if I can.

RADHA: And who's there for you when you trip and fall or have panic attacks or need a ride home?

JAI: Well, I have the director, Nana Veeru, and my family. Winnie and her boyfriend, Dev. Some of the Bollywood Beats team too.

RADHA: And now you have me. I'll be there for you too if you want.

JAI: Yeah?

RADHA: Yeah.

Over a week. It had been more than seven days since he'd seen Radha. He wanted to text her and make sure she was okay, and to ask what she'd meant about being there for him, but it just felt weird. On top of that, he'd been so busy with classes and working the late shift at the store every night. At school he spent every spare moment auditioning applicants for the open spot on the team, and working with some of the other dance teachers to see if anyone could help with team choreography.

Thank God it was the last Friday of the month, he thought. He really needed to let off some stress and steam, and the Final Friday Dance-Off meant he could do just that.

When he walked into the large hall where all the solo dance classes convened, the last thing he expected to see was Radha over by the window, surrounded by members of his Bollywood dance crew.

"This could be good or bad, Jai," he murmured to himself. "Think positive."

He was just starting toward his cluster of friends when

Radha looked over Shakti's shoulder at him. Sunlight glistened around her, and there was a small, amused smile on her mouth. She was like a regal goddess, with her crown of braids and her off-the-shoulder crop top over leggings. Her skin glowed as she watched him and simultaneously said something to his friends.

"Hey, guys," he said, and stepped into the circle and leaned an elbow against Hari's shoulder. "Telling lies about me?"

"Who said we're talking about you?" Shakti snorted. "We're much more interested in Radha. Did you know both of our dads are chefs?"

"I did know that," Jai said. "Radha's a pretty awesome cook herself."

"We're trying to convince her to save us from watching more auditions by joining Bollywood Beats. She'd be perfect for the team."

"Oh, don't bother," Jai said. "I asked and she shut me down."

"Well, maybe you didn't ask nicely," Radha said, crossing her arms.

Hari made an "oooh" sound until Nupur, one of the few juniors present, slapped him on the back of his dastaar.

"Ouch!" he said as he ran a hand over his turban. "What? What did I do?"

Ms. Olga, with her white hair in a severe, no-nonsense bun, clapped in front of the room. "Five minutes left before we begin! All of you better be stretching!"

Jai dropped his duffel bag next to the wall and extended a hand. "Come on, new girl. Forget the nerd herd. Help me stretch, please?"

"You are literally going to be our class valedictorian," Shakti said. "If we're the nerd herd, what does that make you?"

"Captain," Jai said with a grin. "Radha?"

She looked at Shakti and the rest of his friends before she took his hand. "Lead the way, Captain."

Jai grinned. *New girl has a sense of humor,* he thought as he moved to the center of the room, away from his nosy team. Ignoring the people watching, he sat, legs spread in a V, and waited for her to position herself across from him. She scooted until her bare feet pressed against his ankles. They gripped each other's forearms.

"Did you mean it?" Jai asked. "When you said I didn't ask nicely? Because I can."

Radha shook her head. "I was joking. I told you. I don't

want to perform."

"Are you going to be okay dancing in class today?"

She nodded. "You're talking about what … happened."

"Yeah. Have you always had panic attacks?"

"When I was a kid," Radha said as she pulled him forward with surprising strength. Jai leaned into the stretch. "I've had them over the years, but after a while the stage, or dancing, didn't trigger them anymore. It wasn't until the competition in January, the one I mentioned – since then, they've come back."

"How do you manage the stage fright?"

"It's actually performance-anxiety attacks and stress-induced panic attacks. It manifests in different ways. Basically, I'm okay to dance in class or in front of other dancers like me, but if I'm facing an audience, it's a no-go. My mom and I discovered that when I would repeatedly freak out at my last dance school. Instead of Friday dance-offs, they had formal shows. I was a wreck leading up to each one."

Jai pulled her toward him now. "Ah. That explains the Winter Showcase. Did you talk to the director yet?"

"Not yet."

Jai lay flat on his back and lifted one leg. Radha gripped

97

his calf and pushed forward. He relaxed into the stretch.

"Anything I can do to help?" he asked as he looked up at her.

"Thank you, but I'll figure something out. It already sounds like you have your hands full with your team."

"Yeah, things are a bit chaotic right now." Radha helped him stretch his other leg, and then he switched places with her. "Ready?"

She nodded, and he pushed on her calf until her toe was touching the floor above her head. He noticed the delicate lines of her body, while feeling the strength of her muscles under his hands. Jai counted the stretch, and then switched legs.

"What are you going to do about the choreographer?" she asked when they repositioned to work on their backs. "Shakti, Hari, Nupur, and…"

"And Vik."

"Yes," she said. "And Vik. They told me that your choreographer left for the bright lights of Bollywood."

"I think we're stuck choreographing the number ourselves."

"For the last six years of my performance career, I put together my own kathak routines. It sucks."

"Yeah, it does." He waited for her to grip his shoulders with strong, warm hands. "I really wanted to leave the academy on a high. I don't think I can do that now. We're a month behind on rehearsing for the Winter Showcase compared to all of the other dance groups, and now with the added burden of choreography, we're pretty much sunk." When she pushed, he leaned forward until his forehead almost touched the mat between his knees.

"You wanted to make the director proud," she said softly from behind him. "I'm just guessing that's what you were hoping to do. Probably because I would do the same thing. I'd want to show her how much she'd taught me."

Was he that easy to read? He sat up, and then looked at her over his shoulder. "The director means a lot to me."

"Come on, everyone!" Ms. Olga shouted from the front of the studio again. Her black leggings and leotard stood out against the mirrors behind her. "Left and right sides of the room. It's time for a little Final Friday Dance-Off!"

"Come on," Jai said, jumping up and pulling her toward the far wall. The Bollywood Beats crew always tried to stay on the same side during these freestyle classes. "Did anyone tell you what Final Fridays are like?"

"Not really," she said. "Just that all the solo dance classes on the last Friday of the month get together to … what, let loose?"

"Sort of," Jai said. The music started, and the heavy thumping of the bass was a jolt of endorphins. "The purpose of Final Fridays is to learn dance musicality. Listening to the music and interpreting it in dance form. It's also about self-expression, dignity, and honor. Are you ready?"

"Dignity and honor? And ready for what?"

Ms. Olga counted an eight beat from the front of the room, and half a dozen dancers jumped forward. They were freestyling, and then they fed off each other until they moved in sync. Radha's jaw dropped.

"Oh, we're just getting started," he said to her with a grin.

Everyone cheered. The pointe dancers in the room moved into the circle to challenge the first group.

Jai didn't know what was more fun to watch, the escalating dance-off or Radha. Her eyes widened as student after student competed. Almost fifteen minutes in, he leaned over to ask if she wanted to dance with him, but before she could answer, Hari and Shakti hooked their arms under his and dragged him onto the floor.

The music changed, and he called out the combination and jumped into the routine with all his energy. He danced, aware of Radha watching, and enjoying every moment. Before they could back off for another group to take center stage, he saw Radha join from the corner of his eye. Hari gave a sharp seeti, a whistle that only a Punjabi dude at a party could pull off, and the new girl, a beautiful package of surprises, moved past him to Shakti. As if they'd rehearsed it a thousand times, they turned to each other, nodded in sync, and spun across the floor.

"I totally forgot that Shakti used to learn odissi when she was a kid," Hari yelled over the music. "Not like the North Indian style Radha does, but they look great together. You sure Radha won't join our team?"

"Yeah," Jai said. "But, man, I wish she would." Radha and Shakti took an exaggerated bow before returning to their side of the room.

"Did you guys dance together before today?" Jai asked Radha over the sound of dancers and celebration.

She shook her head, her breath a little labored.

"You loved it."

She leaned in until they were only inches apart. "I had dance joy."

"Dance joy?"

She nodded. "It's what I call that feeling that takes over your body, your head, everything, when you're completely consumed by a piece. It's lame, I know, but it happened. Just for a second."

"No, not lame at all. I know exactly what you mean." Jai had danced long enough to understand what it could do to a person.

"Dance joy is the reason I put up with the performances. As long as I could dance, I'd do whatever my mother wanted."

"And then you lost the joy part."

Her smile slipped. "Yeah."

The music stopped, and Ms. Olga clapped in front of the room. "Take a break! Then we'll go again."

Jai led Radha over to the corner of the room so they could talk. "When did you last feel your dance joy?"

She shrugged. "At my performance in January. Maybe for a second at my audition here. And today. This was a lot of fun, Jai. And it wasn't even choreographed."

"Man, I can't imagine how you'd feel if you joined Bollywood Beats for our Winter Showcase number. Choreographing it alone would give you a jolt. If you loved just a little bit of this, then you'd be ecstatic with us."

Her eyebrows made a V; her forehead crinkled.

"What? What did I say?" Jai asked.

She turned away from him and watched as dancers retrieved water bottles, stretched against the bar and the wall, and grouped together to talk.

"Radha?"

She held her hands up. "Jai, has the director let anyone choreograph a dance as their final-grade contribution to the Winter Showcase?"

"Yeah, since choreography is as hard as actually performing... Wait a minute. If you choreograph the dance—"

"I wouldn't have to perform," she said. "If the director approves it, right?"

Jai looked over at his friends and saw how they tried to pretend they weren't watching him. He thought of Masi and how much faith she'd put in his career. Most importantly, he thought of his brothers. Winning the showcase was a long shot, and winning regionals was even more difficult, but the team was going to choreograph a number themselves. Could Radha do better and get them closer to their goal?

"You're a solo dancer," he said. "A classical dancer."

"I've not only choreographed my own routines, but I also worked with the younger students at my kathak school in India. Group performances to Bollywood songs. I've been a part of a dance school for my entire high school life. I know contemporary, jazz, hip-hop. I may not be the best at styles outside of classical, but I can choreograph."

"This is not just any choreography. Our team has very different skills. You'd have to know how to use those skills and position them to fulfill potential."

She stared him down. "You can help me. You're the captain of the nerd herd! And you guys were going to do it yourselves anyway."

"I was just thinking that myself," he said with a laugh. "You'd really do this? You'd really choreograph so you don't have to perform?"

"Yes," she said.

"Do you think you could get your dance joy back if you choreograph, too?"

"No. I think that it comes and goes. I doubt I'll ever feel the same kind of love that I did when I used to dance full-time."

She sounded so sure that he wanted to give her a hug

and let her know that she'd be okay. That he believed her. But still…

"What about cooking lessons with your dad? I thought you were finding a new passion."

"I'll keep doing that," she said. "I can cook and study, and keep up with classes, maybe with your help, and I can choreograph."

He scrubbed a hand on the back of his neck. If she was confident that she could finish a routine, then he'd trust her. There were still others who had to be convinced of her skill too.

Ms. Olga called the two-minute mark.

"So?" Radha asked. "Will you give me a chance?"

Jai looked from Radha to his group of friends, and then to Ms. Olga. "Wait a minute," he said. He waved his friends over, and since they were already blatantly staring in their direction, all four dancers strode over in unison.

"What's up, Captain?" Vik said. "Nice job out there, new girl."

"Thanks," Radha replied.

"Radha," Jai said, "has offered to choreograph our Bollywood Beats routine for the Winter Showcase. She has some experience with group performances, and of course years of classical-dance training."

"That's great!" Shakti said. "I'm all in."

"Do you have any idea what you're getting into?" Hari asked with a laugh.

"We're about to show her," Jai said.

Radha arched one of her perfectly shaped brows.

"Prove that you can lead more than just a person with a classical-dance background, and I'll go to the director and ask for you to be selected as our choreographer."

Her mouth formed an O. "You mean *here*? Choreograph something on the spot, for us to dance right now?"

He nodded. "You know, some people look forward to Final Fridays because they actually prep choreography to try new stuff. It's not unheard of. That's why groups look like they've rehearsed. You don't have a lot of time. Thirty seconds max. But we're good enough to follow your lead."

He saw her jaw tighten and her eyes narrow. "Follow my lead? That's not choreography, that's just – just *following*."

"It's the best way we can test your skill. Think of it as an audition." *And to prove to yourself that this can be more than avoiding a performance on a stage*, he thought.

"Test my skill? Okay, fine. Fine. I see how it is."

She squared her shoulders before she stormed over

to the audio station in the corner. Jai watched her as she had a brief conversation with Su-Jin, who pointed to her laptop screen and the stereo, then gave Radha a thumbs-up. Radha returned the gesture before she turned on her heel.

"You think she can choreograph a ten-minute routine for fourteen trained dancers in a style that isn't really her sweet spot?" Hari asked.

"Yes, but let's see if she really thinks she can do it too."

"Okay, huddle up," Radha said.

She took the lead and talked about the music she'd selected, and an idea that had crossed her mind. The second half of class began, and while they waited for Radha's music to play, they worked through the choreography. Finally the stereo pumped the familiar drumbeats, Radha called the countdown, and Jai did exactly what she'd asked him to do.

They moved in unison, as if they'd been dancing together forever. Part of it was the fact that the moves were ones everyone knew. The class erupted as they brought their whole selves to the floor.

Radha called the last count out loud, and Shakti did a backflip, falling into Jai's and Hari's arms. It timed perfectly with the last beat.

They nailed it, and everyone knew it. They'd barely had a moment to high-five each other when Ms. Olga ended class.

"She's gorgeous and talented," Shakti said to Jai under her breath. "But I can tell she's not into my type."

"What are you getting at?" Jai asked.

Shakti shrugged. "Nothing. Just making an observation. Wondering if you'd made the same observation yourself."

"Shakti…"

Shakti raised her voice so that the team could hear. "All I'm saying is that if you don't ask her to join our team, we're going to kill you." She winked at Radha and rushed out of the studio. Jai decided to ignore Shakti's sidebar commentary and draped an arm around Radha's shoulder. "Are you ready to talk to the director, Ms. Choreographer?"

She nodded. "I have to talk to my mother, too. She's going to hate that I found a loophole in our deal."

"Your deal?"

Radha nodded. "I'll tell you about it later. Jai, if the director okays this and my mom doesn't immediately go into cardiac arrest, we have to start working on a concept, the music, and a schedule. I'll be just as invested as you."

"Yeah. Agreed. In the meantime, I'll help you keep up with classes."

"You'd do that?"

Jai shrugged. "Sure." It might be self-serving, since he'd get to spend more time with her, but he wasn't going to share that bit of information yet.

Radha stepped in front of him and rested her hands on his shoulders. "If you help me with my homework, I'll help you, too."

Jai's pulse jumped. "Aren't you doing that already with the choreography?"

"No, that benefits us both."

"But helping you with your homework—"

"Is selfless. So was catching me from falling and helping me with my panic attack. I may not know a ton about friendship, but I know that what you told me the first time we met was right. You make a good friend." The corner of her mouth curved up. "It's time for me to save you."

"How?"

"You'll figure it out."

Chapter Eight

Radha

Translation of Bimalpreet Chopra's Recipe Book

Ghee

Clarified butter from the cow is the basis for all our
family recipes. To make your own ghee:

First, use only fresh, homemade butter.

Heat the butter on low until it melts and the color changes.

*The whey floats to the top, the milk solids to the bottom,
and the clarified butter to the center. The color should
resemble a dark, clear gold.*

Scoop off the froth from the top, and then strain the melted butter into a container through a cheesecloth.

Let sit until it reaches room temperature.

Note: Unsalted Land O'Lakes. Use a wok. Heat on low for 30 minutes per pound.

RADHA: I tried to make ghee, but black bits start to form in it?

DAD: Heat is too high. You burned the butter.

RADHA: Can I save it?

DAD: Maybe. You won't know until you try.

RADHA: ... That's it? That's all you're giving me?

DAD: 😃 Your cousin in India? She used to do the same thing. You may want to ask her how to strain the ghee right.

RADHA: Simran? I haven't talked to her in years, not since we danced together.

DAD: Relationships, like butter, are worth saving.

RADHA: Cheesy, Dad. That was cheesy. I'll figure it out.

Radha discarded her latest attempt at ghee. In addition to burning the butter, she'd burned off some stress, so at least one good thing had come out of her kitchen disaster. Who would've thought that working with food, even a failed recipe as simple as melting butter, could be just as rewarding as a four-hour kathak class? She dropped the dirty dishes in the sink and surveyed the kitchen island.

"Okay, Friday night," she said with a sigh. "Let's get weird."

The marble surface was covered with her grandfather's recipe book, her textbooks, her laptop, and her tablet. Sticky notes coated everything. Notes for classes, notes for the next recipe she was going to try with Dad, and notes about Bollywood Beats she'd received from the director that afternoon.

Radha picked up one of the sticky notes, which had three song options on it. "You can do this," she murmured to herself. The team needed a choreographer, and Radha didn't want to be on stage for a solo. She'd pointed that out when she spoke with the director. It helped that Radha had a ton of international awards. She was qualified. Thankfully, she got the approval, as long as she also wrote a theory paper on how she'd choreographed the number.

The sound of the front door opening reminded her of the last barrier she had to pass. She now had to tell her mother.

Radha winced as she remembered the fight they'd had the week before when she found out about the Winter Showcase. *Time for round two,* she thought.

"Radha?" her mother called from the foyer. The sound of footsteps followed. "What's burning?"

"Nothing. Well, butter. I was trying to make ghee again and I botched it."

Her mother appeared in a peach pantsuit, her hair perfectly coiled after twelve hours at the office. Her Chanel tote still hung on one arm. "I thought you'd finally gone and burned the house down."

"Obviously not, since you've walked inside and there is no smoke," Radha said.

"Fine." Sujata turned to leave.

"Mom, wait."

She eyed Radha with a cool disinterest. "What is it?"

"I'm sorry for yelling at you last week. I didn't mean to hurt you."

"Does that mean you're going to start rehearsing for your Winter Showcase performance?"

"No. I'm not going to perform."

Sujata dropped her bag on one of the island stools. "If you're not going to perform, then you won't be completing the prerequisites for your grade. That means I'm not going to pay for college, and you'll have to go back to Chicago with your dad. That was the deal."

"No, Mom. The deal was that I do whatever is expected of me to achieve good grades and put in the effort to get into competitive shape again. I spoke with the director today. I don't have to perform in order to meet all the prerequisites for the dance track. There is another option."

Radha's mother gaped at her. "You cannot make those decisions on your own!"

"I'm almost eighteen. I can definitely make those decisions on my own. Instead of performing at the Winter Showcase, I'll be choreographing the Bollywood Beats dance-team number." She crossed her arms over her chest and waited for the explosion, for the judgment and belittling that were sure to come.

"Choreograph a *Bollywood* dance team?" Her voice started to climb until she was practically screeching. "You're going to throw away your classical dance education for that kind of mutilated dance garbage?"

"It's a great opportunity. It's just as good as performing.

I'm in dance school, and I'm keeping my grades up. I'm putting in the effort."

"This is manipulation, Radha. This was not our deal."

"First of all, you're the one who manipulated me. You knew about the Winter Showcase and didn't bother mentioning it. And second, it is part of our deal."

Radha pulled out a piece of paper with her mother's signature on it, which she'd been saving for this exact moment. "I have the original and a copy I can email to you. This is exactly why I wanted it in writing. You laughed at me for typing up our agreement, but I knew something like this would happen. It says right here that all I have to do is put in the effort, get good grades, and complete all my requirements for the academy dance track. It says nothing about performing. You can't pretend that our conversation never happened like you always do."

"So that's it. You're throwing away years of competitions because you refuse to get on a stage. You know the best cure for your stage fright is to perform, right? It's like you're purposely sabotaging yourself. For what reason? Are you trying to punish me?" Her eyes filled with tears, and Radha felt her own burn in her throat. She hated hurting her mother, but she couldn't dance like a puppet anymore. She couldn't be the person that her peers referred to as cardboard.

"This is completely my choice," Radha said. She hid her trembling hands and hoped that her voice wouldn't shake too. "I'm making the best of the situation."

Sujata grabbed her purse. "I'm so disappointed in you. I'll be having a conversation with the director myself."

It wasn't until her mother had left that Radha let the first tear fall. She covered her face with her hands and leaned her elbows on the counter. She knew that her mother loved her in her own way, but sometimes it felt like she only cared about Radha if she was dancing.

Radha leaned against the counter and gave in to the sadness. Pressing a palm against her mouth to muffle the sound of her sobs, she let go.

A few moments later, when her head was clear, and after she blew her nose, she walked over to the sink and splashed cold water on her face. She then went back to her books. Even though the hurt sat in her chest like a weight, she had to ignore it. She had more important things to do.

Like figure out how to make ghee.

She was about to text her father, when she remembered he'd suggested she talk to her cousin Simran.

Simran. They hadn't talked in five years. Simran was twenty-six now, and she posted pictures of her wedding and her baby on social media all the time. The idea of contacting her for a recipe felt odd, but Radha didn't really have any other options. At least not if she wanted to make it just like her grandfather used to.

Logging on to one of her social sites, she found Simran's profile. Her picture was that of a happy, cherubic baby with a full head of jet-black hair and a smudge of kajal eyeliner at his hairline. The last post was about an upcoming Durga Puja sale at the family dhaba. Their grandfather's dhaba.

Without second-guessing herself, Radha sent Simran a quick message.

Hey Simran,

I hope you're doing well. Congratulations again on the baby! He looks so cute. I'm sorry I've been out of touch for the last few years. I have been dancing, and then ... well, I'm sure Dad must've told your dad what happened. Anyway. I'm trying to learn how to cook. I got Dada's recipe book, and I'm starting easy. With ghee. The problem is, I burn it all the time. I tried to lower the heat, but then it doesn't do anything for over an hour. Dad said you may know what to do since you're a ghee master.

Thanks in advance,
Radha

Radha closed the site and was about to review the next recipe in the book when her computer pinged with a video call.

Video call from Simran Desai Walia

It was her cousin. Who did that? Who randomly video-called someone without any warning whatsoever? Was this an Indian thing?

She had to pick up. It would look super rude if she ignored the call, especially after she'd just sent a message. She brushed under her eyes to make sure her short crying jag hadn't smudged any mascara, and then answered.

A glowing face, masked in black-framed glasses and surrounded by a cloud of hair, filled the screen. Radha could see the head of a baby resting against her cousin's shoulder.

"Radha?" Simran said in a low voice. "Is that really you?"

Radha nodded. "Hi," she said softly. "Isn't it like three something in the morning over there?"

Simran responded in Punjabi. "Sahil has an ear infection, so he's not sleeping well. I was so surprised by your message that I had to connect immediately. My goodness, look at you! You have grown so much since the last time we spoke. Your father sends pictures, but in most of them you're all dolled up from dance. The real you is beautiful!"

"Uh, thanks. H-how are you?"

"Wadiya, bahot wadiya. Kiddan?"

I'm great. Absolutely great. How are you?

"Vadiya." Radha picked up her seltzer and took a sip. She saw Simran's response.

"What?"

"Is that *bottled* water? Isn't it time for some chai?"

Radha laughed. "If I knew how to make chai, then yeah. Dad gave me Dadaji's recipe for it, but there are a ton of things that go into a pot of boiling water, and I feel like I'm going to get something wrong."

"Ah. The infamous recipe notebook. Your father sold his half of the dhaba for that notebook."

It was Radha's turn to be shocked. "What? Why?"

She saw the hesitation in Simran's face.

"Please. I'd like to know."

"When Dadaji died," Simran started, "he parceled equal shares of the restaurant to my father and yours. But your mother didn't want to move to Punjab. Chicago was where she had studied, and that's where she wanted to work. She was also expecting you at that time."

"What did Dad do?"

"He chose Chicago over returning to India, but he asked for the original copy of Dadaji's famous recipe book. He said, even then, that he might want to give it to you one day. Over the years, every time he came to visit, he said he made the best choice."

Radha rubbed her sweaty palms against her jeans. Her father had sacrificed his legacy, and her mother had broken his heart. Radha hadn't helped matters by choosing to leave for Jersey too. Hopefully he could see that in her own way she was trying to make up for lost time.

"Thanks for telling me," Radha said. "I didn't know."

"Well, now you do. Have you made anything so far from the book?"

Radha shrugged. "Not really. I figured out how to set up my spice tin. I did blitz together garam masala in a blender. I'm trying to work my way up to the difficult recipes, but I can't even make ghee yet. I keep burning it."

"Medium heat for twenty minutes, then you watch it for another ten minutes on low. The minute it looks golden, you shut the heat off."

"Oh. Really? That's it?"

"That's it. You could triple-strain it through a cheesecloth if you really burned it, but that takes forever. Just make it again, and salvage whatever you can."

"Wow. Thank you. Really, that's so helpful. Hey, Simran? Can I ask you a question? If you know the answer."

"Bolo," she said. "Speak so I can then ask you questions."

"Why did we lose touch? I know you were busy getting married and stuff, and me with my dance … but you never called me, either." Radha had some thoughts as to why Simran hadn't bothered.

Radha was just a dancer without a personality.

She'd had nothing but kathak for years.

She'd been too busy performing to connect with the people in her life.

"What are you asking?" Simran said with a scrunched-up expression. "We have always been friends. You just were very busy, so it's taken some time for us to get together and talk like this."

The answer was sweet and, honestly, the answer she would expect from her Punjabi cousin. "Well, I'm not really performing anymore, so I have time. I know that you still have the baby, but can we try to do this more?"

"Of course! Call me anytime, and I'll SMS you. Okay?"

"Okay. Simran, that is … really nice."

"It's good to see you, Cousin-sister. We can make more of an effort now."

Effort. There was that word again. "Yes. I would like that."

"Acha, now my turn." Simran adjusted the sleeping baby in her arms and leaned closer to the monitor so her eyes took up most of the screen. "My friend who has been with me since the fifth standard moved to New Jersey after marriage. She's visiting her parents and will be going home next week. Do you want me to send anything from here? Masala for your cooking? Clothes?"

"Uh, sure," Radha said. "To the masala, anyway. Whatever was used in Dada's recipes for the dhaba. As for clothes, I don't really have any events coming up, but I appreciate the offer. Let me know if you want anything from here the next time your friend visits India. I'll send something … for the – for the baby."

Her cousin had a baby, and she'd never sent anything,

she thought.

"Yes! I will give you my list too. Okay, now tell me more, chutki."

Radha muffled her laugh so she wouldn't wake the baby. She liked that Simran had used the endearment for the youngest girl in the family, the same her father used. "Well, I'm working on choreographing a group Bollywood dance routine."

"Oh!" Simran's eyes widened, and she wiggled closer, baby in arm, to lean toward the screen again. "I love Bollywood dancing. Tell me. Do you have Indian boys in your group?"

Radha felt her cheeks heat. "Sure. The captain of the team is a boy, actually. He's really nice. Jai is also super smart, but complicated."

"Jai? I want all the details," Simran replied. "Is he Punjabi?"

"Uh, half, I think. His dad is Gujarati."

"Ahh. Well, it shouldn't matter anyway. In India each region is like a different spice tin. We use different spices, but in the end, we're all using the same dabba. What else, chutki? I have time."

Chapter Nine

Jai

JAI: Hey, did you tell your mom?

RADHA: Yeah. She's thinking of ways to send me back to Chicago because she's being a dance mom.

JAI: Yikes. Do you think you're going back?

RADHA: Hopefully not. Until then, I'm going to do whatever I can to choreograph this dance. Any chance we can start this Sunday?

JAI: I'm working at the store all day. Want to come over? I may have to stop to help customers, but for the most part, mornings are quiet.

RADHA: Sure. Eleven okay?

JAI: Yeah, sending you the address now.

Since the start of his shift, Jai had been getting ready

for Radha's arrival like an Indian aunty expecting distant relatives for chai. His father had come to visit in the morning and had laughed at Jai as he swept and mopped the floors, cleaned the glass windows, and dusted every exposed surface. Jai even rearranged the hot dogs so that the good ones were the most noticeable in the warmer. After his mom picked up his father, Neil arrived to work the rest of the day shift with him. Thankfully, Neil hadn't witnessed Jai's … prep work. He would've never let Jai live it down.

Right before Radha was supposed to show up, he managed to calm down enough to complete his AP Calc homework and finish the draft of his admissions essay for Dr. O'Hare's class. Not that he would submit the essay, but an assignment was an assignment.

He'd just emailed the draft to Dr. O'Hare when a white Audi pulled into the parking lot. Radha tossed her braid over one shoulder and grabbed her leather backpack from the passenger seat. As she strode toward the entrance, Jai rushed to do something, anything that would make him look busy. Unfortunately, his brain wasn't working as fast as it should've been.

"Hi," he said at her entry, and held up some blank Powerball cards.

"Um, hi there. Are we playing the lottery?"

He looked down at the stack in his hand and shoved them into their container on the countertop. "No. No, not at all. I'm not even supposed to sell those until I turn eighteen. My brother is in the back working on delivery stuff, and he's the only one who can approve the sale of that, so … yeah."

"Oh, that's right. You have two brothers."

"Yeah. Neil usually does the day shift and Gopal, my oldest brother, does the night shift."

Radha's mouth quirked in a half smile. Jai wondered about the flavor of the thin sheen of gloss on her lips.

"Jai?"

"Yeah?"

"We should get started."

"Right! Yes. Of course." He rounded the counter, grabbing two folding chairs along the way. He placed them facing each other in the small space next to the employees-only door. "Your mom was cool with you coming today?"

Radha shrugged. "She wasn't home. Probably went to the office or something. We've been avoiding each other."

"Ah. Sorry."

"It's okay. Some things are what they are."

"Right." He motioned to the open chairs. "Is this okay? I don't know how you want to do this. Our last choreographer used to have something ready before the school year even started."

"We'll make up for lost time," Radha said. "I think."

"Did you get a chance to watch the videos I sent you of our past performances?"

"I did," Radha said as she sat in one of the chairs. "I watched them all. You guys are good. Really good. But then I watched videos of your competition, and the winners of regionals for the last six years, and they are, unfortunately, better than you."

Jai winced. Even though he knew she was right, he hated the criticism. "Next time, be a little gentler when you stab me with the knife."

Radha took her rose-gold wireless headphones out of her bag. "We have to step into the competitive mindset. I've lived with that mindset for most of my life, and I can tell you that it has its advantages."

"Like what?"

"Like exploring concepts no one else has done." She opened her laptop and, after a few clicks, handed it over to him, along with the headphones. "Here. When I wasn't studying the competition, I was making this mix. Give it a listen. I'm a little rusty, but I think it can work."

Jai fastened the headphones over his ears and pressed play.

Classical North Indian music. Drums. Chimes. Harmonium.

And then ... dubstep?

He raised an eyebrow at Radha, watching her now as the music played. His body could feel the beat, his feet itched to dance and move, and then he felt his pulse quicken as the music changed again to classical against a hip-hop beat, and finally reached a crescendo.

Ten minutes and eleven seconds later, Jai handed the headphones back.

"Holy shit."

She flushed. "Not bad, right?"

"Uh, that was *amazing*. You did your own mixes?"

"Yeah, my mother made me learn how, because she was worried if we asked anyone else to do it, my music would leak."

"I can't say I hate her for it," Jai said. "The only thing is, it sounds like so much classical."

Radha shrugged. "What's the root of Bollywood dance? Classical and folk melded together for the movies. Then hip-hop and contemporary came in later. Now people focus so much on the hip-hop and bhangra that they forget the other roots that made up the art form. Not one performance at regionals in the last three years included classical. Even the Rutgers High all-girls team used contemporary, and they're the dance team to beat, I think."

Jai flinched at the mention of his ex's school. "They do win more than us."

"But they win with ballet or jazz or contemporary as the main form of dance, with bhangra, raas and, okay, I admit, some steps from Bollywood movies. I am one of the best kathak dancers in the world right now … well, I used to be. I can help you with a classical-focused routine. It'll be hard if not everyone has a classical-dance background, but in the end we'll deliver a performance no one has seen before."

She was glowing while she talked, Jai realized. Truly glowing. He didn't want to pull her from her mood, but man, he wished he could take away those moments of sadness from her so she was like this all the time when she talked about dance.

"So, what story are we going to tell with this piece?" Jai asked.

"You couldn't tell?"

He shrugged. "Sorry."

Radha rested a hand on his knee. "We're doing an Indian wedding."

"W-what?"

Radha laughed. "Holy cow, you look like I just told you we're getting married. *Relax*. I'm talking about telling a wedding story."

"How?"

"In pieces," she said. "Choreography is, surprisingly, like building a recipe. There are the ingredients, which are the dancers; the instructions, which are the song and the concept; and the steps, which is where I come in. We're building a recipe together that is going to tell the story of a wedding in a messy, fun family. We'll start by dramatizing a mehndi and a sangeet."

"Okay," he said. His brain began working in overdrive as he tried to think the concept through. "The mehndi is when the bride and family gets mehndi done, and the sangeet is the Indian karaoke party night. Both events usually have a lot of singing and dancing. Now that I think about it, a wedding is a pretty perfect setup."

"Exactly. There are a bunch of Punjabi songs – I couldn't help myself. It's in the blood, I guess. We can also add garba in there if we want to make it a wedding between a Punjabi and a Gujarati."

Jai grinned. "As a bicultural Punjabi Gujurati desi whose parents had a loving marriage, I think that sounds amazing. After the sangeet is the wedding day, right?"

"Right. We'll even tell the story of the groom's procession – the baraat is where we can introduce bhangra. Following that is the wedding ceremony, with hip-hop and funk. For that scene I envision that you each do something different, and then you freeze. One person moves, then another, and then you're all in sync again."

Jai could picture it in his head, and he knew that she was onto a brilliant idea. He'd never seen something like that before, and he doubted anyone at the showcase would've seen a performance with so many moving parts either. "The climax – it's the wedding reception, right?"

"Exactly. You all do the same choreo. That'll make the biggest impact. The whole routine will be ten minutes with multiple moods and tones. We'll record a talk track to intro the dance, and close it with a bang. If we can nail this—"

"Then we're going to win." He opened his arms, and when Radha flushed and leaned forward, he embraced her. She smelled like vanilla, and her hair had the faint scent of kiwi.

The employees-only door creaked behind them, and Jai and Radha jerked apart.

Neil gaped and shot him a questioning look. *What is this?*

"Neil, meet Radha. She's going to be helping Bollywood Beats with the choreography."

"Hi," Radha said.

"Hi." Neil smiled at her in the disarming way he used with any female who walked into the store. "It's nice to meet you. If I'd known that we had company, I would've said hello sooner."

"That's why I didn't tell you," Jai said.

Neil leaned against the doorjamb. "I'm sorry that you have to work with my brother. Mr. Cranky Pants here knows that I'm the best brother."

"Jai's not so bad himself," Radha said as she looked over at Jai.

"Yeah, I bet," Neil said. "You know, I think most of his team has come through the store, and my older brother,

132

my mom, and I have seen all of Jai's performances, but you don't look familiar."

"That's because I'm new. To New Jersey, the school, the team, everything."

Neil scanned the store and then did a double take when he saw the Audi outside. "Wait, is that your car?"

"That's my mom's car," Radha said. "I just use it."

"That's great, that's great." Jai watched his brother's goofy grin slip from his face. "Hey, Jai, I need your help for a second. Do you mind?"

"Um, sure. Radha, can you give me a minute?"

"Yeah. Take your time."

Jai followed his brother into the narrow back room between metal shelves stacked high with supplies.

"Dude!" Neil said. He gestured toward the exit door. "What are you doing?"

Jai shook his head. Sometimes he felt like he needed a translator to talk to his brothers. "Didn't I just tell you?"

Neil gripped Jai's shoulders and shook. "You are a great kid. You're smart, and kind, and always giving more of yourself than you should. That is why, as your older brother, I'm going to ask you a couple questions. First. Is the pretty rich girl out there related to someone at Columbia University?"

"Uh, I don't think so? Why does it—"

"Second question. Is the pretty girl out there with the Audi connected to some scholarship fund to get you money?"

"No. What is going on Neil?"

"Are you going to benefit in any way from her connections or money?"

Jai felt as if his brother had just shoved him. "What? It's not like that. I don't care about her money. She's helping me with the routine for Bollywood Beats, and hopefully we'll be able to save face at the competition this year."

"And you're sure that's what she's going to help you with in the end? Win your showcase, and maybe cash in that prize at regionals?"

Jai looked at the door, and then at his brother. "Why do you care?"

"Because you dated a girl who was just like that and didn't make you happy!" Neil whisper-yelled. This time when he gestured, he knocked a box of tissues off a shelf. "Have you forgotten your ex, Tara with the good hair?"

"She's nothing like Tara. And did you seriously just make a Beyoncé reference?"

Neil pinched the bridge of his nose, which was confusing since Jai was the one who felt like he was frustrated.

"That girl? She's probably nice, but if she loses the Winter Showcase, I bet you she'll be fine. Even if she says she needs some cash like you do, it's not the same. Her parents will give her the money that she wants. But you? If you lose, then yeah. You'll be working here. And maybe we can get you to take classes part-time, and maybe you'll get to medical school, but we all know that it's going to be a big fat maybe."

"You're telling me that if I mess with Radha, I'm not going to focus on winning and I'll screw myself over."

"Yes!" Neil said. He immediately shushed himself and then cuffed Jai on the neck. "Focus on the prize. Focus on the game. I know you've always done that, but you're in the fourth quarter. I remember how sad you were after you and Tara broke up for the final time. Even though you're over it now, and both of you are friends, I don't want my baby brother to lose sight of his dreams, especially since people like us have so few chances to chase them."

"My dreams are to help you and Gopal and Dad build the legacy Dad started."

"No, Jai," Neil said. "When Dad decided to buy this

store, and Gopal and I were in college for business, it was our collective dream. That was something we wanted to do. You were just a kid. And when you started to think for yourself, Columbia became your dream. Don't put more roadblocks in your way than you already have to get to your dreams. I'm going to say it one more time. Tara."

"Dude, Tara wasn't a roadblock."

"Uh, let's see. After you guys broke up, you were so distracted because you thought you were the problem that you almost missed your SATs."

"That doesn't mean Tara was the roadblock. She's a cool person, Neil. We just didn't work out."

Neil tapped his head. "But your relationship took your eye away from your one and only shot. Our family doesn't get second chances, Jai. Remember that."

Jai winced. The more he thought about it, the more Neil had a point. Radha could technically leave him in the dust, especially if her mother sent her back to Chicago. Winnie was surprisingly good at judging a person's character, Bollywood obsessions aside, and she had vouched for Radha as someone Jai could trust. But if he had feelings for the new girl … well, things could get super complicated.

Then there was the future. Even if something were

to happen between the two of them, what future would they have after school? Radha would go off somewhere while Jai would be working the night shift with Gopal. They were from two completely different worlds. She was an Audi-driving, pink-headphones-wearing, McMansion-living dance princess, while he was the son and brother of convenience-store owners living one town over from Princeton.

"Shit."

Neil shook his head. "Now you're getting it. Protect yourself, Brother. That's all I'm saying. And I'm telling you all this so I can protect you."

Jai nodded. "Thanks, bhai. I can always count on you to screw the mood."

"I'm here to help, kid."

When Jai returned to his seat next to Radha, she smiled at him. "Everything okay?"

He shifted his chair away and hated himself for the way she looked at him with confusion. "Yeah," he said as cheerfully as he could. "Yeah, it's fine. Uh, okay, how about we see what we need in terms of choreo for an intro, and then set up the regular practices with the team? We're going to have to bring the whole group together in, like, a week at the latest. Maybe we can start with Shakti and Hari on Monday since you've already danced with them, and we'll see how they feel first."

Her brows furrowed, and Jai felt like a tool. She pointed to her laptop screen.

"Okay. If that's what you want."

It wasn't, he thought. But, as with most things in his life, he didn't know if he had a choice.

Chapter Ten

Radha

Translation of Bimalpreet Chopra's Recipe Book

Suji Ka Halwa

New beginnings should always start with something sweet. A palmful of suji ka halwa and a prayer to Lord Ganesha will bless you with success.

Mix atta and ghee over medium heat. Stir until toasted to a golden brown.

Reduce flame to low and add boiled water. Pour in slowly to avoid lumps.

Increase heat to medium and stir until water is absorbed. Add sugar and cardamom until dissolved. Top with raisins and cashews.

RADHA: So my dad taught me how to make suji ka halwa yesterday in v-chat.

SIMRAN: How did it turn out?

RADHA: It tasted like flour.

SIMRAN: Ah. You just need to practice. Once you get the right combination of ghee, flour, and sugar, you'll be great.

RADHA: I'm super familiar with practice, but this is a whole different type of routine for me.

SIMRAN: And doesn't that make it all the more exciting?

After Radha left Jai's store, she knew something was wrong. That night, he didn't respond to her dumb dance-meme text message, and when she met with the senior dancers on Monday, he skipped the session. By Friday he'd sent her a total of five texts and had said hi only once to her in the hallway. Luckily, she'd connected with the seniors right away, so she didn't really need his help, but she'd thought they were ... well, friends. He was treating her like a total stranger now.

"I don't understand what I did wrong," she told Shakti.

Shakti sat on the floor of the studio they occupied and waved a water bottle around. "I've dated people with different gender identities, and even though noncommunication is universal, I still don't know how to deal with it. You're on your own, Radha."

"First, we're not dating. We're just friends. How do friends fix things?"

Shakti shook her head. "If I knew, I wouldn't be single right now."

"We're not dat— You know what? Never mind."

"Hey," Shakti said as she got to her feet. "Haven't you ever dated someone who decided to ghost you? What did you do in other situations?"

"Shakti, I've never dated, or been ghosted, or anything. I was in twenty-four/seven, three-sixty-five, competition mode for, like, most of my life, remember? No one wants to be a friend with that, let alone a boyfriend."

"Wow, super lame."

Radha rolled her eyes at her friend, even though Shakti was snickering. "You're the one who's going to pay with practice."

"Hit me with it," Shakti said with a laugh. "I have to be the best I can be. The Winter Showcase is really important. There are going to be a ton of recruiters there, and even if I don't get into a dance company, I want to know that I did my best to try."

Radha threw herself into refining the intro with Shakti for the rest of the day; then she spent hours in the kitchen that night cutting vegetables and learning knife skills to tamper her anxiety. By Monday she swore to herself that she wouldn't be awkward about Jai's sudden disinterest. Maybe he'd never liked her in the first place, and he was just being nice. He had called her a friend on more than one occasion. That meant she'd have to ignore him the same way he'd ignored her, even if he had been the first person she'd felt connected to since moving to Jersey.

She was still thinking about him when the halls cleared after last bell on Monday. Radha changed into her workout gear and hurried to their first two-hour practice. She was halfway there when she started to hear the thumping bass, and it only grew louder as she closed in on the practice studio.

"What in the holy Gita is going on?" Radha approached the door and peeked through the clear glass pane.

Jai, in the middle of a circle, surrounded by the male dancers on the team, was completely consumed in a freestyle bhangra party.

When she'd first met Jai, she'd thought he looked like a younger version of Ranveer Singh. Now she realized that he might look like Ranveer, but he danced like Hrithik Roshan. Not that Ranveer was a *bad* dancer. But Hrithik was … well, he was just better. Jai didn't have a stiff or inflexible bone in his body, and he appeared so carefree as he laughed with his friends. He looked so happy.

He was happy, while she'd been miserable and anxious for eight whole days. The pit in her stomach hardened.

She had to stop thinking about Jai. Channeling every guru she'd ever had, Radha watched the chaos in the studio. That was *not* how kathak dancers warmed up.

She was just about to enter when the door flew open and a familiar face smiled at her. "Are you just going to stand here all day?" Hari asked.

Radha scanned his workout gear and loved that his dastaar matched the accent colors on his shorts.

"Hari, you don't want me in there."

"Why is that?"

She patted him on the shoulder. "Because you're going

to be so sore by the time Shakti and I are done teaching you the intro of the routine."

"Radha!" Shakti said from the other side of the room. "You're here!"

The music cut off abruptly. Every head in the studio turned in her direction, including Jai's. He was breathing heavily, but he hadn't broken a sweat yet. His T-shirt stretched against his chest, and a little dampness had started forming at his collar.

"Hey," he said, the smile slipping from his face.

"Hey," she said. *You jerk.*

Someone nudged him in the arm, and he rolled his eyes before cupping his hands around his mouth.

"Team! This is Radha. She's the new student in our senior class, and for those of you who don't know her, she has a classical-dance background and will be choreographing our Winter Showcase routine. She's already started with the seniors, who are going to assist today."

The entire team called out hellos.

Radha laughed. "Uh, hi," she said. She scanned the expectant faces, waited for the few cheers to die down. She held up her tablet. "Jai, can you connect this to the speaker, please? I'd like to start with a warm-up track."

"Oh, we're warmed up."

"From what I saw, that was a circus, not a warm-up."

Hari made an "oooh" noise before Vik shushed him.

"Fine," Jai said. "We'll do it your way." He took the tablet from her.

Radha put her bag down at the front of the room, ignoring Jai's glances in her direction as he plugged her device into the speaker system.

He'd promised to help her with schoolwork, with getting through this choreography, but how could he if he was going to ignore her like she was contagious? Well, she wouldn't break *her* promise. She'd agreed to choreograph the Bollywood Beats dance routine, and she would. In the end, she'd still be able to get out of performing.

"I need two rows, seven dancers each row," she said, her voice echoing against the mirrored walls. "The seniors have heard this, but for everyone else: I learned kathak for, well, forever. I went back to India every summer starting when I was seven to take intensive classes. I attended a performing arts school in Chicago, and although I'm not as strong in other styles, I am familiar enough with them to choreograph."

I think.

"As for our concept," she continued, "who's attended an Indian wedding?"

Someone snorted. "This is central Jersey. Practically everyone in this school has been to at least one Indian wedding."

"Oh, shove it," Anita said from the right front, closest to the mirror. "Radha, you should give him the jumps at the thirty-second mark."

There was a round of laughter. Radha had to remember that Bollywood dance class wasn't as … strict as her kathak classes have been. The joking was not something she was used to, but she could adjust.

"You should've all received the music clip by now, and if you haven't, then do your best to keep up." She looked at Jai, who stood to the side. "To win the Winter Showcase, I'm going to use your strengths in this routine, but kathak is my strength, and you'll have to learn it, too. The elements of kathak we'll focus on are nritta, which is dance technique, and katha, which is story or the act of storytelling. The story we are telling is from the perspective of a bride, a groom, and two different families."

"We've mapped the intro already," Shakti added. "It's amazing."

"We'll teach the intro in hour two. First we'll do assessments. I need to know skill levels in this room to finish the routine. Ready?"

Thirteen heads nodded at her.

"Okay. I'll go first, and then I expect all of you, seniors included, to repeat what I did when we play the music again. Basically, what you'll hear is a group of bols, beats repeated three times. I'm going to use a mix of footwork and mudras, hand gestures with footwork."

She unzipped her sweatshirt, kicked off her flip-flops, and touched the floor with the tips of her fingers before pressing her hand against her chest. Dance was a prayer, and even when she wasn't wearing her ghungroos, it was important to her that the gods knew she was still honoring them. Normally, she'd do a full namaskar, but it didn't feel right just yet.

She took her place in the middle of the floor and viciously tamped down the bubbling anxiety in her throat. Nope, not a performance. Not an audition. Not anything but a demonstration to her peers.

The music began, and the familiar tabla beat centered her.

One two three four, one two three four.

Her feet slapped against the tile, and her hands moved in rhythm. Her chakkars were solid, one of her strengths, which was most likely why she felt stronger each time she spun.

She repeated the combination two more times, and when the music ended, she stopped and held her pose. The team clapped.

"I'll break it down for you all now," she said. "Jai, can you play it from the top? Let's see if we can do it together."

They faced the mirror, and after counting down, she watched in awe as the majority of the dancers were able to complete most of the moves she'd demonstrated. The tihai was not easy, but overall the team had so much more potential than she'd thought. Their last choreographer had been under-utilizing their skill.

"Okay, let's try something a little harder to warm up." She'd have to freestyle, but it would be worth it. They started again, and Radha showed a faster piece.

Half of the team was still able to keep up. If she'd been judging on technique, they wouldn't have scored that high, but they were able to move and follow along better than she'd expected. That in itself was mind-blowing.

"Let's add the two pieces together," she said. This time

when she stood in front of the room to lead the dancers, her eyes met Jai's through the mirror, and he gave her a thumbs-up. She nodded, and the track started over.

That was when Radha felt it again. The dance joy that had been so elusive. Happy expressions reflected in the wall mirror in front of her, and the moves that lay dormant inside slipped through like sunlight through opening blinds. Her muscles ached with a familiarity she'd always loved.

As the music ended, she was sure her dance joy would leave her again too, but when she faced her new students, it was still there. The joy was still inside her, and Radha wanted to cheer, because it had been so long since dance had made her happy.

"Hey, Radha?" one of the students said. "What if we add a little, I don't know, sex appeal to it too? Bollywood has a little bit more swagger."

The room echoed with laughter. Radha couldn't help but smile too. "We'll keep it simple for the warm-up, but let's see what we can do with the intro."

"From the top, Coach?" Jai said.

"From the top. Five, six, seven, eight!"

*

Class ended far too soon in Radha's opinion, but she could see that she'd exhausted most of the team. They were starting to stagger. T-shirts were removed, hair was tied, water bottles were emptied.

They'd start again tomorrow, though. Radha couldn't wait.

Jai walked over with her tablet. "Great practice. Do you have an idea of skill level now?"

"Some, but I'd appreciate a little more insight into individual dancers."

"Okay." Was he offering to help her? Maybe she'd been reading into things. "I'm sure Shakti wouldn't mind helping."

"Shakti?"

"Yeah," he said. "I mean, I'd do it, but I have the store, and a few quizzes coming up."

She definitely had not been reading into his cold-shoulder routine after all. The words were out of her mouth before she could stop herself. "Are you sure school and your store are all that's stopping you?"

He looked away. "What do you mean?"

"I mean, one minute you're texting me every day and promising that we're working on this together, and the next you can't get rid of me fast enough. If you don't want to, I don't know, hang out with me anymore, or want me to choreograph, then just say so."

Before Jai could respond, Shakti called Radha's name. "Are we on for free period tomorrow? Maybe we can talk about the stage entrance?"

"Sure, that works for me."

Before she could ask Jai to wait, he was already using Shakti's interference as an excuse to escape. "I have to go to work. See you guys later." Jai saluted a few other dancers but never once looked back.

"Radha?" Shakti said.

"What? Yeah."

Shakti's lips quirked. "I was just going to ask you if you were planning on going to the Diwali festival this Saturday."

"The what?"

"The Diwali festival! Most of us go because our parents are part of the Indian American Coalition of Central New Jersey. The group hosts a big party with the Princeton University South Asian Students Association. Diwali is in a couple weeks, so this weekend is supposed to start the festivities. You should come!"

"Oh," Radha said. "Uh, yeah. Let me think about it. I don't think I've ever gone to a Diwali festival unless I was performing, so I don't know if it's going to be my thing."

Shakti's eyes widened. "You're kidding. You've never actually celebrated Diwali? I feel like you've missed so much."

"Well, we do the puja thing at home, and my mother usually buys me new pajamas, but the Diwali season was always about heritage-event competitions. And my father, well, he was always cooking for Diwali parties at the restaurant…"

Shakti snorted. "Yeah, my dad runs a restaurant too, remember? No excuse."

"Your dad doesn't run an Indian restaurant, Shakti."

"Yeah, which is why it's fun that he's way into it. He went to his first Diwali celebration when he started dating my mom, or so I'm told. He hasn't stopped celebrating since. I feel like you could be the same way."

"Getting really into a Diwali celebration? Yeah, I doubt it, but hey, stranger things have happened to me lately."

Shakti and Radha waved at the lingering dancers and left the studio for the parking lot.

"You know," Shakti said, "I'm really surprised that Jai didn't invite you. He's going with his family this year."

"He is?" The pang hurt more viciously than she'd expected.

Shakti seemed oblivious to her feelings as they continued walking. "Maybe he's seeing his ex-girlfriend again. She'll definitely be at the Diwali festival."

"Ex-girlfriend?"

"Oh yeah. Tara. Don't let her first impression turn you off. She's actually really nice. I've known her for years because our parents are friendly. She leads the Bollywood dance team at Rutgers High."

Holy Vishnu. Jai had dated the *competition.*

She felt like such a fool. She had talked to him about how Rutgers High had a better team, and he hadn't said anything.

That was definitely the nail in the coffin.

"Thanks for the invite," she said. "I don't know if I'll go, but I'll keep you posted."

"Sounds like a plan. See you tomorrow, Radha!"

"See ya." Radha slipped into her mother's Audi, which she'd borrowed for the day, and headed home. The whole way, she wondered why she'd been so stupid about a boy. She'd started to like Jai – really, really like him. She was such an idiot.

Chapter Eleven

Jai

To: JMuza@PAAS.edu
From: JPBollywoodBeats@gmail.com
Subject: School list

Hey, Masi,

I know exactly what you're doing, but because you're doing it out of love, I'll go along with it. Here is a list of the schools that I'd apply to IF AND ONLY IF MY LIFE WERE DIFFERENT AND I HAD MONEY.

Totally a hypothetical list. Columbia, my number one school and Nana Veeru's favorite, is so expensive that even if I got a scholarship, and had some money set aside, I would still have to take out student loans to afford it.

Which is why I refuse to send out applications.

Also, I'm sorry it took me so long to get your father home last night. We were joyriding. He wanted to "talk," which basically meant that he spent his sweet ol' time lecturing me, and I had to keep circling your block until he was done.

Happy early Diwali from this desi boy to his Zimbabwean adopted masi.

Jai

Jai did not want to go to the Diwali party. It was an Indian association event, which meant that even if he was hanging with his friends, every aunty in a ten-mile radius would try to introduce him to their daughter. Either that or they would ask him where he was going to college, and that question was infinitely worse.

At least his friends would be there. And Tara. Maybe he'd ask her what he should do about Radha.

"My boys look so handsome," Jai's mother said. She brushed a hand down Jai's shoulder, smoothing the lines in his sherwani. She'd dressed up. Instead of her usual tracksuit or thrift-store jeans and a shirt, she'd put on a bright red-and-orange salwar kameez with her cherished gold wedding jewelry. Her short hair was styled, and the small amount of makeup she owned was judiciously used to highlight her happy lines.

"Can you please refrain from saying stuff like that when we get there, Mom?" Neil grumbled from the back seat. "It's embarrassing."

"Not as embarrassing as Gopal drooling all over himself," Jai said. He glanced in the rearview mirror to see his older brother snoring with his mouth open. He felt sorry for the guy. He worked the night shift, so he'd normally be sleeping for at least another hour.

"Neil, wake your brother up," his mother said. "*Gently.* I'm just so happy we all can celebrate together."

And there it was. The reason he was willing to put up with just about anything. Because of their schedules, they were never in the same place at once. It meant a lot to Mom to be together. They would've brought Dad with them, but he'd become agitated and upset when it was time to get ready. He was happier at home reading with the nurse tonight.

"Yo, drool-zilla. Get up, man."

"Neil! I said *gently.*"

"What? That is gentle."

Jai rolled his eyes at his older brothers, as he pulled into the parking lot of the Hyatt Regency. The Princeton South Asian Students Association banner was out front along with the Indian American Coalition of Central New Jersey flag. People wearing way too much jewelry and sparkly clothes were crowding into the hotel entrance.

"Let me check with the nurse one more time," Jai's mother said.

Jai listened as she made the call and talked to their regular caretaker. He heard the worried tone in his mother's voice as she asked for an update. A few minutes later, she hung up with tears in her eyes.

"Your father would've *loved* coming with you boys. He feels so unhappy at these events, though."

Jai held out his arms for a hug. "Don't worry, Mom. We'll take him out next weekend. All of us. We'll have Nana Veeru take over like tonight or shut down the store if we have to."

His mother leaned in for barely a second before pulling back, and patting Jai on the cheek. "You're a good boy, puttar. Your father would never let you shut down the store, and you know it. He's a stubborn mule. Like his sons. Now. Let's go have some fun tonight."

Jai shot his brothers a look before they walked under a storm-cloud-covered sky and entered the ballroom together.

"I'm going to get a drink," Gopal said after they'd gotten their entrance hand stamps.

"Gopal!"

"Nonalcoholic, Mom. I would never." He kissed her on the cheek and walked toward the bar.

"Oh, look," Neil said, motioning to a group of girls in the corner. "Someone has a question about store milk prices over there. I better go help them."

"Do your brothers think I immigrated here yesterday?" Jai's mother said after they'd left.

Jai laughed and looped an arm over her shoulder. "This is why I'm the smartest. Because I know that I can't fool you."

"No, my baby. You're my biggest idiot."

"Hey! What did I do?"

She reached up and pinched his chin. "You underestimate your own worth and skill. You got that from me. It's okay. I'm here to tell you when you're being foolish."

The doors behind them opened with a rush of air, and

Jai turned just in time to see Radha enter the banquet hall.

Her hair hung loose around her face and fell in curls to her waist. She wore a shimmery gold-and-black sleeveless anarkali with a Nehru collar. She was stunning in a classic, golden-age sort of way. But the bigger question was, why was she here?

"Jai?"

"Mm-hmm? Yeah?"

"Do you know her?" his mother asked.

"Who? Oh, *her*? Uh, yeah. She's Winnie's friend. Radha Chopra. She transferred to the academy. She's nice, you know, in that distant, we-don't-really-talk-because-I-never-talk-to-girls kind of way."

His mother tapped her fingers against her temple and pointed at him, palm up. "This is one of those moments, my baby, where you're being foolish. Go say hello."

"But I'm here with you. Didn't you want to spend some time together?"

"We're all here at the same time instead of at the house, or the store, or school. That makes me happy. Say hello to your friend, and then introduce her to me later. Acha?"

"If you're sure."

His mother was already walking away.

"Okay, then," he said, but by the time he left his mother's side, Radha was gone.

She'd seen him, though, hadn't she? But even so, he wouldn't expect her to wait for him. He'd been acting like a tool by avoiding her, and she knew it. The one thing that she didn't know was that his avoidance had become a necessity, because in the short amount of time he'd spent with her, it had become clear that he really liked her. Neil was right. Their lives were on two completely different paths. But man, he wished things were different.

Jai scanned the crowd and found her across the room meeting Shakti next to the buffet tables. Shakti wore bright lemon yellow and stood a head taller than most of the people in the room. She embraced Radha like they were long-lost friends.

He should go to them.

Before he could move, Jai felt a tap on his shoulder.

"Nice seeing you here," Tara said.

"Tara. Hey … I was just about to go find, uh, someone."

She gripped his arm just as he turned to walk away. "Hey! I literally came searching for you to see how you're doing."

"Sorry, it's just … a lot is going on."

"Why don't you talk to me about it? We haven't caught

up in forever."

"Sure." He looked over at Shakti and Radha one last time before focusing on Tara's face. Her eyelids mimicked a sunset and the colors matched her lehenga. She always looked like she was in portrait mode.

"So. Tara. How is school?"

"Great. I already submitted my college applications. We're finished with our routine, too, for our Winter Showcase. Did you guys find a choreographer?"

"Sort of," he said. "She's new to our school. A friend of Winnie's."

"Winnie Mehta? You mean the Bollywood girl who hates me?" Tara asked.

Jai smiled. "Yeah. Because you were a jerk to her when you guys first met."

She rolled her eyes. "Sorry. Can I help it if people don't bother getting to know the real me? I'm not a villain in anyone's story. And, in my defense, you had really pissed me off that day. Who tells a girl that you're going on a nice date, sees her in heels, and doesn't say anything about a carnival until he parks in a muddy field?"

Jai winced. "I had a lot on my mind that day too."

"Yeah, well, tell me something new."

The DJ transitioned into a fast-paced Bollywood dance number, and the lights dimmed in the banquet hall.

"Want to dance?" Tara asked. "Like old times. You missed the navratri garba a few weeks age, so you owe me one since I didn't have my partner."

Dance? No, he didn't really want to dance. Unfortunately, not dancing would hurt Tara's feelings. Jai looked over to where Shakti and Radha had been standing. They were no longer there.

"Jai!" Tara shrieked. She grabbed his hand. "One dance?"

"Yeah. Sure. Like old times."

"Just like old times." She shimmied as her full lehenga skirt billowed around her in a swirl of pink and lime green. They stepped onto the large parquet platform with a handful of other people. The music changed again, and even though he went through the moves with her, something didn't feel right. Jai felt out of sync.

"Come on!" Tara said, and moved in closer.

He tried. He spun her until they were chest to chest, but even with the familiar moves, he just wasn't into it. He wanted to dance with Radha.

Tara wrapped around him, and when her fingers dipped into his hair at the base of his neck, he stopped moving and backed away off the floor. "I'm sorry," he said. "I can't do this."

After scanning the room, he found Radha and Shakti heading toward one of the bar stations. Jai squeezed between chairs and tables, cutting around clusters of curious aunties, until he intercepted them.

"Captain," Shakti said, when he stood in their path. She looked over his shoulder and raised an eyebrow. "Aren't you *busy?*"

"Hey. No, I'm not. Radha, do you have a minute to—"

"Jai? You got lost! Were you getting us drinks? They're over that way," Tara said as she stepped up next to him. She rested a hand on his shoulder. "Oh. Hey, Shakti."

"Hey, Tara," Shakti said. "How's it going?"

"Same old. My parents said they went to your dad's place the other day and loved the food. It's one of the best restaurants in town now."

"Thanks."

Tara turned to Radha, her smile slipping. Jai's stomach knotted. *Damn it, Tara,* he thought.

"I don't think you and I have met, but you do look … familiar."

Shakti motioned at Radha like she was on display. "Tara,

Jai's ex-girlfriend, meet Radha. Transfer student and brilliant choreographer. She's going to lead us to victory."

"Wait a minute," Tara said to Shakti. "Radha, you said?"

"She did," Radha replied. "And I'm standing right here."

"I see that," Tara said. "Sorry, I didn't mean to be rude. I know you from somewhere... Wait. Are you Radha Chopra? The kathak dancer? And your mom. Sujata Roy, right? You're kathak royalty."

Jai watched the color drain from Radha's face.

"Oh my God!" Tara clapped her hands together like a seal. "It is you. I take classical dance. Shakti and I started together, actually, before I moved from odissi to bharatanatyam and kathak. Your story is *everywhere*. You know, after the whole London thing."

"What London thing?" Shakti asked.

"Radha reached the semifinals and then she quit," Tara said. "Radha, there were so many rumors that you got disqual— Oh. Um, never mind."

"Disqualified?" Shakti asked. "Is that what you were trying to say? How?"

"Nope," Tara said, shaking her head. "I screwed up one of these meetings with Jai's friends once before.

I've learned my lesson. Your mother's affair with a judge is not my business."

Jai swore.

Radha took a step back.

"Tara," Shakti said with a sigh.

"What? She was representing Chicago. I have friends in Chicago who study kathak, and that's all they talked about. That she let the whole US down or something. I didn't believe it, though. I swear."

Jai couldn't control his shock. "Is that true?" It was all starting to make sense. She hadn't competed since January. She didn't want to go back to her dance school in Chicago. Her mother and her father had just gotten divorced. That explained the performance anxiety. The panic attacks. Not that anxiety was ever clearly the result of one thing, but her family situation was a pretty good reason to him.

Radha's expression cooled. "I was the last one to find out about my mother's relationship. That's when I left. But it was really great meeting you. Jai, for the last week, you haven't wanted me around. Now here's your excuse to tell the director that you want a new choreographer. And now I think I've enjoyed enough Diwali celebrations for one night. I'll see you at school, Shakti." She strode to the exit.

"Radha, wait." Shakti whirled on Tara. "Girl, we need to have a chat about women supporting women. That, or your timing."

"Ugh, that was bad. Honestly, I should just lead with my bitch face. It's less awkward for everyone."

Shakti turned on Jai and drilled a finger into his chest. "Go fix this, Captain. Now."

Jai didn't need to be told twice. He ran after his girl.

Jai didn't catch up to Radha until they were at the far end of the parking lot near her car. "Radha!" he shouted into the shadows. "Radha, hold up for a second." He raced ahead of her and blocked her path. The sky was darker, and rain clouds blocked the night sky.

"Oh, *now* you want to talk to me?"

Jai winced. "I deserve that."

Radha crossed her arms over her chest. "Well? Are you going to tell me that you want me off the team or not?"

"No, of course not. But why didn't you tell me what happened? We could've talked about it. I feel like I was blindsided back there."

"Tell you what, that my mother had an affair with

a judge she used to dance with when she was younger? Or that for every competition that I've ever danced in, I'm now thinking that my mother had a hand in my winning it, and I'm actually not that great a dancer after all?"

"You're a phenomenal dancer," he said, even as it began to drizzle. "You have to know that."

"No, Jai. No, I don't know it." She gripped the chuni draped over her shoulder with white-knuckled fists. "Now, every time I try, I fall apart. But it looks like I'm going to have to figure something out for the Winter Showcase."

"I didn't say you shouldn't choreograph anymore!" He'd never messed up this badly with someone, but all he wanted to do was comfort her, and nothing was going right. "Look, I'm sorry I haven't been around." His hands were disgustingly sweaty. He tucked them in the pockets of his sherwani. There was no way he was making sense.

Radha marched toward him. Her heels brought her closer to his height, which was enough to make him cower. "I've been competing for years, so I'm pretty smart when it comes to people. That's why when you first approached me with the whole 'hey, let's be friends, let's trust each other' thing, I believed you. Do you know how hard it was for me to say yes? I don't make friends easily, Jai. And then, after agreeing to this friendship, you totally blew me off!"

"We are friends. But we're so freaking different. I mean, look at you! You're like the Indian maharani, flush with cash money, while I'm … well, the court dancer in this situation, I guess. The cliché poor kid of immigrant parents."

"Are you serious?" she said, her eyes widening. A droplet clung to her lashes. "You dropped me like third-period French because my parents have money and you don't?"

"No, because there is a good chance you're going to graduate, go to college, and forget that we ever met! I'm stuck in New Jersey, Radha. We're here for ten more months together and then we're done."

"Who says I'm leaving New Jersey? Who says that we can't talk to each other after we graduate? Do I seem that shallow to you?"

"No, of course not—"

"Then *why*? I deserve the truth."

"Because I *like* you!" he shouted. "Because I like you and

I can't risk it. God, it was so selfish of me to treat you that way and not talk to you, but what else was I supposed to do? If I freak you out, then I screw my team over, because they lose a choreographer! So I tried to keep my distance, and I'm sorry, okay?"

He turned away from her stunned look. "My brother reminded me that, I don't know, I'm supposed to keep my eye on the goal. That I have so few shots, and if I get distracted... It's nothing to do with you. I was just—"

"A complete idiot," Radha said.

"I was? I was. Yes, of course. But you think I'm an idiot for the same reason I think I'm an idiot, right?"

Radha shielded her face from the steadily increasing drizzle. "This is absolutely ridiculous. I can't believe I like a guy who is as clueless as I am when it comes to relationships."

His brain fried, and before he could filter his thoughts, he blurted out, "You like me?"

Radha propped her hands on her hips. "How could you ghost me like that? I spent days wondering if you even wanted to be my friend. And then you danced with your ex in there, and I still want to be with you. For as long as this thing is, I don't know, a thing."

"Radha?"

"Yeah?"

"I'd like to kiss you."

"P-people don't go around *saying* things like that!"

"How would you know? You've spent your entire life dancing."

"Jai!"

He stepped toward her, swung her into a dip that would've made a Bollywood hero proud, and pressed his lips to hers. His head spun, but he held her close, even as Radha's hands wrapped around his neck. Jai sank deeper into the kiss, as the slight drizzle turned into a downpour.

And then his heroine ran.

Chapter Twelve

Radha

Translation of Bimalpreet Chopra's Recipe Book

Paneer

To create homemade paneer, you need a large pot,
a colander, whole milk, lemons, a cheesecloth,
and a lot of patience.

*Bring eight cups of milk to a boil over medium heat. Stir
frequently to avoid burning.*

*Add lemon juice and turn heat to low. Continue stirring
until solids form.*

Place colander in the sink, line it with cheesecloth, and pour in curds and liquid.

Rinse gently to remove lemon flavor.

Tie ends of cheesecloth together and squeeze out extra liquid. Hang to drain, then shape into a disk and chill.

FOUR MISSED MESSAGES

DAD: Hey, chutki. Just checking in on you. I talked to your mom and she said you were getting back into dance. Something about mtg your director who was pretty convincing? Either way, I hope you're happy. And I know Chicago isn't your favorite place, but maybe you'd want to visit me sometime.

SIMRAN: Hey!! I wanted to know how your paneer recipe turned out. Don't worry when you add lemon. Sometimes adding something that seems completely wrong can be a wonderful treat.

SHAKTI: I'm so sorry about Tara. For what it's

worth, she apologizes too. There is nothing between her and Jai anymore, and she wants you to know that she knows she stepped in it big-time. Also, if you ever want to talk, I'm here for you, dude.

JAI: I'm so sorry if I did something that you didn't like. You ran away pretty quickly, so I'll give you whatever space you need, but maybe when you're ready, we can talk?

Radha knew that she was a coward, but she'd never been in this particular situation before. When she finally stopped kissing Jai, she was soaked from the downpour.

Her heart was pounding so hard that it began to hurt, and she knew that the slicing pain was going to get worse. Without another word she rushed to her car, dove in, thanked God for keyless ignition, and peeled out of the parking lot.

By the time she pulled into the driveway, she was gasping for air, and her chest ached. Spots were starting to form in front of her eyes. Her hair frizzed around her ears, her outfit was damp, and she was trembling so hard from the cold. She hadn't experienced a panic attack this vicious before, and no matter how hard she concentrated, Radha couldn't get it under control.

Can't breathe, she thought. *Can't breathe.*

The tears started as she pushed into the house.

"M-Mom," she croaked. She sobbed, even as she heaved for more air. Her chest hurt so much. She was going to pass out. "M-Mom."

Her mother rushed into the foyer, her eyes widening. "Radha!"

She couldn't remember what happened after that. Radha sat on the tiled floor in the foyer, her back against the front door, while her mother held her rescue inhaler to her mouth. Sujata talked, made her count, made her use her stress techniques to clear her head, then held Radha while she cried.

It was almost an hour later when they climbed the stairs to her room.

"You know that you're supposed to carry an emergency inhaler now that you're dancing again," Sujata said. "Even when you're going to some party."

The inhaler. Right. Radha hadn't touched it since she arrived in New Jersey. Had refused to. She held her hands up as her mother pulled off her blouse. She was exhausted.

And she was scared. Jai was the first boy she'd kissed, other than a dancer in India when she was fourteen. It was amazing and terrifying all at the same time. And now she'd probably ruined it.

Radha stepped out of her lehenga and waited as her mother tugged a cotton nightie over her head. "Mom?"

"Yes?"

"I know you're mad at me, but do you, uh … do you think you can make an appointment for me? With a therapist? I think it's time."

Her mother's eyes softened. "Okay. First thing Monday morning."

"Thanks." She was ushered into the adjoining bath, where her mother helped her take off her jewelry, comb her tangled hair, and wash the remaining makeup off her face.

Radha didn't have the energy to protest when her mother tucked her into bed before nine and then turned off the light.

*

Radha couldn't have been asleep for long. Her head still ached a little, and her eyes were blurry as her vision cleared and she tried to read the time on her bedside clock.

Eleven. It was still dark outside, so she'd only been sleeping for two hours. Her body felt infinitely better, though. A little achy, but she could breathe more easily.

When she turned on the bedside light, she saw the glass of water and the emergency inhaler within arm's reach. Radha scrubbed a hand over her face and then got out of bed. She'd just go to the bathroom and climb back in bed.

That was when she heard Sujata raising her voice downstairs. Her mother rarely yelled, even when she was fuming mad at her. She could pee later, Radha thought, as she opened her bedroom door and started downstairs.

"It's as bad as when she was a kid, and you want me to send her to Chicago for Christmas break? No way. Did you know she made me sign this ridiculous agreement that I wouldn't ask her to perform? Then when I told her she had no choice and I was going to send her to live with you, she actually *fought* me on it because that's how badly she didn't want to go to Chicago."

"I blame you for that," her father's voice snapped through the speakerphone. "You keep pushing and pushing all the time. Now she doesn't want to visit me. I think her break is far enough in the future that she'll be ready."

"No way," her mother said. "For once, think about your daughter."

"I always think about my daughter! *You're* the one who has this twisted dance fantasy when she's made it clear she's not interested anymore! She can't rewrite your history, Sujata."

The voices were coming from the kitchen. With a sigh, Radha walked down the hallway. When her mother spotted her, she immediately switched off the speakerphone.

"Radha, is everything okay? You didn't sleep long. Do you want to go to the hospital?"

Radha held out a hand. Apparently, she'd have to do more emotional labor tonight that wasn't her own. "I'm fine. I want to talk to Dad."

"Later. We're discussing—"

"Christmas, I know. I'll talk to him."

With a grunt, Sujata passed the phone over. "Hi."

The gruff voice on the other end sounded tired. "Hi, chutki. Your mother just told me what happened. Want me to fly there? I have a couple friends in New Jersey. One of them is a doctor. We can get you checked out."

The fact that he was offering to leave his restaurant

to visit her had tears stinging her eyes. When was the last time her father had put her before his restaurant? He'd even stayed away the day she moved out.

And wow, wasn't that some negative stuff taking up her brain space? Therapy couldn't come fast enough, she thought. If she didn't figure out a way to process her emotions, her anxiety was going to keep getting harder to manage.

Radha cleared her throat. "You don't have to come. I'm okay. Just a lot of stress. Classes, my independent study, and this show that I'm choreographing a dance for."

Sujata's eyes narrowed at the mention of the show.

"Mom is going to find me a therapist. Cooking is helping, and I don't want to stop, but I think I need that therapy after all."

"Ah." Her father cleared his throat again. "Good. But if you need me, I'm here for you. Radha, I know I've always been busy, but I'll come."

"I know. I'm lucky you guys are so cool about therapy."

Her mother gave her a questioning look just as her father said, "Oh?"

"Yeah, my friend from school said her guidance counselor suggested therapy for her to manage her stress, and her mother said that she just needed to drink more water."

"Well, we're lucky that some of the friends we went to college with chose to pursue psychiatry," her father said. "Do you remember Uncle Vinod?"

"Isn't that one of your poker friends?"

"Yes, that's him. He has his own practice. Maybe he can teleconference with you if you want to talk to someone familiar until your mom connects with a therapist there?"

"I can wait a little while longer, but thanks."

"Okay, chutki. But remember, drinking water is always a good idea too."

"I'll keep that in mind, Dad."

"I'm glad you're okay."

The gap between them closed a little more.

"Happy early Diwali, Daddy," she said softly.

"Oh, yes, things are already festive here! I know that Diwali season was always busy growing up. You with your shows, me at the restaurant. But how about I teach you something special tomorrow to celebrate? We'll do a dessert. You and me."

"Sure, what is it?"

"Mango kulfi."

"Ice cream?"

Out of the corner of her eye she saw her mother

frown, but Radha was already thinking about how kulfi was made, and whether she saw it in her grandfather's notebook. "Is it one of Dada's recipes?"

"This is my recipe. You up for it?"

"Yeah. I love ice cream. Sounds like fun." The mention of food had her stomach rumbling. She stepped around her mother, who was still watching her like a hawk, and opened the fridge. "Maybe you'll have more time to teach me some of the harder recipes if … if I come for Christmas break. The most complicated things I've made are Maggi, paneer, and halwa."

"You mean it? You'd like to come home to visit?"

The idea that Chicago was still her home made her queasy. New Jersey was now her home. But, honestly, she had to put aside any thoughts of running into old dance-community members and see her father. It was important.

"I'll come visit. Don't worry about taking days off. I'll go to the restaurant with you. I've never done that before. Would that be okay?"

Her father cheered. "Of course! This makes me so happy. Send me your break schedule, and I'll send you a ticket, okay?"

"Sounds good. Talk to you soon, Dad."

"Bye, chutki."

She hung up and passed the phone to her mother. Then, without another word, she took out a small container of cubed paneer that she'd drained and dried, along with a small bowl filled with a mustard-yellow batter.

"I thought you didn't want to go back to Chicago ever," her mother said. "In fact, you've fought with me multiple times about this."

"I don't want to *move* back to Chicago, but Dad is there." She'd made fried paneer yesterday as an experiment with the air fryer. She hadn't planned on repeating the same recipe, but she was in a pink nightie on a Friday, and she'd just been kissed. Her circumstances called for fried cheese.

"Well, I don't think you should go, Radha."

"What? Mom, yesterday you were ready to send me back there permanently. Now that I am willing to visit, you've changed your mind?"

Sujata crossed her arms over her chest. "Your father doesn't have the time to watch you. This has become the best place for you until we can make sure you've learned how to manage your anxiety."

Giddiness danced in her stomach. She doubted her

mother would keep the same opinion for long, but it bought her some time. "I'm sure I'll be fine by the time I get on the plane for Christmas break. Besides, my biggest worry was seeing my old dance peers, and I'll definitely be staying away from them when I'm at Dad's house."

"Radha," her mother said with a sigh. "They never mattered."

It was true, Radha thought. The gossipmongers didn't matter. But being judged fairly for her skills, and not for her mother's affair, or even her mother's dance career, did. She couldn't say that, though. She'd already said too much to her mom.

Radha dropped the paneer cubes into the batter. "Want some?"

"Fried food? Radha. That doesn't give you enough energy to dance. Oh, wait, you're not dancing anyway, and you're throwing your performance career away for *Bollywood* dancing."

Radha rolled her eyes. "You make it sound like I'm giving up kathak and joining a circus. Which also wouldn't be a bad thing."

She set a single layer of coated paneer in the base of the air-fryer container. "What did you do when you were growing up in India? How could you avoid all this amazing food?"

"Easy," she said, and sat on one of the barstools. "I was dancing and was on a strict athlete's diet, pretty much the same as yours *should* be. When I came here, the comfort food from home wasn't that easy to find. At least until your father and I married."

"And he never made it for you?"

Radha's mother shook her head. "By then I was used to living without it. He made a few other things that I enjoyed, but trust me, our arranged marriage wasn't based on food."

She had a wistful smile on her face, and while she enjoyed her memories, which were probably few and far between, Radha sprayed the top of the paneer with cooking oil. After flipping on the machine, she leaned against the counter and wiped her hands.

"Why did you agree to marry each other?"

Her mother's forehead scrunched in confusion. "What do you mean?"

"You had nothing in common. Cooking and dance. They don't exactly make sense together, right?"

"My baby girl," Sujata said, reaching out to cup Radha's

cheek. "There were so many other factors that went into our marriage, and just as many that played a part in our separation. Cooking and dancing were the least of our problems. Sometimes, passions don't have to make sense together. Sometimes they just have to … exist."

Radha nodded, remembering the letter her father had sent her with the recipe notebook. If dance was no longer her passion, then she had to find another. It didn't have to make sense, though.

However, she was learning that dance was something she was still passionate about.

"I guess both you and Dad are inside me. Right?"

"Right."

As Radha checked on the paneer, her thoughts went to Jai. He existed in a space where dance was one of his passions, but so was biology. The only difference was that he knew which one he wanted to pursue professionally, and which one gave him joy. Radha was still clueless.

They sat in silence while Radha cleaned the bowls and the countertop. When the fryer finally beeped, Radha pulled out perfectly browned pieces of cheese.

"Yes!" she cheered. Her headache, the one that had lingered after her panic attack, was nearly gone.

Paneer was like a medicinal miracle. Well, except to vegans and lactose-intolerant people, she guessed.

One by one, she put the pieces on a plate.

"Baby girl, can I talk to you about something?"

Radha looked up at her mother from across the counter. "Yeah?"

"How would you feel if … if I started dating?"

"D-dating?" Okay, not what she expected her mother to say. "I don't exactly have hopes that you and Dad are going to get together again. I mean, after what happened, we have to move forward. Is there someone at work? Please, God, don't tell me it's your spin instructor."

Sujata chuckled. "No, definitely not. It's Tarun Bhosle. He—"

"Was a judge during London classics," Radha said, her jaw dropping. There it was. The feeling of betrayal. "He was the one who…"

"Yes. I've known him for years. We danced together."

"You told me, but are … Are you serious?"

Her mother nodded. "Tarun and I connected online prior to us even flying to London. I know you don't want to talk about it, but I would never date a judge for you to win. That was not what happened. You're the best.

You're a prodigy, a shining star in your generation. The whole kathak community knows you. You don't need anyone's help."

But she'd never know that for a fact, would she? That was what hurt the most, and what Radha couldn't get over. Now no one would know if she was truly the best.

"Is this guy in the US now?"

"No, we're long-distance. He writes me emails, and maybe I'll go see him after you're done with high school, but only if that's okay with you. I, uh, I already spoke to your father, and we're making peace with each other about it. But your opinion means the most to me."

If her opinion meant the most to Sujata, Radha thought, then her mother would listen to her when she spoke her mind. "Okay. I mean, if it makes you happy."

"He does," Radha's mother said. "We have shared history. And we're older now."

Radha snorted. "A *lot* older."

"Radha!"

"What?" She didn't know why she found it so funny, but Radha laughed. It wasn't like she could do anything about her mother's decision other than crack up about it. Also, maybe this guy would keep Sujata occupied long enough for Radha to finish her choreography for the Winter Showcase. It was probably selfish of her to think that way, but her mother needed to focus on more things than Radha and dance.

She picked up the plate with the fried paneer and put it on the kitchen island between them. "Mom? I'll give you my blessing if you do one thing."

Her mother's eyes brightened with hope. "Yes. Anything."

Radha picked up a paneer cube. "Eat this. The whole thing."

"Are you serious?"

Radha nodded. "And you can't spit it out."

Sujata glared but took the cube. She stared at it, disgusted, before taking a small bite. Her mouth moved as she chewed, and then her throat worked with a swallow.

"Happy?" she said.

"The whole thing."

Radha grinned at her mother's miserable expression.

"I'm only doing this because I care," Sujata said.

"And I'm only daring you so you'll remember how hard it is to make someone else happy. Hopefully, we don't have to do that for each other anymore. Want another?"

"No way."

Radha popped a cube in her mouth. "More for me. Now, about my trip to see Dad."

Chapter Thirteen

Jai

RADHA: Hey, I'm sorry I jilted you like that last night.

JAI: Are you okay? Did I do something wrong?

RADHA: No. You were awesome. You were great. I just panicked.

JAI: Yikes. The kiss was that bad?

RADHA: Lol. No, it was perfect.

JAI: So ... do you still feel the same?

RADHA: Yeah. You?

JAI: Yeah. I want to take you out. Like on a date.

RADHA: I'd like that too.

JAI: Awesome. How about tonight?

RADHA: Okay.

JAI: I'll pick you up. Radha? Wear something you can dance in.

Jai sent Radha a quick text that he was parked at the curb. She'd told him she'd come out to the car in case her mom was in the house.

He could respect that. At this point, he'd do whatever she asked. He hadn't been able to sleep, thinking he'd done something that had scared her. He'd played the kiss over and over in his head for hours, picking it apart. He dipped her, his mouth met hers, she kissed him back, it felt amazing, and then, in true Bollywood fashion, it began to rain. When he pulled away for a breath, she bolted.

No, that wasn't exactly true.

She went bug-eyed and then bolted. He'd barely backed up enough before she was speeding toward the exit.

It had taken all his willpower not to call her or text her a gazillion times. And then her text had come in. She'd said she wasn't going anywhere. She'd said she liked him back, and he trusted her. Radha was different.

She was also incredibly forgiving for the way that he'd kept her at a distance. He'd thought it was best for both of them, but really, it had only hurt her, and that was the last thing Jai wanted.

He heard the sound of a door opening and saw Radha appear in a pair of black jeans and an off-the-shoulder sweater. Her hair was in one of those high ponytails, and she wore ballroom heels. He'd never seen her in ballroom heels before.

Jai remembered just in time to get out of the car and open the passenger door for her.

"Hi," he said.

"Hi." She smiled shyly and slipped into the passenger seat.

Smooth, Jai. Really smooth. He rounded the hood and got in the driver's seat. "Uh, you look great."

"Thanks." She fumbled with the seat belt. "You said to wear something I can dance in. Is this okay?"

"You're perfect. I mean – you look perfect. Your clothes are perfect. And your shoes. Ballroom shoes, right? The weather's not bad, so your feet won't get cold. If they do, we can leave. Whenever you want. Hey, how about we get going?"

She smiled, her fingers twisting together with the nerves he felt. "Yeah. I think that's a good idea."

He merged onto the local roads that would take them straight to the downtown area. A full two minutes passed in silence before he blurted out, "I scared you."

"You didn't," she said. From the corner of his eye he saw

her hesitate, and he almost swallowed his tongue when she rested a hand on his knee. "You know I have attacks. Not scared at all. It was all in my head."

"Okay. So, hypothetically…" His pulse sped up. "If I, uh, kiss you good night. Would you be okay with that?"

She jerked her hand back, and he felt the ghost imprint of where she'd touched him.

"Hypothetically," she said, "I'd be okay with it. But if I panic again, I promise I won't run. My mom shoved my emergency inhaler in my bag, so I'll suck down a couple gulps and probably ask you to try again. Oh my God. I can't believe I said that. I'd ask you only if I haven't completely freaked you out."

"No, not at all. No freaking over here. I guess we're just going to have to get to the point where you're not … you know … panicking."

"Wait, how do you propose we do that?"

"Practice."

She gasped and let out a bubbling laugh.

It had been way too long since he'd heard her laugh, and even though they were new friends, he'd missed that sound.

"Come on. We're almost there."

They parked on Nassau Street, a couple of blocks from their final destination. Jai opened her door for her, then took a backpack from his trunk. He slung it onto his shoulder, ignoring the curious expression on her face. In an effort to distract her, and hopefully ease some of the tension in his shoulders, he clasped her hand in his and led her down the sidewalk. When she linked fingers with him, he felt the softness of her grip against his callused one.

He used to worry that Tara hated his calluses, but Radha wouldn't mind. He knew that.

They strolled a block and a half until they reached their destination: Princeton Burgers, one of the best downtown burgers-and-fries places. Jai led Radha to the counter and motioned to the extensive menu. "I know this is not exactly the same as all the awesome food you've been cooking, but I think you'll like it."

Radha smiled at him. "I'm not exactly an expert in fast food, but this looks pretty good."

He pointed to the first two options. "Honestly, basic is best. Either of those are my favorites but pick whatever you want. Oh, and the cheesy tots. And the milkshakes. I think we should get all three."

"That sounds pretty ambitious," she said, smiling up at him.

"We can handle it."

"Okay, well, then why don't you go first? I'll follow your lead."

He greeted the woman behind the counter. "Double bacon cheeseburger with cheesy tater tots and a chocolate ripple milkshake, please. To go."

"To go?" Radha asked. "We're not eating here?"

He shook his head. "But don't worry, we'll have a chance to sit."

"Okay, I'm curious now." She ordered a plain cheeseburger and tots with a vanilla shake. A few minutes later they carried their food out and started down the street again. She was quiet.

"What is it?"

"What is what?" she asked.

He nudged her arm. "I know you can't still be nervous. Are you?"

Under the dark skin of her cheeks, he could tell that she blushed. "I just keep waiting to see if you're going to ask me about what happened in January."

And there it was. The reason for the fidgeting, he thought.

"You don't have to talk about it if you don't want to."

She picked up a tater tot dipped in cheese. "What if I do?"

"Then I'll listen."

They turned a corner and entered an area the downtown used for outdoor movie nights. A projector was set up in the distance, and people were lounging on chairs and blankets on the grass. There was a parquet floor in front of the projector, bracketed by two speakers.

"Welcome," he said, "to Bollywood Movie Night!"

Radha's face lit up. "This is the film club's project, right? Winnie told me she used to do this when she was president."

"Every week. Tonight, the theme is best Bollywood couples' dances. We're watching two movies back to back."

"Two?" She gaped at him.

"Don't worry, they're abridged. We're not sitting through six hours of Hindi cinema."

"Ah, okay, that makes more sense."

Jai set down his backpack and handed her his food. In a few moments he had a blanket laid out. He helped her get comfortable on the grass next to him.

"Now," he said. The movie was starting, but they were far enough to the side that they could still have a conversation. "What were we talking about?"

Radha opened the lid of her tater tots container. "I keep waiting for you to tell me that because of my reputation, you don't want me to choreograph anymore. I know you said you weren't going to do that last night, but … I can't help it."

He cupped a hand under her chin. Her eyes met his.

"I'm not going to do anything. And neither is the team or the school. We can just pretend that the interaction with Tara didn't happen. You aren't completely powerless, Radha. You have the team supporting you now. A lot of people have your back."

Her expression became rueful. "That's what my therapists used to say."

"Well, they're right."

She twirled her straw in her milkshake. "Your ex. I couldn't help but think that on the surface, we have some similarities."

"Ha. You guys are nothing alike."

"Well, her outfit was definitely designer. She studied classical dance. And she's about my height and has my hair color."

"We're Indian. All of us have the same hair color. Black or brown."

"Fine, I'll give you that. But the money thing, and the classical-dance piece. You guys broke up ... what, a few months ago? Shakti said you were a little torn up over it. Then I told you I might be leaving the academy, and ... well. You stopped texting me."

The movie soundtrack blasted through the speakers as the hero entered the scene. Jai spared it a glance before turning to Radha. "I'm not going to lie. My brother reminded me that Tara and I didn't work out for a lot of reasons that you and I may not work out either."

"You could've just talked to me."

She said it with such frustration that Jai laughed. A couple on the next blanket over glared at him. He sent them a look of apology. "But you have to admit, Radha, that—"

"That, what, you're going to stay in New Jersey after high school and I'm going to end up wherever my parents decide to pay for my ticket? That we're going to dance, and you're going to become class valedictorian? That I'm going to keep learning how to cook and studying kathak while having no clue what to do with either, while you know exactly what you want to do but can't pursue your dreams? We're the *same,* Jai. The same."

Moved, he cupped her cheek, leaned in, and kissed her. Her lips were soft under his and tasted like mint. His pulse sped up, and then he was pulling back, giving her space.

"Okay?" he asked.

Her pupils were dilated, and she was breathing a little fast, but she nodded. "Okay."

They watched the movie in silence and shared their food, one delicious bite at a time. When they finished, Jai got up and tossed their garbage in the nearest receptacle.

He shifted closer to Radha so he could drape an arm over her shoulder. "I'm sorry," he said in her ear. "I know I said it already, but I'm sorry. For not texting you as much as I wanted to. For not showing up to practice with the seniors. For leaving you confused. I won't do it again. Just promise me something?"

Radha turned to him, their noses practically touching. "Yes."

"You'll talk to me about your stuff when you're ready. I'm not going to ask you before then."

She nodded, and then kissed his chin.

He was still grinning when the speakers crackled

and the first dance number started. A few people from the audience jumped up and started dancing. Others ascended to the parquet floor in front of the screen.

Jai stood and pulled Radha to her feet. "I promised you we'd dance," he said.

"Well, the stage looks a little crowded now."

"That's okay. We don't need it." They slipped farther into the shadows so they weren't blocking anyone's view. Under the canopy of a tree at the edge of the lawn, Jai slid a hand up the side of her body until it fit below her shoulder blade. His shoulders squared, and he looped her other hand around his neck.

"Try to keep up," he said with a wink.

"Oh," she said as she wrapped her right leg around his waist. "So that's how it is."

He danced with her to the music, and she moved her hips, then slipped in and out of his arms over and over again.

She fit him, he thought. She fit him like a perfect pair of dance shoes. Like the perfect music. Like the perfect partner. After she told some of her secrets, and he shared his own, he spun her in circles. He'd never done this silly, ridiculous thing before, where he felt compelled to dance with someone at movie night. But here they were, and he was truly happy.

When the music ended and the hero and heroine started a heated conversation on the screen, Jai wrapped his arms around her and kissed her like there was a chance that this was the last time they'd get to be together in this way.

Chapter Fourteen

Radha

Translation of Bimalpreet Chopra's Recipe Book

Aloo Tikki

You will need potatoes, red chilies, green chilies, coriander, cumin, chaat masala, ginger, grated onions, cornstarch, and oil for frying.

Cook the potatoes, let them completely cool, and add spices and all other ingredients. Shape into patties and fry on each side until golden brown.

Note: Make sure potatoes are completely dry and cold; otherwise, they can get gloopy. Coat in panko bread crumbs at the end to make crispy. (Dad suggests whole onions instead of grated onions, and Simran is convinced frying in ghee is better.)

RADHA: Hey, Dad, got the plane tickets. Thanks!

DAD: Good! Excited to see you, chutki. What are you making today?

RADHA: Well, after our disastrous attempt at making mango kulfi, I'm going to try something a little bit easier. Aloo tikki.

DAD: Technically, tikki is harder than kulfi. We talked about the onions, remember? Want to video-chat through it?

RADHA: Rain check on the chat. I talked to Simran last week, so I think I want to give it a go myself. If I need help, I can ask my … friend. I'm sort of seeing this boy.

DAD: Oh? Is he Punjabi?

RADHA: Holy Vishnu, Dad. I'll talk to you later. I have to meet my advisor.

DAD: That doesn't answer my question. What if he has horrible taste in food? What if he thinks salt is the only spice he needs?

DAD: ... Radha.

Radha knocked on the office door. When she heard the soft "come in," she entered Director Muza's domain. The woman sat like a queen behind a large wooden desk. Her dhuku was a crown that matched the bold print of her blouse. She had a couple leftover pipe-cleaner spiders hanging from the ceiling in memory of Halloween, and what looked like a pretty Diwali diya at the corner of her desk. Radha wondered if Jai had given that to her.

She inched forward, realizing that it was the first time in more than a month that they'd met in person, even though the director religiously checked in with her every few days.

"Director?"

"Yes, Radha. Goodness, is it the end of the day already? Please close the door and take a seat. We'll have a quick chat, and then you can head on over to your team practice."

Radha nodded and slipped into one of the chairs facing the desk. She put her backpack on the floor at her feet, and waited, hands clasped together.

The director typed something, then swiveled to face Radha. Her smile was kind. "You made it two whole months! We're already in early November, and I've heard nothing but good things about you from the teachers."

The slippery nerves in her stomach eased a little. "Thank you. I've been trying hard."

"Yes, I can see that. Your mother said that you might have some anxiety and sent me a note recently to inform your dance teachers about your emergency inhaler. They're all aware, as well as the school nurse. We're so sorry we didn't address that right away with your health questionnaire."

Radha barely controlled her eye roll. "I'm managing my anxiety. It didn't become a problem until early this year. Now it's my new normal. My mother is being a little careful."

"As she should. Now we will too. Regarding your general requirement courses, as your advisor I received a report of your grades. Solid B's and A's. Much better than your last year in Chicago."

"Yes, Director." She worked her butt off for her classes. Last night alone, she'd been up late practicing and then studying for a quiz. She had no choice. The last thing she was going to do was mess up her second chance with a bad grade.

The director watched her with steady assessment, as if knowing what was going through her head. Funny that she didn't make her nervous, Radha thought. Maybe she was able to deal with the stare down because of all her years in front of gurus who used to bark if she literally stepped out of line.

"Why don't we move on to your kathak independent study? Your paper is due at the end of the school year, but you're supposed to finish your preliminary research and present your topic soon. Have you decided yet?"

Radha reached in her bag for her tablet. "I, uh, think I want to look at kathak from an evolutionary perspective. How did it start, and how does it appear in mainstream media today? Like, we see so much of kathak in Bollywood dance."

The director nodded. "Good, that's very good. But remember. This is a thesis, with requirements for page count, bibliography, and properly cited sources. I need you to make a statement and provide evidence to prove that statement. What statement are you going to make about kathak's evolution? Do you think that, over the years, Bollywood has made a positive impact on kathak?"

She wanted to say yes. How could it not? Every time she danced in a studio with the Bollywood Beats team, she felt alive. She felt like everything she'd ever learned about her classical art form had renewed purpose. Radha felt like she had found purpose again too.

But that wasn't the right answer. No, she'd done papers on kathak before, and the years of theory classes were permanently burned into her brain.

"Kathak as an art form should be preserved the way it was intended to be studied."

"Why?"

"Because it's a classical art. Like ballet, or the Viennese waltz. Kathak has mythology, and history, and tons of theory. It's beautiful in its pure form."

"And so it shouldn't be affected by evolution?"

"Well ... no," Radha said. *Yes*, she thought.

The director stared at her, and the only sound between them was the gentle ticking of the wall clock.

"I'd like for you to see a show," she finally said.

"A show?" *Not a kathak show – please, not a kathak show,* she thought.

"There is a Bollywood dance symposium at NYU." The director grabbed a sticky note off the corner of her desk and scribbled something on it. "Here. If you can make it, I recommend attending. You can use it as a source for your paper. If you're unable to attend, we'll figure something else out."

Radha looked at the words on the bright square piece of paper. The director wanted her to see a Bollywood show, not a kathak performance.

Her brain was in overdrive.

Paralysis by analysis, her new therapist had said. Radha had to break that cycle of thinking; otherwise, she was never going to deal with the anxiety.

"Radha?"

"Yes, Director. I'll attend the Bollywood show."

"Good. And if after that you truly believe that kathak needs to be preserved, I'd like your draft thesis statement and a list of research texts you'll use by the end of November. Okay?"

"Yes, Director."

"Good." Director Muza leaned back in her leather chair and crossed her arms. "Now. I had one more thing I wanted to talk to you about that's part of your grade. The second independent study."

"Are you talking about the Bollywood Beats choreography?"

"I am. How is the routine coming along?"

"Really good, Director." She smiled, thinking about how much she looked forward to rehearsals.

"Really?"

"Yes. Actually, Jai and I were talking about having you come and visit one of the practices if you have some time. We're almost done with teaching the routine. The art department is going to help us with some of the props and the backdrop."

The director picked up a pen and wrote something down on the desk calendar in front of her. "Next week?"

"Uh, sure."

"Good. I'll send you both an email about your schedule."

Radha nodded and put her tablet in her book bag. She stood and was ready to leave the office when the director motioned for her to sit down again.

"There is one last thing. College applications are due within a week if you're applying Early Decision. Your letters of recommendation – have you talked to any of your former teachers? Do you have them lined up yet?"

Radha shook her head. "I-I don't know where I'd even go to college, or what I want to do. I wrote an application essay as an English class assignment, but college ... I'm sorry."

The director leaned forward, tapping the table between them. "There is absolutely no need to apologize. Or to look so terrified of me, Radha. Sometimes college isn't for everyone. If you don't want to go, then no one at the academy is forcing you to. My nephew is also undecided."

She was talking about Jai, Radha realized. The director probably didn't even know how close Radha was to her adopted family.

"Director, I want to go to college, but I just haven't really thought about when and which one. I feel like I need to know what I want to do first, but every time I sit down to figure that out, I feel overwhelmed. I thought that maybe I'd just get through one day at a time first."

Jai was one of the rare ones who knew exactly what he wanted to do. He'd finally told her that his dream school was Columbia. His voice pitched low, like it was his dirty secret. In the two weeks they'd been dating, she'd learned about how he'd inhaled medical journals with his nana and father when they were in rehab. How he used to study abnormalities and knew all these random facts. He subscribed to every Reddit group about dance injuries.

Jai should be thinking about college, not her.

"Why don't you come and talk to me when you're

ready?" the director finally said.

"Okay. Director, maybe I could wait until after the Winter Showcase to make my decision?" Hopefully her feelings about dance would magically clear up by then too.

"Absolutely. Just know that I'm here to help if you need it."

"Thank you."

"And don't forget to schedule an appointment with me after the Bollywood show in New York. If you don't go, then meet with me when you have your thesis statement ready."

"Okay." Radha picked up her bag and was halfway to the door when she decided to shoot her shot. "Director?"

"Yes?"

"I have a question. It's personal. About Jai."

She hadn't thought she'd ever see the composed head of the dance department look surprised. "What about Jai?"

"Well, we're dating, and he told me how close you are, and how you're the reason he started dancing in the first place."

The director's surprise intensified. "He told you?"

"Yes, ma'am. He also told me about Columbia, and I

know we shouldn't be talking about him behind his back, but do you know if there is anything I can do to help?"

The director sighed. "I'm sorry, Radha. I can't discuss another student with you. Confidentiality reasons."

"Yes, Director. Maybe just a yes-or-no answer then?"

The director sighed again.

"I'm going to take that as a yes. If a student has money issues, is there a scholarship connected to the academy? Funds that could help for other stuff outside of tuition?"

The director shook her head. "Not that I know of, but I like what you're thinking. There may be private grants or scholarships for this sort of thing. But, Radha, a student would have to send those applications on his own. He would have to take the initiative. More importantly, if the student is your friend, I think your position is to support whatever he decides."

"Really?" She took a step back. "But I agree with you that he needs to go to Columbia."

The director shook her head. "This *student's* family and I appreciate the help. But I know that if you don't support him, it'll do more harm than good."

Radha nodded. The director had known Jai longer than she had. The last thing she'd want to do was hurt him.

"Well, I hope he changes his mind."

"Me too."

Radha adjusted her backpack again and waved one last time before closing the office door behind her. She'd support Jai just like the director had recommended, but it wouldn't hurt for her to research grants or funding opportunities. There were also, of course, grants for business expansion. If she couldn't find money for Jai, there was always the chance she could find money for his brothers.

She was striding down the dance wing when she saw Jai walking toward her.

"Hey!" she said.

He grinned. "Hey yourself. You finished your meeting with the director?"

"I did. She's coming to see us next week."

Jai leaned down and pressed a kiss against her cheek. "Awesome. I was headed to the vending machines to grab a snack before you put us through the wringer. Want to walk?"

"Oh, I actually bought some aloo tikkis with me. I know you said you wanted to try them if I got around to making them."

His eyes widened. "Yes. You are seriously the best girlfriend ever."

"I feel like the bar is set really low."

"Or maybe I just think that everything you do is fantastic."

Radha wrapped an arm around his waist as they walked together. She'd help him, she thought. She'd do everything she could to figure out a way to make sure he was happy.

Chapter Fifteen

Jai

To: JMuza@PAAS.edu
From: JPBollywoodBeats@gmail.com
Subject: Bollywood Beats status update

Masi,

We're ready for you on Tuesday. Also, no matter how many times you call my mom, or tell Nana Veeru to try to convince me to apply to college, I'm not changing my mind.

Jai waited for Radha to give the cue.

"I know we've done this a few times already," Radha said from her spot next to the director, "but it's the first time the director is watching, so energy up, please."

She lifted a hand in the air and counted down.

"Five, six, seven, eight!"

The music began, and Jai swaggered forward to the rough-cut dialogue that started their skit. Shakti met him halfway across the studio floor. They moved together, mirroring each other, and then backed up, before running in slow motion toward each other again.

He heard the director laugh. Yes, he thought. Jai picked Shakti up, and she tossed her head back, arms widespread.

The music changed again, and Radha cued everyone for a second time. The lyrics were about a family pressuring the bride into accepting the groom's proposal. The team circled them, left, then right, and then everyone except for him and Shakti faced front.

Their feet slapped against the floor, echoing together in rhythm. Backs straight, shoulders dropped, heel-toe, heel-toe.

Then the team circled again, this time with more speed. Shakti spun counterclockwise, while Jai anchored her.

"And … stop!" Radha said. Everyone froze at the exact moment the music changed.

Dancers raced offstage and then four reentered, their hands graceful. Shakti moved to perform the narrative piece, where she acted as if she were serving tea. The dancers portraying fathers stepped to stage left and faced off while the mothers did the same to the right. Jai continued to count sixteen beats in his head as he danced with Shakti in the middle.

He kept getting distracted by her expression. She looked stressed and was already starting to sweat. She could barely keep up, but she was the only other person on the team who'd even had a chance to memorize Radha's choreography for the lead. Jai didn't have too many complicated steps as the groom, but Shakti was onstage for most of the performance.

She missed a step, then two, before she said to Radha, "I need to stop for a second."

"Everyone, keep going! Shakti, switch with me."

Shakti stepped aside, and Jai's arms were instantly filled with Radha. She smiled up at him, taking over the bride's role for the rest of the eight minutes they'd choreographed.

Radha moved with an effortless grace that elevated his performance and every dancer's performance in the room. She had an energy that fed the beating heart. She glowed as she finished the scene; then, while she crossed the floor with him, she called the next cue.

This was what she was meant to do, Jai thought. She always appeared confident to him, but she was on a whole different level when she danced.

Radha counted down again. "Final push! Shakti, switch with me."

Jai waited for the music to change, and then he stepped into the organized formation with the entire dance team. There was so much floor work that Jai's knees ached from sliding across the hardwood and then jumping up again, but he kept going until the piece stopped.

When the music ended, Radha called time, and everyone cheered and clapped.

"We haven't reached the climax of the song yet," Shakti said, heaving for air. "I'm never going to make it."

"We just need more practice," Jai replied. He watched as Director Muza leaned in to speak in Radha's ear. She nodded and then shook her head. They spoke with animated hands and in tones he couldn't quite understand.

"Hey," Shakti said, quieter this time. She was still out of breath, but her words were more discernible. "I feel like I'm letting everyone down."

Jai squeezed her shoulder. "You can do this. If Radha and I have faith, you have to believe too."

Shakti's brows furrowed. "Are you sure? I mean, Radha makes it seem so easy."

"That's because she choreographed it. You'll kill it. I know you will. Just give it time. We still have a couple months before the showcase."

Shakti nodded. "I need to nail this for the dance scouts."

"I know. You will. We good?"

"Yeah," she said. "We're good."

She tapped his shoulder lightly with her fist and waved to Radha before grabbing her things. She, along with some of the other team members, were already saying their goodbyes and leaving for the night.

Jai walked to Masi and Radha, who were still talking in hushed tones.

"... There isn't enough transition time at around the two-minute mark. Switch the style up if you can."

"If I show too much variation during that scene, then the reception is going to look dull in comparison."

"It won't. If you don't build up that part of the routine, it's going to be disjointed."

"Okay, I'll talk to the team tomorrow," Radha said.

"Great. You're doing fantastic."

"She's awesome, isn't she?" Jai said as he bumped

Masi's shoulder.

"She is, even if the dancer playing the groom has heavy feet."

"Hey!"

"It's true, you have heavy feet," Radha said with a shrug.

Vik and Hari said her name from across the room.

"I'll be right back, Director. Franken-foot."

Jai grinned as Radha walked away to correct Vik's and Hari's form.

"You know, I thought that since she'd been out of classical dance for most of the year, she'd need a lot more training to get back up to speed," the director said. "This has been good for her."

"It was fate," Jai replied. "We needed a choreographer, and Radha joined the school at the right time. I don't think the team ever really had this kind of chemistry before. Payal would just tell us what to do without modifying anything to skill level. Her stuff was also much easier than this, so I feel like we were bored by the time the Winter Showcase came up."

The director sighed, and Jai faced her.

"That sigh, Masi. I know that sigh. Why are you sighing?"

She shook her head. "What you and Radha are trying to accomplish is inspiring. You're chasing your dreams, and that's what I want not only from my students but from my adopted nephew. I think Bollywood Beats has a fifty-fifty chance of winning the showcase."

His jaw fell open. "That's it? After all we've done? Is that sugarcoating for we're still terrible?"

The director took his hands in hers. "When have you ever known me to sugarcoat?"

"True, but I feel like there is something you're not telling me."

She nodded. "You have a chance at winning the showcase, but ... I don't think you'll win regionals."

That hurt more than he'd expected. Although he was only focused on making Masi proud, on ending high school with a bang, he'd secretly hoped that winning regionals were a possibility. The window was small, true, but he was beginning to believe it was there. And with regionals came the hope for scholarship money.

Masi squeezed his shoulder. "It's not the choreography, or even most of the team, that'll cost you the prize."

"Wait, what?"

"Jai, I know you're not into sports, but for the sake

of discussion let's use a sports analogy. Right now? Bollywood Beats is benching their MVP."

"Our MVP? Oh … *Oh*."

Radha did three quick spins in the middle of the floor without even spotting.

"You want *her* to perform? No way. There is no way that I can convince her to dance."

"She's your key, though."

"No. She can't perform. She's finally feeling healthy again. She's enjoying classes now instead of being nervous that her anxiety is going to find her here too."

"Maybe performing is a way to address her fear," the director said softly.

"Why does she have to address her fear at all? I don't get why people say that. Why can't Radha do whatever she wants? I don't want to force her. That's really shitty, Masi."

"Radha's reasons are her own, but she is the key to winning. Shakti is a solid performer. But there is a distinct difference between Shakti's and Radha's abilities in this dance form. The whole studio felt alive when Radha was front and center. That's her power. If you want to guarantee your win, you have to convince that girl to be up on that stage with you. I don't see any other option."

There was no way he'd hurt Radha by putting her in that position. More important, she didn't care about winning. Sure, she wanted to help him with the showcase, but they hadn't even talked about the cash prize available if they won regionals.

Jai scrubbed his hands over his face. "I don't want to say anything. About what you think of the routine. Let me just get through the choreography first, and then—"

"Jai," Masi said, shaking her head. "As captain of the team, you have a responsibility to Radha and everyone else in the room to be honest with them. If you don't tell them, then as your advisor I will."

"Masi—"

"Their dance careers are affected too."

"Okay. Can I have some time? I want to tell them my way."

"Fine, but if you wait too long, I will speak to them myself." Masi patted his cheek. "You are a sweet boy for thinking of her and trying to protect her."

"Masi, we're in public."

She laughed. "Yes. And now for some more advice. I told Radha she has to go see a Bollywood show at NYU. She's going to examine how kathak may have transformed

Bollywood routines. Many different college Bollywood teams will be performing. I think you should go with her."

"Bollywood show, huh? I wonder if it's their annual dance showcase." It would give Radha the type of exposure that she needed to really understand what the competition would be like. As a choreographer only, of course.

"Showcase or not," Masi said, "it'll be good for both of you."

"I'm back," Radha said. She stepped between them and pushed a strand of hair out of her face. "Sorry about that."

"You have nothing to apologize for," the director said. She smiled at Radha and then squeezed Jai's shoulder. "I'm happy with what I've seen today. Keep up the good work. Let me know if you need anything from me when you start to finalize the number for the showcase."

"Thank you," Radha said.

The director exited the studio, her orthopedic shoes clipping against the floor, leaving silence in her wake. The other dancers had already deserted the studio. Radha and Jai were finally alone.

"So," Radha said. "What did I miss?"

"The director thinks I should go with you to the Bollywood show at NYU."

Radha's expression brightened. "You'd come with me?"

"Uh, yeah. As your official boy, though, I would expect you to ask me first."

"Expect, huh?" She looped her arms around his waist and tilted her head. "In that case, I have a date. And here I thought we should ask the whole team if they want to come."

"Seriously?"

"Yeah, why not? It'll be fun. Right?"

"Yeah. It'll be good for all of us."

Jai wanted to tell her about the director's prediction. The words were on the tip of his tongue. It was just that she looked so happy now. She used to have worry lines around her mouth, which he'd never noticed until he saw the difference between how she acted in class and how she laughed with him.

Jai pressed a kiss to her nose as he replayed Masi's words in his head. Regionals was his problem, not hers. He'd tell her about the director's prediction some other time.

"Jai?"

"Yeah?"

"You're staring."

"It's because you're so pretty," he said.

She laughed, and her cheeks darkened with a blush.

"Radha?"

"Yeah?"

He leaned in, heard her swift intake of breath, and pressed a kiss to the corner of her mouth. It was as soft as he remembered. Thoughts of regionals, his college applications, everything slipped out of his brain.

"Let's go for burgers," he said.

"Now? You want to go out?"

"Why, yes I do. Thank you for asking."

Radha laughed. "I have a quiz to study for."

"I'll help you. As long as you promise that I won't be late for my shift."

Her eyes sparkled as she linked her fingers with his. "I promise."

Chapter Sixteen

Radha

Translation of Bimalpreet Chopra's Recipe Book

Parantha Dough

To make parantha dough, you'll need:

Wheat flour
Water
A little ghee

Add water to the flour a half cup at a time, consistently kneading between applications. When it starts to come together, add palmfuls of water as needed to continue building pliability, and work the dough until it is soft.

Add ghee at the end to ensure an easily workable texture. Do not add salt. Let it rest for three hours under a damp cloth before use.

Dough can also be used for roti.

DAD: Ready for your parantha recipe tonight?

RADHA: What?? I thought you were busy?

DAD: I hired another chef for the dinner shift. I'm ready to go when you are!

RADHA: I can't. I'm going to NYC with some friends. Tomorrow?

DAD: Do these friends include that boy?

RADHA: He's one of them, and DON'T TELL MOM. I haven't told her yet.

DAD: Chutki. I was married to her for almost twenty years. I have no intention of telling her anything that could get me killed.

RADHA: Well, that's comforting.

DAD: Want to make paranthas tomorrow? For breakfast. Exactly when paranthas are supposed to be eaten. Get some potatoes. We'll make stuffing for it, too.

RADHA: Can I use the same potato mix I make for tikkis for aloo paranthas?

DAD: Oh. Yeah. You can. I didn't even realize that.

Radha put her phone back in her cross-body bag. "I'm making paranthas with my father tomorrow," she said to Shakti.

"Wow, that sounds awesome. You talk to him at least once or twice a week now, right?"

"Yup."

"Do you think it's because he's trying to make up time? You know, for all the years you guys didn't spend in the kitchen. I know you said that when you were performing you weren't that close."

"I don't know. I can tell you that now, things feel different. They feel right. I even told him about Jai, and I've never felt close enough to tell him things like that before. My mom has no clue yet, and I always used to tell her stuff first."

Shakti pulled her legs up onto the torn leather seat and tucked her chin over her knees. "Do you think she'd be mad?"

"Mad?"

"Yeah," Shakti said. "These days you never know with Indian moms. It's like they're on a dating spectrum. Some moms are totally cool with dating – they even slip a twenty and a packet of gum in your purse before you go out on a date. Then you have the other moms, who may have grown up in the States, who are still horrified that boys exist before marital age. Those moms are still flabbergasted that bi people like me exist. I can't imagine what a mom with a disciplined dance career like yours would be like."

"Ah. Honestly? I have no idea how she's going to react. My best guess is that Sujata would have a meltdown, but not because I was seeing a boy or anything. She'd probably be mad at how it's interfering with my dance, or with classes."

Radha turned in her seat. Jai sat a few rows behind her in the train car. He was surrounded by his friends, laughing at something Hari had said. He must have felt her staring and looked up.

There was that easy smile that spread into a grin.

And if she wasn't in love with him already, she was halfway there, Radha thought.

Jai winked at her before returning to his conversation.

Shakti tugged Radha's hand until she leaned forward. "Have you hooked up yet?"

"Oh my God. Shakti!"

"Don't play the prude with me. Remember, I'm the one who taught you on Monday how to use red lipstick to hide hickeys on dark brown skin. As your wing woman, I want to know if you've run the bases. Done the deed. Gone all the way, as my mother said in her sex talk."

"You promised you'd never bring up the hickey thing again." Like she needed to be reminded of that mortifying experience. Thankfully, she had friends now who could help. Nosy friends, but they were still amazing. "Jai and I are dating."

"Yes, this has been established over the last few weeks."

"And that's it. Dating him is better than I ever, I don't know, pictured it could be."

"You didn't do it yet," Shakti said, shaking her head.

Radha laughed and put her feet up on the empty bench seat next to Shakti. "Can I ask you a question?"

"Sure."

"Was he like this with Tara?"

"Oh no," Shakti said, forming an X with her fingers. "I am not going there at all."

"Why not?"

"Because trying to compare yourself to an ex is bad, Radha. You are a beautiful, unique person who is at a different point in Jai's life."

"You need to stop watching TED Talks," Radha said. "I'm just curious. Sometimes when I want to talk about after high school, he closes up on me, changes the subject, anything. I just think that maybe the people he dated had something to do with the way he treats the subject with me."

There was sympathy in Shakti's eyes, and Radha hated that it was there. She didn't want to think that there was something about Tara that made him happy, that she couldn't do. "Give me something."

"Fine," Shakti said. She looked over Radha's shoulders and then leaned in. "Tara and Jai didn't connect the way you two do, which is why they're way better as friends. He was always, I don't know, *surface* Jai with everybody I've ever seen him with. But now? He's something more. As for his future … well, you probably know about that more than anyone. He doesn't talk to us, either."

"You promise me you're not just saying that?"

Shakti nodded. Her large hoops brushed her shoulders. "I mean it. And if it makes you feel any better, Tara keeps texting me, asking me to call her about something that she, like, can't text. Apparently, she texted Jai and he's ignoring her."

"I mean, that's rude, but a small part of me is okay with it too."

The train screeched to a halt, and static echoed through the intercom. "We're stopping here for a moment, folks," the conductor's voice said. "Once the train in front of us clears the platform at Jersey Avenue, we'll be moving again."

"Ugh, we're going to be stuck on this train forever," Shakti said.

As soon as she said the words, the familiar opening bars of "Chaiya Chaiya" burst through the car.

Simon, one of the freshmen, was holding up a speaker the size of his palm over his head.

"Ohhhhh, damn!" Shakti shouted.

Radha's jaw dropped as her team cheered and started dancing. They began to move into the aisles, ignoring the fact that they were on New Jersey Transit. Jai grabbed the metal rack overhead and vaulted forward, moving swiftly toward her.

"Nope, not happening, not gonna— Jai!"

He dipped her in the center aisle before spinning her

out. One of the other team members grabbed her by the waist and lifted her up. She laughed, dizzy with spinning and moving from one partner to the next.

Then the chorus began, and everyone moved in unison.

Radha hadn't lived under a rock. She knew the steps just like everyone else. She laughed when she realized one of the most famous train songs in Bollywood history was playing, and she was on a train with a group of people who had the choreography down.

Somehow Radha ended up near Jai, and they took the lead.

"Shah Rukh Khan has nothing on you two!" Shakti yelled.

Radha had to agree. As the music continued to echo from the small speaker, and the train car rocked from the force of everyone jumping, Radha felt dance joy grow inside her. It came all the time now, whenever she was with the team. When the music started to fade, Radha wrapped her arms around Jai, squeezing him with all her strength. He squeezed her back with the same force.

She hoped that she could always see him this happy, and held on as long as she could.

*

The Bollywood Beats dance team found seats in the middle of the NYU auditorium. When the curtains opened and the lights dimmed, Radha squeezed Jai's hand. Countless performances flashed in front of her eyes. Thankfully, the setting was where the similarities ended. This was nothing like a classical-dance competition. There were cheers and whistles from the audience. Some had even brought signs.

And the dances. If this was the caliber that her team had to be in order to win, then Radha was on the right track.

By the end of the show, she was bursting with ideas of how to tweak the routine. With a final wave to her team, she turned to Jai in the small lobby alcove. "That was amazing. I know we're here for my independent study, but there is so much more we could do that I didn't even think of! I'm talking a lot. I'm a little hyper. I need to calm down before we meet Winnie and Dev for dinner."

Jai laughed. "Well, you don't have long. Winnie said she'd meet us here in a minute." He peered over the crowd.

Radha spotted Winnie first. Her childhood family friend stood in a pair of ripped jeans, a leather jacket, and Converses that had … was that Shah Rukh Khan's face all over a white background? Her French braid swung in a perfect Bollywood-heroine-like arc.

"Hey, guys!" Winnie threw her arms around Radha first.

The hug felt right. Even though she and Winnie would go months, sometimes a year without talking, Winnie always welcomed Radha with open arms. Sometimes literally.

The guy she assumed was Dev stood behind her.

"Hey," he said. "How's it going? Radha, right?"

"Yes. It's nice to finally meet you."

He nodded, then looked over her shoulder at Jai. His polite smile morphed into a grin. "What up!" He then opened his arms just like Winnie had, and Jai hugged him the same way Radha had responded.

"Totally unnecessary," Winnie replied, even though she was laughing.

"Oh, you want one too? Okay," Jai said, and he picked Winnie up and spun her in two quick circles.

Their relationship was close, Radha thought as she watched the three friends embrace. But that was okay. She was making her own lasting friendships now, and they were just as amazing as what Jai had with Winnie and Dev. Hopefully, one day her connection with them would be as strong.

"I can't believe you got away from the store on a Saturday, man," Dev said. "Did your brothers hire some more help?"

"No, but Nana Veeru is there. My dad wanted to go stay with him during the shift, but God knows what trouble they would've gotten into together."

"They're both doing great?" Winnie asked. "Healthy?"

"Both are fine. I haven't been on the same shift as Nana for a while, but my brothers told me he's been acting a little funky, so this may be the last time we let him get away with being on his own." Jai shrugged. "But that's probably more than you wanted to know."

Winnie squeezed his arm. "I *always* want to know. You can tell us the rest of the stuff that's going on at the store when we're at dinner," Winnie said. "The restaurant is just a few blocks away. I hope you like it. Dev and I are obsessed."

"Radha? Radha Chopra?"

Radha whirled at the sound of her name. An older woman with dark black eyeliner and a large red bindi stood in the distance, padfolio in hand. She wore a sari, and her hair had a severe part down the middle with frizzy waves that fell to her waist.

Oh my God.

"Didi," Radha said. The respectful term she'd used for her dance instructor was out of her mouth before she could even think about her response. Radha approached Guru Nandani Modi, professor and celebrated kathak dance instructor, and bent to touch her feet. She had gone to India and sweated through classes at Guru Nandani's school for countless summers. Guru Nandani had always been gentle with her, even though she was a tyrant around everyone else.

"Betia, it's so good to see you. You're in New York?" she asked in Hindi. "What a lovely surprise."

Radha looked over her shoulder at her three friends before responding in the same language. "I live in New Jersey now. I was here just to see Bollywood Blowout. But why are you in New York? What about your school?"

"My graduates do most of the teaching these days," she said. "I've been in New York for about two years now, since shortly after you graduated from your last summer intensive. I teach kathak at Tisch."

"Well, New York is a dance hub."

"I also judge a few dance competitions."

Radha could see it on her face. Didi knew what had happened. Her hands began sweating and her throat began to close up.

"Didi..."

"Betia, you were always my best student! What happened in London?"

"I ... I learned that there was a possibility I wasn't being judged on my skill, and I couldn't stomach staying in the final round thinking there was a chance I really wasn't good enough and was going to win anyway."

Guru Nandani gently cupped Radha's cheek. "Radha Chopra. I never thought you were such a coward that you would let fear decide your fate."

"Wh-what?"

Didi shook her head, her hand falling away. "How can you not know your skill? You were fourteen years old and dancing with masters in my studio. Even your mother, who was my other longtime student, couldn't compare to your skill."

"But that doesn't mean I'm good enough to—"

"No," she said. "It doesn't mean you're good enough. That can only be measured by your inner strength, and if you believe you've put everything into your performance."

"I have! I *did!*"

"Then why did you run away?"

"Didi, it was so much more complicated than that."

"It always is, betia. You are in an industry where other dancers will do or say whatever they need to in order to make you feel small. It is your responsibility to be bigger than that. If you can't do it, then you were never meant to be a kathak dancer in the first place."

The thought was revolting. Never meant to be a kathak dancer? No, no she was *always* meant to dance. It had been a long time since Radha had truly embraced her love for kathak, but it had never gone away.

Instead of voicing her opinion, she counted backward in her head and folded her hands in front of her. The sweat was beginning to form on the back of her neck. Her skin felt clammy under her light jacket. She was going to start hyperventilating any second. She could feel it.

"Now. New Jersey you said? Princeton Academy for the Arts?"

"Yes, D-Didi."

"I've heard wonderful things about that institution. Are you happier than you were in, where was it? Chicago?"

She nodded.

"You'll do well, then. And I may see you soon. Oh, and if you're applying to college, let me know. I'll write you a recommendation. Email Geeta at my school office in India – the same one your mother used to register you with – and she'll get in touch with me."

Radha nodded again.

Guru Nandani patted Radha's cheek once more and then left in a cloud of rose perfume and fluttering locks of black hair.

The trembling started. Seconds later, she felt a familiar arm around her shoulder.

"Let's go," Jai said.

"No, I can't—"

"I told Winnie and Dev to leave without us. We'll meet them at the restaurant. Why don't we take a moment?" He led her into a hallway off the lobby. It was blissfully deserted.

Radha leaned against the marble wall, closed her eyes, and wheezed. If there were a way to die of embarrassment, Radha would have already been cremated, her ashes strewn into the Raritan River. She tried to take a big deep breath, then another, but it wouldn't come. She'd forgotten her inhaler again, too.

Come on, Radha. This is a bodily function. You should be able to breathe!

She was good enough, she thought. She was meant to dance. Her mother had ruined everything. No, *Radha* had ruined everything. She'd left. She'd left because she was a coward.

"Hey," Jai said, stepping closer. He took her hands and pressed them against his chest.

"She called me a coward," Radha said, gasping for air. "I'm not a coward. I just don't want to dance, because of my panic attacks. My p-panic attacks. They. Don't. Make. Me. A coward."

"Look at me," he said, pressing her hands harder against his chest. The muscles under her fingers expanded and contracted. "Do you feel that?"

She nodded.

"Close your eyes and try to match your breathing with mine. Ready?"

She nodded even as more tears rolled down her cheeks. Jai rested his forehead against Radha's. "Your panic attacks are part of you, Radha," he said. "And no one has the right to judge you. You just dance and be whatever you want to be."

242

Radha inhaled with him, then exhaled.

She didn't know how long they stood like that, or how many tears seeped through her lashes. It didn't matter. Nothing else mattered for her other than the realization that she finally loved someone who knew everything about her, who was watching her at her worst, and who still wanted to be with her anyway.

Chapter Seventeen

Jai

JAI: Sorry I missed your call.

WINNIE: Sorry I missed yours first! I am always in class! I'll be home for Thanksgiving, but I wanted to check in and see what's going on. Is everything okay at home?

JAI: Sort of. I wanted to ask you something when we visited you in the city. Director Muza and I think that we can probably win the Winter Showcase with our routine this year, but we don't have a chance in regionals unless Radha performs with us. She's amazing at it.

WINNIE: Okay ... what's the problem?

JAI: She won't dance in the showcase. Can't.

WINNIE: Yikes. Okay, and why is winning regionals

a thing?

JAI: It's selfish so I feel like a jerk for even talking about it.

WINNIE: Spill it, Patel.

JAI: There is a cash prize with regionals this year. It's a lot for a smaller team of our size. My share of the money would mean that I'd have a chance of going to college. PLEASE DO NOT TELL ANYONE I TOLD YOU THIS. I AM TRUSTING YOU.

WINNIE: Holy Vishnu, no need to be melodramatic. That's my department. 😃

WINNIE: Look, the only way you're going to be able to deal with this is talking to her. My other suggestion would be having a dance-off, but since you guys do that all the time, my good advice is wasted on you.

JAI: Sigh. Thanks a lot.

WINNIE: You're welcome! Talk to her soon, though. The more you wait, the harder it'll be for you to explain why you didn't come to her in the first place.

Jai eyed the box drawn with sidewalk chalk on the pavement behind the convenience store.

He took his position. "You ready?"

"Yeah," Radha said. "I'll count it down." She pressed play on her phone. Music filtered through the small portable speaker sitting next to them on a discarded delivery crate.

"Five, six, seven, eight."

He started on the left side of the mandap-shaped box.

Radha cued his transitions as she stepped into the bride's role. She helped him navigate over and over what he needed to know in order to lead the team.

The music changed, and Radha called time.

"Good," she said. "You got it!"

"It only took forever," he said. "You okay going through it again before we do homework?"

"Are you kidding me? Dance will win over equations any time. I want to see the routine again anyway. I think with some tweaks to this part, the team will find it easier to pick up, too."

"When we do this onstage, we're going to have to mark a box that's at least twice this size; otherwise, it's not going to make an impact with the audience."

"Definitely," Radha said. She rubbed her gloved hands together and then tucked them into the puffy vest she'd put on over her clothes. He hated that they had to practice outside in November weather, where she'd be cold, but he'd been hovering over Nana since the start of the shift, so Nana had kicked them outside.

This past week, he hadn't been communicating well. Masi was supposed to take him for a full blood panel and some other tests, but until that happened, he insisted on going to work.

The last thing Jai expected was that he would be worrying about his honorary grandfather on top of everything else ... like Bollywood Beats. They'd been working so hard, he thought. It would really hurt if they didn't at least win the showcase. Jai still hadn't told the team or Radha about Masi's recommendation for regionals, either. He had no idea how he was supposed to bring it up.

Radha's voice pulled him out of his thoughts. "How is the art department doing with the wedding backdrop?"

"It should be done by next weekend. And Anita said that her sister had a DIY Indian wedding, and she has a ton of leftover decorations we can use for the stage too."

"That's awesome," Radha said as she bent over to do a quick stretch. "It's all coming together."

Jai hummed in agreement. "Yeah, thank God. I don't know what I'd do if I had to work on college applications and keep up with choreography, AP classes, and working."

She stopped mid-stretch and then turned away from him.

"What? What is it?"

"Nothing."

"Radha…"

She jerked upright, her body wound as tight as a rubber band around a ball. "I'm sorry. I just don't know why you won't apply to Columbia."

"*Columbia?*" He backed away from her. Talk about a question from left field. "I don't understand why you'd even ask me that."

"It's your dream school, isn't it? Fine, you've missed Early Decision, but Regular Decision is still open. I know your Common Application is done because the director made you fill it out. You told me that she and your AP Bio professor wrote recommendations. You showed me your essay, and it's amazing. I'd bet that there will be absolutely no other person who writes a story on medical abnormalities and the history of dance. All you have to do is apply!"

Her words hurt like a knife wound. Why couldn't anyone understand how important it was for him to be there for his family? He'd been too young when his father got into the accident to do much more than sit by his bed and worry with him while his mother cried and his brothers figured out ways to make sure they wouldn't lose everything.

"I'm sorry," she said when Jai remained quiet. "I didn't mean anything … it's just that you're always taking care of me, and I want you to be happy, so—"

"Radha, I *am* happy."

"But you'd be happier if you could study medicine, right? Maybe even join the Columbia Bollywood dance team?"

"Radha, please leave it alone."

"I asked the director and—"

"You talked to *Masi* about me? Radha, why would you go behind my back like that? Does anyone else know my business now?"

She paled. "No, of course not! I never meant to make you feel that way. I was just asking for advice on how to help you!" She stepped into the chalk-drawn box. "Jai, let me help."

"Why don't you focus on yourself and your own applications?"

"I don't— What do you mean?"

He waved a hand at her. "Half the time you don't know if you want to cook or dance, and you're questioning yourself because almost a *year* ago a jealous competitor said you didn't have a personality."

The words ricocheted between them, accompanied by her gasp. "Trying to figure out what you want isn't a bad thing."

"You know what you want, Radha. You just can't admit it yet."

She looked like he'd slapped her, and he'd never felt lower in his life. *Oh no,* he thought. *You screwed up. You screwed up, Jai.*

"Wait, I'm sorry. I didn't mean that—"

Radha held up a hand to stop him. "I think I better go."

Fix this before she leaves you.

"No, no, not like this. Radha, please. I didn't mean it."

"I think you did."

He followed her, close to her heels. "I didn't. I swear. I'm sorry. Please don't go this way." He followed her to her car parked a few feet away. She got into the driver's seat, and he held the door open, crouching so he could remain at eye level with her. As much as she'd just hurt him, the thought of her breaking up with him had his gut churning. "Radha, please don't leave me. Please."

She'd reached for the ignition but froze at his words.

He gripped her thigh. "Talk to me."

Finally her beautiful eyes turned to look at him. "I'm s-sorry I asked the director about you."

"You were just trying to help. I'm in the wrong. Don't be mad. Don't be mad, okay?"

Radha sniffled even as she leaned over and kissed him. "I shouldn't have brought it up. I promise I'll leave it be from now on. Whatever you want to do."

Even though you think it's wrong.

"I'm sorry I said what I did," he replied.

"You're right, though," she croaked. "As much as it hurts, you're right."

"I'm not. I'm not. I was just … I don't know. Please forgive me?"

She nodded, but didn't look at him. He leaned forward and pressed a kiss to the corner of her mouth. "Why don't we call it a day? We did a lot, and I should really help Nana in the store. Besides, we've been at this for a while."

"Okay," she said, and pressed the start button on the Audi. It hummed to life. "See you at school tomorrow?"

"Yes. I'll call you."

Radha nodded again. Jai shut the door behind her and watched as she drove out of the lot and onto the street. He walked to the back entrance, twisted up inside.

Panicked. He was panicked that she was going to leave him.

Eventually she would. He had to come to terms with that.

After he reentered the store and locked the back door behind him, Jai took a deep breath. He didn't know if he could handle any more stress for the rest of the day.

His phone buzzed and he checked it, hoping that it was Radha. Instead it was another message from Tara.

TARA: Hey, Jai. I know it's been a while since the Diwali party, but I really need to talk to you. Can you call me when you get a chance?

He'd have to talk to Radha first, he thought.

But maybe later, since he'd almost screwed up his relationship on his own over not applying to college, of all things. He wondered why there weren't more movies about South Asian kids and their quest for higher education. He had nothing to reference in his time of crisis.

Jai shoved his phone in his pocket and pushed through the employee entrance to check on Nana. The store looked empty. Nana wasn't behind the counter, where he usually sat.

"Nana?" Jai called out.

There were three aisles. He walked past the first one, then the second.

Halfway down the third aisle, he saw Nana on the floor, surrounded by rolls of paper towels.

"Oh my God. Nana? Nana!" He scrambled forward onto his knees at Nana's side. "What happened? Did you fall?"

Nana slowly turned to look at him.

Nonverbal.

Half his face was drooping.

Fear gripped Jai's whole body. "Nana Veeru? Can you smile for me?"

Only one side of Nana's face responded.

"Hold out your hands?"

Nana looked at him with confusion on his face.

Okay, that wasn't going to happen, Jai thought. Was that all he was supposed to do? He was too afraid to remember Masi's directions.

Jai ran his hand over Nana Veeru's neck and along

his back, checking for any injuries. His nana sat there, swaying.

Okay, forget this. He jumped straight to calling 911.

"What's your emergency?"

Jai went into autopilot. Name, location. Patient name and age. Stroke survivor having another stroke. He guessed at his weight. He didn't know medications. Nonverbal. Paralysis.

He sat on the floor, praying harder than he ever had in his life, as he continued to talk to Nana in a soft, even tone and waited with 911 on the line to report if there were any changes. Every thirty seconds, Jai asked Nana to react to instructions. Minutes later, paramedics burst through the glass doors. Everything happened so fast, and in a blur. It was surreal, and Jai could barely keep up. He followed the paramedics outside, locked the store, and climbed into the ambulance.

Nana was strapped in, fear and confusion reflected in his eyes.

"It's going to be okay," Jai said. "I'm here. Masi is on her way."

Please don't let me lose him.

The minute he was seated next to the gurney, Jai texted

his brothers, his mother, and Masi. They were going to meet him at the hospital.

His thumb hovered over Radha's name. He should let her know.

The ambulance hit a small bump, and his phone almost slipped from his fingers.

He'd tell her later, he thought, as he gripped Nana's hand. Nana didn't squeeze back.

Everything was going to be okay. It had to be.

*

The sickening hospital smell was exactly what he remembered from years ago. He hadn't moved from his waiting-room chair since the moment he'd arrived, and all he could think about was the smell.

"Jai?" He jerked at the sound of his name. Masi rushed into the waiting room, her dhuku slipping, her jacket hanging open. "What happened? Where is he?"

Jai stood. "They took him inside. I-I don't know. I did everything I could, I swear. Masi, I tried everything, and I'm so sorry – this is my fault. I wasn't—"

Masi clasped his face in her hands. "Jai, be calm for me. This is not your fault, you hear me? I'm going to go get

255

as much information as I can about what's happening. Stay here."

He wanted to tell her to stay and sit with him so he wouldn't be alone. Instead he watched her disappear through the swinging double doors and rubbed his dry eyes. If he had been in the store, and not so consumed with his performance, maybe he would've found Nana Veeru faster. Jai knew how critical it was for a person who'd had a stroke to get treatment quickly. All that mattered now was Nana Veeru's life.

"Jai!"

His mother and Gopal rushed down the hallway toward him.

"We came as soon as we could," his mother said. She was still wearing the faded salwar kameez she preferred when she was at home.

"Who's staying with Dad?" Jai asked. "Were you able to get a nurse that fast?"

"No, Neil is home. Is Jammie here yet?"

"Yeah." Jai waved toward the double doors. "She's trying to find out what's happening."

"Okay. I'm going to check on her." She hurried off in the same direction as Masi.

Gopal sat down next to Jai. "What happened?"

Jai shook his head. "I – I, uh, was practicing outside in the parking lot. Radha and I got into a little bit of an argument over something stupid. She left. I went inside to check on Nana. I found him sitting on the floor surrounded by paper towels."

"Shit," Gopal said. He cuffed Jai's neck. "This is not your fault, kid. Don't think for a second that this is on you."

"As a stroke survivor, Nana Veeru has a higher chance of suffering a second stroke. If he's not taking his medications, or eating right... Bhai, we can't lose him. We can't lose Nana."

"And we *won't*. We're going to take care of him. That's what family does. Right?"

Jai swallowed the burning in his throat. "Right."

They sat in silence while Jai rehashed his afternoon. If Radha had stayed, he didn't know if she'd have been able to help. He was familiar with hospitals and stroke units, while she'd probably never even stepped into an emergency room in her life.

She was kind, but would she stay calm through that much chaos? She had a lot on her own plate, too much to be borrowing his problems.

"Are you going to tell me what's wrong?" Gopal finally asked. "Besides Nana."

"It's Nana."

"That's it? That's all?"

Jai slumped in his seat. When his brother wanted him to talk, he was like a government interrogator. After Dad's accident, Gopal had taken on the role of hounding him when something was wrong.

And because he knew he couldn't change his brother, Jai leaned back, closed his eyes, and told him everything. About Radha, about their fight, and about what he'd said after she tried to help.

After he finished, Gopal shook his head. "Well, you're an asshole."

"Yeah." Jai ran his hands through his hair. "Yeah, I know."

"How are you going to fix it?"

"No clue. I'll tell her about Nana Veeru, but I don't want her here. She'd try to support me. Gopal, we only have a year together. She's this bright light, and my memories with her shouldn't include hospitals."

Gopal nodded. "Fair. But maybe you'll have more than a year with her. And maybe you need to have hospital memories too. That means she cares enough to accept you during the good and bad times."

"No," Jai said. "I don't want to hurt her or, like, burden her with my problems. I'll explain why Columbia isn't for me. She deserves an answer. But that's it. She's better off far away from this stuff."

"Wait a minute," Gopal said. There was ice in his voice. "What do you mean by *burden* her? With what? With Nana having a stroke? With Dad?"

"No way, bhai." Jai's stomach dropped at the thought of his grandfather and father being anything but important and vital in his life. "Nana and Dad are not a burden. Ever. That's not what I meant."

Gopal stood, his hands fisted. "You can't just play the 'my life is shittier than yours' card without people thinking that you're treating two elderly people with disabilities like a burden."

"What is wrong with you?" Jai snapped. He stood now too. "Neil tells me that I should stay away from her, and now when I'm trying to figure out how to keep her at a distance, you're telling me not to?"

"No, not like this! We have more than so many people have. We still have Dad and Nana. They're right here.

Yeah, things sucked for a while when you were younger, because we were out of money, but we're doing better now! You have a future, but you're too stupid to see that."

"No, I'm the only one who isn't stupid in this situation," Jai said. "Why can't any of you see that the family needs me to stay right here in New Jersey instead of going off to college? I'm doing the right thing with Radha."

"By using Dad and Nana as an excuse, you coward. They're not a convenient excuse for your high school bullshit." Gopal shoved Jai back into his seat. "Mom was right. For someone so smart, you can be incredibly dense."

Gopal stormed through the double doors and left Jai sitting in the waiting room by himself, with his head cradled in his hands.

Chapter Eighteen

THANKSGIVING

Radha

Translation of Bimalpreet Chopra's Recipe Book

Punjabi Samosas

Samosas are the food of friends and family.
Serve as a snack for some gup shup conversation.

To make the samosa dough, start with all-purpose flour, carom seeds, salt, ghee, and water (as required). It is important to know the ratio between flour and batter. Kneed and set aside.

To make the potato filling, you'll need ghee, cumin seeds, ginger, garlic, boiled potatoes that have been mashed, green peas, dried mango powder, red chili powder, coriander seeds, garam masala, pomegranate seeds, and half a red onion. Dry-roast the pomegranate seeds and cumin seeds. Crush the pomegranate seeds. Melt the ghee, then add all seasoning first. Then add potatoes and peas on medium-low heat until combined.

Once the potato mix is ready, and the dough has rested, pinch a ball of dough, dip it in a little oil, roll it into a circle, and shape a cone. Add potatoes to the cone, then wet the edges of the cone with water to seal. Deep-fry samosas in medium-hot oil.

Note: Can use sweet potatoes, corn, or lentils as substitutes. Let filling cool completely before shaping cones and frying. A hot mixture will make the dough soggy.

JAI: My brothers think I'm becoming cranky because I haven't seen you in a week.

RADHA: I can come to the hospital!

JAI: That means a lot to me, but don't worry. Listening to me being cranky and taking care of my team is more than I can ask for. How is the routine coming along?

RADHA: It's under control. I'm working extra with Shakti. Jai, are you sure there isn't anything I can do?

JAI: I promise. Thank you for putting up with me.

RADHA: Well, you're cute so that helps 😃

"I don't understand why you would do that!" Simran's voice screeched from the laptop as she yelled at Radha in a mix of Hindi and Punjabi. "You are desecrating the samosa, chutki!"

Radha held up the triangle of stuffed dough so that her cousin could see it clearly on the video-chat screen. "Right out of the oil. I bet you that you'd love it if you tried it."

"I don't think I'd ever want to try a samosa stuffed with sweet potato and marshmallow."

Radha shrugged. "I made the dough more like a pastry dough, so it's actually pretty good. I think this is my best Indian-fusion recipe yet." She remembered digging her fingers into the dough, smelling the sugar and the salt, and feeling the tension in her shoulders slip away. The sizzle of frying had reminded her of foggy moments with her father, in her childhood, before dance had taken over her life. Before the restaurant had taken over his life and become his main priority. As she bit into the hot, triangle-shaped dessert, an amalgam of sweet and soft and creamy textures, she felt connected with her family.

Simran's voice radiated through the computer speakers, breaking her out of her food-love trance. "Why are you cooking all these samosas before – what time is it over there?"

"Two. It's Thanksgiving in America today."

"Samosas were one of the first things Dadaji learned how to make for the family. You're spitting in the face of tradition, Thanksgiving or not."

"I'm making some new traditions." She wondered if Dada would've liked her samosas, despite Simran's complaining. He'd passed away before she was even born.

Jai's grandparents had passed away when he was young too, but he had Nana Veeru. Even though the sweet old man she'd met only a few times was a chosen-family member, he was just as important. Sometimes chosen family could understand things blood relatives didn't.

She sighed. There she was, thinking about Jai again. She was a fool. It had only been a week, for God's sake.

The sound of a baby fussing came through the speakers. Simran's gentle voice followed.

"Do you need to go feed the baby?"

"Yeah, let me go. It was good catching up with you, even though you're doing unspeakable things to perfectly good recipes."

Radha laughed. "I'm sorry, but not really. Sweet-potato samosas are delicious."

"Well, you'll have to come and visit and make some for me. It's the only way I'll know whether or not you're lying."

"I'll see what I can do," Radha said. And waved before she disconnected the video chat.

A message popped up on the screen before she could shut down her computer. For as long as she could remember, she'd never spent hours talking to people. Until now. It was kind of nice.

SHAKTI: Hey, Happy Thanksgiving!

RADHA: Happy Thanksgiving! 🦃 Is your Indian-Caribbean Friendsgiving event happening?

SHAKTI: Yes! That's actually why I'm messaging. I know you were supposed to go to Winnie's house with your mom, but why don't you come over and celebrate with my family and our friends? You have to admit, I'm a lot more fun.

RADHA: LOL, true but I actually don't think I'm going anywhere. I feel like staying home today.

SHAKTI: Lame. On a holiday?

RADHA: More food for me. And I don't have to watch sportsball.

SHAKTI: If you change your mind, we can eat amazing food and also practice. I can't believe we're at the end of November and I still don't have the dance.

RADHA: You'll get it!

SHAKTI: You'd be better at it than me. You should've just done the lead role.

"Radha?" her mom called from upstairs. Radha jumped at the interruption. She had to read Shakti's last line again.

"Radha, I've said your name three times now!"

"Oh. Sorry. I was talking to Simran. And texting. I'm in the kitchen."

The click of heels grew louder until her mother appeared. Sujata wore dark-wash jeans and a burnt-orange cashmere sweater. Her hair was styled around her face in a short bob.

"I needed you to come to the stairs."

Radha motioned to her samosas and open laptop on the island. "I now have commitments, Mom. I've become popular."

Sujata struck a pose with her hands on her hips. "Okay, Ms. Popular. How do I look?"

"The heels are ridiculous."

Her mother looked down at her feet. "What? They go with the outfit!"

Radha thought about Winnie's mother, and how the woman probably spit-shined her floors when company came over. "Aunty isn't going to let you wear them in the house. You're the only one who has forgotten your desi roots and tromps dirt in here."

"We don't have dirt in this house. I pay for a cleaning service."

"The gods are still judging you. Wear the brown boots that are easy to slip on and off."

"Okay, I can do that. Can you take my picture, too? I want to send it to Tarun."

"Well, I'm no longer hungry," Radha said as she put down the second samosa.

"You'll survive." She waved at the food. "Are we taking your food with us?"

Containers of saag paneer, cranberry chutney, mango pie, plain paranthas, masala mac and cheese, and her sweet potato–marshmallow samosas were lined up in a single row. She'd not only cooked and packed the food; she'd also washed the dishes, cleaned the countertops, and sprayed down the oven and stovetop.

Stress cooking and food-culture exploration at a whole other level.

"I may have gone overboard," Radha started. "But you can take this with you to Aunty's house. I'll stay home."

"It's Thanksgiving! Don't you want to see Winnie? She'll be there with her boyfriend."

"I just saw her a couple weeks ago. I'll text her, but I'm pretty sure she'll understand."

"Well, I'm not leaving you here by yourself," Sujata said. "Why did you change your mind? Are you feeling okay? Have you been doing your new exercises?"

Radha picked up the leather-bound notebook her mother had bought her and waved it in the air. "I am writing down all my feelings like I'm supposed to."

In reality she was compiling recipes. The shape of the

book, the softness of the cover and the binding, made it like a newer version of her dada's recipe notebook, and she couldn't help but use it in the same way. Fortunately, her mother would never find out. She practically slept with it under her pillow to make sure of that.

Sorry not sorry.

"Okay, well, if you're sure." Her mother stopped mid-turn. "You know, why don't I come home early? We'll leave the food here and eat some of it together when I get back."

"Seriously? You're going to have Indian food with me?"

Her mother shrugged. "It is Thanksgiving."

Miracles do happen, Radha thought. "Yeah. We could do that."

"And then maybe we'll watch some of your old routines so you can turn your Bollywood dance group into something a little more dignified. I don't know how you convinced your doctors to advocate for you teaching that routine instead of getting back on the stage. Don't think for a minute you're off the hook for that. Since you've put yourself in this horrible situation, and you have no choice but to stay in this school, the least you can do is make the best of it."

On second thought, miracles were a lie.

"Just go, Mom," Radha said, "and don't worry about coming home early. I'll take your picture later."

It took another five minutes of fussing before her mother was finally out the door. Radha relaxed in the silence and solitude. She'd do the responsible thing and work on her kathak thesis statement. She was almost done with it, which was a good thing since she had to hand it in next week.

Radha put the food away and was opening up her textbooks at the kitchen island when her doorbell rang.

Her mother had probably forgotten the front-door keypad code again. The woman had a mind as sharp as a Japanese chef's blade, but she couldn't remember what her Netflix password was or how to get back into the house.

Radha peeked through the glass pane at the side of the entrance door, and her jaw dropped. She yanked it open.

"What are you doing here?"

"Hi," Jai said. "Happy Thanksgiving." He stood in a button-down shirt and dark-wash jeans, holding out a bouquet of orange and yellow flowers.

He looked amazing.

"I don't understand. Aren't you supposed to be at the hospital?"

"I just left. Now I'm visiting you."

They stood on the stoop, staring at each other.

"Well?" he said. "Are you going to kiss me or not?"

The knot that had formed in the pit of her stomach loosened. On impulse, she vaulted up so that her legs wrapped around his waist and her mouth fused to his. When his arms banded around her and he kissed her, she sank into the kiss.

"No, seriously," she said, a little breathless, when she finally pulled back. "What are you doing here?"

"You're here."

Radha let him carry her into the house. She shut the door and then pointed down the hall.

"Mom is going to stay with the director tonight," he explained. "I did some recon, talked to Shakti, and found out that you were here." He effortlessly carried her and the flowers into the kitchen.

"Well, great timing. My mom left like fifteen minutes ago."

Jai set her on her feet. "Uh, yeah. I was parking across the street when I saw her leave. Then I waited to make sure she wasn't coming back. I wasn't sure if you'd told her about me, so I figured that was the safest solution.

Hey, nice place."

"Thanks," Radha said. "I do appreciate an Indian boyfriend who understands potential parent pitfalls." She picked up her plate of samosas and held it out. "She'll probably hate that I'm dating and say that it's taking away from my chances of performing ever again. I didn't bring you up yet, because, well, I didn't want to argue with her. I have other stuff to focus on."

Jai picked up a samosa and took a bite. His eyebrows made a V, and then his eyes went wide. "Holy Vishnu. This is a Thanksgiving samosa!"

"Yup," Radha said with a grin. "Not bad, right?"

"Not bad? It's *great*. If you have more of those, you can pack them up and bring them with us."

"Uh, where are we going?" Not that she was going to say no. Her vision of a quiet Thanksgiving with her thesis statement went right out the window.

"What do you say," Jai started, "to having Thanksgiving with me, my brothers, and my dad? Neil is already home, deep-frying a tandoori turkey. Gopal is closing up shop and visiting Nana for a bit, and he'll be joining us in a couple hours. We could also use some fresh blood around when we watch *Sholay* for the millionth time."

"You want me to celebrate with your family?"

Jai nodded. "Like I said. I missed you."

He reached for her, and Radha was ready to reciprocate the hug when he changed course and grabbed another samosa.

"Hey!"

Jai wiggled his eyebrows. "What do you say? Thanksgiving Punjabi-Gujarati style? Well, mostly Punjabi style, because my mother is the one who taught us how to cook."

"It sounds great. I'll text my mother and let her know I'm going to be at a friend's house after all. Give me a second to change and we can head out."

They froze at the same time.

"Oh," he said.

"Oh."

The house was empty, and they were alone. Together.

"Your mom isn't—"

"Yeah."

He looked like a deer caught in the headlights. Like he didn't know what to do, but also wanted very much to do the things that were left unsaid between them.

And wasn't that sweet? Her heartbeat was pounding

away again, but now it was from love and excitement – not even a hint of anxiety. Radha leaned in and kissed him. If anyone was going to be the one, it would be him, she thought as she pulled away. "There are more samosas on the counter over there. Help yourself."

"Yes. Great. I'll stay here and eat samosas. By myself."

*

When he pulled in front of a small two-story colonial home with a wide ramp leading up to French doors, Jai's easygoing smile faded.

"Ready?"

Radha nodded. She picked up the large insulated bag of Tupperware. "Anything I should know before I walk in there?"

Jai froze. "What do you mean?"

"Like does your dad know we're dating? I don't want to say something if…"

"Oh. Uh, yeah." His shoulders relaxed. "They know about you. Come on. I'll help you with the bag."

Radha brushed her fingertips over the Ganesh door knocker as she followed Jai into the small foyer and kicked off her shoes after him.

One point for Radha, zero for Sujata. Everyone takes their shoes off.

To the left of the foyer was a large, open living room.

The house was spotless. Framed candid shots of Jai and his family sat on bookshelves bracketing a TV. A painting of an Indian village scene was mounted on the wall. Under the painting was a large gray sectional. At the end of the sectional, a man sat in a wheelchair tilted back on a power base motor. Next to him on the couch was a blue foam mat and a blanket.

"Let me introduce you to Dad," Jai said. "Don't let his smile fool you. He's sneaky."

Radha squeezed his arm. "Like father, like son, they say."

"Truth. We moved him from the blue mat on the couch to his chair so he could watch a movie before I left. I think he'll like this interruption."

Radha followed Jai, realizing that she'd never met the parents of someone she was dating before. She knew from the way Jai talked about him that his dad was kind and funny. Swallowing her nerves, she smiled at the man wearing a T-shirt that said I LOVE BOLLYWOOD. His eyes darted from the screen to Jai, then to Radha and back.

"Dad? This is Radha, my girlfriend I was telling you about. She's spending Thanksgiving with us."

Jai's father's smile was full of teeth, laugh lines, and crinkling eyes. It was the sweetest expression, and Radha knew where Jai got his charm from.

"Hello," he said, his mouth moving slowly to shape the word.

"Hi, Uncle," she said. "It's nice to meet you."

"Nice. You're pretty."

"Hey now," Jai said, stepping in front of Radha. "There is no need to charm my girl."

Jai's father grinned at him.

"Neil is checking on the bird in the backyard, right?" Jai asked.

"Yes. It's going to burn."

"Yeah," Jai said. "Just like last year. Radha and I are going to take care of the food, okay? I'll check on you in a bit." He motioned to the TV, which was playing *Sholay* on low. "The movie is almost at the good part."

Radha winked at Jai's father, who chuckled in response. She followed Jai into the kitchen. They began unpacking the bag of food they'd brought in from the car.

"Sometimes he'll watch in my parents' bedroom,

which is down the hall over there," Jai said. "We had it reconfigured years ago for his quadriplegia. But he wanted to watch it on a bigger screen today for some reason."

"Quadriplegia?"

"Paralysis from the neck down, including torso. His injury didn't affect his ability to breathe on his own, but he was diagnosed with some cognitive impairments, like with speech. He needed a lot of rehab and speech therapy. That's where he and Nana Veeru spent a lot of time. Most of it was watching *Sholay*."

Radha froze. "Wait a minute. Jai and Veeru. Those are names from the movie *Sholay*."

"Yeah, they are." Jai laughed. "You're just figuring that out? Dad loved the movie way before the accident too. I was named Jai after the film."

"And Veeru. Nana Veeru?"

"Yup. Dr. Vimbai Muza, from Harare, Zimbabwe. Masi and my mom used to say that we were two peas in a pod from the start of our relationship, kind of like Jai and Veeru from *Sholay*, so the name change stuck."

"Jai, is your nana going to be able to work with you at the store again?"

Jai's smile slipped. "I don't think so."

"What are you guys going to do?"

"We're going to have to hire someone." Jai grabbed Radha's hands and faced her. "There's something I want to tell you. Something that I haven't explained. Maybe if you know it, you'll realize why going to Columbia is not an option."

She was already shaking her head. Columbia was the reason they'd fought last time. She didn't want to ruin today, especially when it had been so long since she'd seen him. "You don't have to explain. I'll let it go. I promise."

"No," Jai said. "I really want to talk to you about it."

Radha looked at their hands. "I'll listen, but whatever it is, I'm with you."

"I … thanks. Look, when my dad got into the accident, I was ten. I couldn't really do anything to help him, my mom, and my brothers. I saw how hard Dad worked in rehab, how my mother worked two jobs, and how my brothers dropped out of school to run the store. My family functioned as a team to survive. We have no other family in the US. It's just us, so it was drilled into me that all we have is each other. The medical bills practically wiped us out, and we were in really bad shape, and I couldn't do anything to help while my parents and my brothers did everything for me. Now my brothers want to open a second store. If I go to school—"

"You won't be able to help."

Jai nodded. "My brothers will have to hire two people instead of just one, and my family's goal to open a second store will be so much farther away. With my help, we'll get it done."

Radha pinched the bridge of her nose and tried to count to ten. "Jai Patel, you did *not* bring me here for Thanksgiving so you could try to convince me that you can't go to Columbia."

"What?" he sputtered. "No, I wanted to explain things to you, though. You know, because it's only fair."

She paced the small kitchen. Nope. She couldn't keep her promise after all. There was no way she could support this martyrdom.

She clasped his face in her hands. "You have a family that loves you, and that wants you to be happy. They support you in whatever you want to do. And the most amazing part is that you know what that is! Take it from someone who has a ton of regrets, and who has to carry around an emergency inhaler now, who sometimes stays up until two in the morning stress cooking just to deal with the fallout."

Jai dropped his forehead against hers. "You're not cooperating. You're supposed to listen to me and think that I'm such a great guy for wanting to put his family first."

"No, I think you're being selfish by putting your family in that position, actually."

"Have you been talking to my brother Gopal? Because he pretty much said the same thing."

"You know, Shakti says you're supposed to agree with everything I say. I feel like that's dumb advice, but in this moment, I don't hate it."

He pulled her in closer. "How about we shelve Columbia? If you want to talk about it later, we will. Maybe after you figure out *your* college situation."

"Sneaky, Jai. That's really sneaky and underhanded." She rubbed the tip of her nose with his. "Look, if there is one thing I've learned from my new therapy sessions, it's that we're seventeen years old. We don't have to know exactly what we want to do, but we have to be willing to take chances to figure it out. We are the product of our parents' immigrant dreams. Like my father once told me, it's not about picking a stable job, it's about following the right dream."

"You know," Jai murmured as he brushed his lips against hers, "I actually believe that. Because I took a chance with you. And I am so freaking lucky that no matter how many times I mess this up, you're willing to give me the benefit of the doubt. I'm trying really hard not to make any more mistakes."

"That means a lot." Her mouth tingled, and her heart did one slow roll in her chest. "You were a chance too. Maybe that's a sign that we should take some more?"

Jai closed the space between them with a kiss that melted every last thought out of her brain.

"Hey!"

Radha jumped at the same time Jai jerked and hit his elbow on the counter.

Jai's brother stood at the back door with a long pair of tongs and heat-protectant gloves up to his elbows. "No hanky-panky in the kitchen," he called through the screen.

"Hey, bhai, your bird is on fire," Jai snapped.

Neil's eyes went wide; he spun around and raced across the lawn.

"How do you know? We can't see it from here," Radha asked.

"I don't know, but there's a good chance it's true." Jai leaned in and kissed her again. "I'm thankful for you today. I'm glad you're spending Thanksgiving with me this year."

"Me too," she said. Radha wanted to add that there could be more Thanksgivings together in the future, but she stopped herself. Neither of them was ready for that yet.

Chapter Nineteen

DECEMBER

Jai

MASI: Can you come by my office tomorrow after practice?

JAI: Sure, everything okay? Is Nana okay? I know it's been a few weeks since we ran into each other at the hospital, but he looks like he's getting better?

MASI: Yes, he's okay. I want to talk to you about applications before winter break.

JAI: Masi, we've talked about it already.

MASI: You've done all the work. There is no harm in hitting send. I'm texting you as your aunt, not as your teacher.

JAI: There is no point.

MASI: There is still a chance with regionals. And I'm saying that as your teacher now.

JAI: I don't think that's an option either.

MASI: Have you asked Radha to perform?

TARA: Hey, I don't know how many times I've tried to call and text you. I know that you're mad at me, but I'm trying to do the right thing here.

JAI: Sorry, I've been busy. I'll call you later. Promise.

Jai rushed down the hall toward dance practice. He was running late, and on the last day of school before winter break, too. It had been like this all week. He missed his advising session with Masi and hadn't been able to talk to her since. Then, he'd gone to the store in the morning to help open because their part-time help had called in sick, and then his car had broken down in the parking lot. The Lyft driver had taken forever to get to him, and by then he'd been late for his first class.

Now he was supposed to meet Radha before practice, and he was a minute away from the studio when his phone buzzed in his pocket.

MASI: I know you have practice this afternoon, so I wanted to tell you that I had a few advising sessions today and I addressed the team about the showcase and regionals. You haven't mentioned to your team about my recommendation. That's what we were supposed to discuss on Monday, but you missed our meeting.

Masi's message stopped him in his tracks. What did she mean? He shot back a quick message.

A slick uneasiness churned in his gut as he quickened his pace to the studio. Masi had warned him he had to speak to Radha about performing in the showcase, but there'd been no easy way to do it. If Masi had really said something before he could, it would make him look bad as captain of the team.

He opened the studio door and stepped inside.

Radha was sitting on the floor with an arm around Shakti. Shakti had tears in her eyes, which did nothing to lessen the impact of her glare when she spotted him.

To her left, Hari and Vik stood with their arms crossed, like soldiers waiting for direction as to who they had to throat-punch.

The throat-punchee would be him, he thought. He dropped his dance bag, and before he could take another step, Shakti swore at him.

"I never thought you'd lie to us like this, Jai."

"Lie?"

She wet-snorted. "I almost got into a fight with Radha, because I thought you were both in it together. But she had no idea that the director didn't think we were a slam dunk for the showcase or for regionals because I'm the one dancing lead! What were you going to do? Try to Jedi-mind-trick us into coming to that decision on our own?"

"The last thing I wanted to do was lie to any of you, Shakti," he said. "I hadn't told you yet because there was a lot to consider. Radha, you know that, right?"

Her furious expression knocked him a full step back. "I never thought you'd do this," she said. "The showcase and regionals. Some of the team are depending on their performances for dance scholarships or getting into troupes."

"What she's saying is the team is not just about you," Hari said. "We trusted you!"

Jai felt his own anger spike as Hari got in his face. "And I'm trying to do the right thing by all of you! The director wanted Radha to dance the lead, but she is choreographing because she doesn't want to perform in the first place."

"That's a cash prize at regionals. You may be done after high school, but some of us are going to college," Hari said.

"That was a low blow," he said quietly. He'd never thought his friend would try to hurt him that way.

"Jai, I deserved the right to make the decision for myself," Radha said as she got to her feet.

"You made that decision," he said, rounding on her. "On the very first day we started working together. You were going to move back to Chicago because you didn't want to perform."

Shakti gasped. She got to her feet as well. "Is that true? You were going to leave us, Radha?"

"If my mother had had her way, then, yeah," Radha said. "Jai, that doesn't mean you get to decide what I'm going to do without asking me first! The director said she's been able to gauge the winning team for the last ten years. If we win the showcase and regionals—"

"But we're not," he said. "Because you refuse to dance again because of something that happened almost a year ago, and I was trying to do what you wanted."

"There are recruiters coming to the showcase!" Shakti shouted. "But guess what – the director doesn't know if I look good enough, because I can barely keep up! And you're here making decisions without even consulting people like me who are putting their futures on the line!"

"Then what should we do, quit now and say screw it?" he shouted back. "You all want to write papers instead?"

"We may have to if we kick your ass and you can't dance anymore," Vik said.

"Stop it," Radha said. Her voice was like a whip. "We need some privacy, guys. Since I'm his excuse for not telling everyone, I want to talk to him."

It wasn't true, he thought. He wasn't using her or anyone as an excuse. He was just ... Jai didn't know. He had a lot on his plate, and talking about something that could potentially hurt his girlfriend wasn't exactly high on his list of priorities.

When no one made a move to leave, he snapped, "Clear the room!"

"I'll tell the rest of the team that practice is canceled," Shakti said. She was the first to storm out of the practice studio. She ignored Jai as she passed. Hari and Vik followed her, glaring at him.

"I don't know how I can trust you after this," Vik said,

and closed the door behind him.

The studio echoed with their footsteps as Jai and Radha circled each other.

He wanted to tell her so many things. That she should've understood why he hadn't said anything. That this was what Radha had wanted, and it wasn't his fault that she didn't want to perform.

"How dare you?" she shouted, and the words cut him. "I never thought that you'd think of me as someone you needed to save."

"What? What are you talking about?"

"You thought that I was so pathetic I wasn't capable of hearing the director's feedback? That I was so weak because of my anxiety that you had to keep information from me? From your *friends?*"

"Yes!" he burst out. "Yes, I kept that information from you, not because you're weak or because of your anxiety, but because you *literally* said that you refused to perform. How could I ask you to dance after everything you've told me? For fuck's sake, Radha. What do you think would've happened if I'd said something? You'd have felt like I was forcing you into a corner!"

"No," she said, pointing at him, jabbing him in the

chest. "You don't get to make assumptions about me and my reactions. You're trying to blame *me* when this is all *your* fault. What you did was turn this around and make me feel small, make me feel like I'm the reason fourteen dancers won't get a shot at something important at regionals, when this was really all about *you*."

"This has *never* been about me," he said, pounding a fist against his chest.

"No, it's *always* been about you, Jai." She walked to him, but instead of touching him, hugging him, she looked at him with pity, and that hurt so much more.

"You were too young when your family was going through something really terrible. You blame your brothers for needing you to open another store. You blame me and my performance anxiety because it's stopping us from going to regionals. Not once, Jai, not once have you looked in the mirror and blamed yourself for refusing to look at all the options you have to pursue your dreams and go to a school like Columbia. People would kill to be as smart as you."

"You have no idea what you're talking about," he shot back.

"Well, let me put it to you this way," she said as she

grabbed her dance bag. "If I don't dance in the showcase, and maybe even the regional competition, then there is zero chance you'll get that cash prize you can use for school. That's what you've been telling your family and the director, isn't it? That I'm the reason we won't win? I could've helped you, Jai!"

"With what?" he shouted. "How were you going to help me when you can't even help yourself, Radha? You're so busy cooking when you're not at school that you're not even giving yourself the chance to remember that you've found your dance joy again!"

She paled. "That's not true."

"You know it's true. You love it just as much now as you did when you first started kathak classes. But you're hiding." He motioned to the empty studio. "Every day you come in here and pretend that you're doing your part, but you're really just scared to take the next step, and every therapist, every person who loves you, is waiting for you to freaking see it. You're not managing your anxiety now; you're using it as an excuse because you're afraid."

She looked like he'd slapped her, and then he realized that he'd repeated the words of the dance teacher who'd berated her at the NYU show.

He didn't step down, though. He couldn't – otherwise he'd end up telling her how much he was hurting too. "And yeah. I screwed up. I screw up a lot with you, and I own that. But what you can't see is that you've messed up too, by not even trying to understand me. You're so privileged, you don't know what it's like to be poor, to be truly scared and helpless. To listen to your mother cry in the middle of the night, wondering where the money is going to come from. To think that you might have to go back to India because there isn't enough money for food and for your dad's treatments in the US. To watch your brothers quit college because they have to work instead."

"And you don't know what it's like to wonder if anyone has ever wanted you for who you are!" she shouted. "Or, better yet, even knows who you are!"

Jai watched her loop her dance bag over one shoulder and her backpack over the other. She straightened her back and sailed past him, then twisted the door handle with a vicious yank.

"I guess both of us are cowards, then, Jai. You don't want to admit that you're afraid of failing if you apply to Columbia. And I don't want to lose anyone again if I go back to dancing. But it looks like I've lost you anyway."

She was gone before Jai could stop her.

Her words, and his, raced through his brain like a bad movie reel.

What he should've said was that he loved her and that he was really sorry.

Jai drop-kicked his dance bag across the studio floor. He had no idea how he could fix things that had been inherently broken from the beginning.

Chapter Twenty

Radha

Translation of Bimalpreet Chopra's Recipe Book

Dal Makhani

Dal makhani is Punjabi comfort food. Served hot
and fresh with bread or rice, it can make any pain
go away. When my children are upset, I make dal
makhani for them.

*To create this most delicious and comforting dish, you
will need:*

Urad beans (whole and split) and red kidney beans
Ginger, garlic, onions, tomatoes, and tomato paste

*Cumin, green and black cardamom, salt, green chilies,
mango powder, cinnamon bark, bay leaf, and nutmeg
Butter or ghee
Heavy cream*

*Soak the beans overnight, then cook them in the same
water. Panfry the seasonings, the onions, and then the
tomatoes. Add beans and let simmer for at least one
hour on low. Mash the beans to create a thick stew
consistency. Add cream at the end.*

Note: Soak beans overnight, then rinse. Dry-roast
seasoning, crush in mortar and pestle, then panfry
in ghee the ginger, garlic, onions, tomatoes. Put
everything in an Instant Pot for 30 minutes. Let
pressure release naturally. Pour cream at the
end in small increments until the color changes to
medium brown.

Best served and eaten when you're pretty sure
you've broken up with a boyfriend.

Radha watched the taxi pull out of the driveway before

she walked up the cobblestone path to the front door of her childhood home.

She braced herself against the bitter Chicago cold, punched her birthday into the front-door keypad, and let herself in. She felt a strange sense of nostalgia, walking in. She'd become a dancer in this house. She was returning as so much more.

The lights went on as she passed the sensors and dragged her bags and coat up the curving staircase to her bedroom. The bed was freshly made, and her furniture was the same.

Her dance trophies were crammed into a wide built-in bookshelf. Six rows of metal and glass statues that served as a reminder of how different her life used to be. She still wondered if she'd deserved all of the trophies she received over the years, or if her mother had been responsible for some of the wins. After London, she'd probably think about that all the time. But now she knew the trophies didn't matter. They'd never mattered, and seeing them again didn't bother her as much as she'd thought they would.

Radha rubbed the heel of her hand against her chest, remembering how Jai did the same thing, and then unpacked her clothes into her old dresser. She changed into yoga pants and a sweatshirt, grabbed her recipe notebook and her grandfather's, and headed downstairs.

Her dad was supposed to be home by six. She wondered if being with him would be as easy as it had been over the last four months through video chat, or if they'd go back to acting like strangers again. Hopefully things would be easy. She needed easy.

Radha walked barefoot across the glistening floors into the chef's kitchen. All the appliances and surfaces gleamed as if they were brand-new, the cabinets fully stocked like always. She spotted a large cream-colored bowl in the corner and lifted the kitchen towel to see black whole and split urad dal soaking inside.

She wondered if her father knew something was wrong and was making the comfort food for her. She hadn't told her mother anything other than that she'd had a fight with someone at school. Maybe that had been enough for her to say something, and for Dad to soak the lentils overnight.

Deciding it was time she cooked for her father, Radha opened Dada's recipe book and hers in tandem so she could refer to the notes, then raided the fridge and the pantry, locating the remaining ingredients she needed.

She found the Instant Pot and spent the next twenty minutes putting together Bimalpreet Chopra's famous dal makhani recipe. Well, famous according to her cousin.

After setting the pressure cooker, she cut onions, cucumber, and tomato for a quick desi salad, then deftly covered it with plastic wrap and put it in the fridge.

The counters were wiped down and the dishes, pans, cutting board, and knife she'd used loaded in the dishwasher or hand-washed. When she finished, the dal still had another twenty minutes to cook, so she wandered through the house, feeling out of place and oddly at home at the same time. Her father had put up a three-foot Christmas tree in the corner. There was a plastic container next to it labeled 'Decorations'. She'd have to do that later.

After she circled the living room, touching the art that her mother had left behind, the framed picture of her first recital that her father kept on the mantel, she stood in front of the basement door.

Her dance studio was downstairs.

Radha grabbed the knob, and, her pulse racing, she opened the door and slowly descended into the personal space where she'd spent countless years of her life. The lights flickered on when she reached the bottom, and she faced the wall of mirrors.

"Surreal," she whispered to herself. "Surreal that this was four months ago." She remembered all the details as if it were yesterday. Her music system was still in the same place. A rack of clothes that she'd worn during competitions leaned against the far-left wall of the room. A towering display of her stage makeup stood in the corner next to the bathroom on the right. A small altar, covered in red silk and displaying murtis of Lord Ganesh, Goddess Saraswati, and Lord Krishna, butted up against the wall of mirrors. Her practice ghungroos sat in a basket on the floor next to the altar.

Radha touched the two frayed cotton cords, each with over two hundred bells in a single row. When she tapped one of the brass bells, it rang like crystal-clear music.

She sat down and tugged off her socks. She wrapped each sock around an ankle, then took the ghungroos from the basket and began tying them over the socks. If she'd had any clean ankle pads, she would've used those, but this would have to do. Then she was knotting the ends of the strings.

It was as if her whole body had been waiting for her to wear her practice ghungroos again. They felt different from her stage pair, because she'd spent so much more time with them over the years. Everything inside her lifted and sighed.

Radha got to her feet and gave one testing stomp. The sole of her foot slapped against the tile. She stood with her shoulders pushed back, her hands flat at chest level with fingers pointing toward each other, and started her namaskar. She needed blessings, and this time she wanted to do a more formal and respectful version than simply touching the floor with her fingertips. When she was done and had returned to her first position, she pulled her phone out of her sweatshirt pocket and plugged it into the stereo system. She scrolled for the right track, and when she saw a dance piece she hadn't played in nearly a year, she selected it from her kathak playlist. Radha increased the volume and took her position.

The first strains of the sitar were like welcoming arms. She listened and counted the beats before her cue.

This composition was supposed to be her big moment at the Kathak Classics in London. It was the routine that she'd never gotten to perform, in the final round.

Tatkaar.

Ta thei thei tat, aa thei thei tat, ta thei thei tat,

aa thei thei tat...

The intro was deceptively simple. And then the track changed into a paran.

Radha's muscles relaxed, and her feet hit every step like she'd been practicing the choreography all this time.

The track changed again, and she spun across the floor in chakkars. She grounded herself and completed two chakkars per beat until she spun a total of one hundred and eight times in the tarana. She was awash with relief when her body responded as it should.

She let go of her chaotic thoughts and embraced the dance joy as it washed over her. She pushed herself harder and faster, immersing herself in the piece she hadn't been able to perform. Even when her eyes blurred with unshed tears, she didn't stop.

This was why she loved kathak so much. Why she'd let her mother push her into being her best. Because she wanted it just as much.

The music ended, and she stopped in the exact same spot where she'd started. She was breathing heavily, and her muscles trembled with exhaustion. When she heard the clapping, she turned to see her father at the base of the staircase, leaning against the railing. He wore jeans and a button-down shirt. His hair was a little grayer, and he looked tired, but he smiled, and Radha knew he was really happy to see her.

"You've always amazed me, chutki," he said. "You have so much happiness when you dance."

She couldn't hold back anymore. She burst into sobs and ran into his arms.

*

Radha put her ghungroos away and washed her face while her dad finished the dal. He made a quick batch of rice and set the small table he'd added in the kitchen. They drank cans of orange soda, the only beverage in the fridge for some reason, and ate with their hands.

"Vadiya, Radha," her father said. "I normally don't use the Instant Pot for dal makhani, but I'm so happy you did."

He leaned his forearms on the table as if getting closer to the plate. That was how she knew that he loved the food he was eating, and it warmed her that she could make something her father would enjoy with such enthusiasm.

"Dal is literally one of the best things to use it for. There are group forums dedicated to Instant Pot dal."

"Recently I've used it to make yogurt. I can't wait to see what else you make in the kitchen."

"Since I haven't been performing, I've had a lot of time to learn and explore. You'll be surprised at what I can do. More than what you've seen when we video-chat."

Her father took a minute to chew and swallow before responding. "You know," he said, "I was thinking of turning the basement into a gym, but if you're going to use it when you come and visit, I'll use one of the bedrooms instead. You said you're not performing, but it looks like you still like to dance."

Radha scooped up more dal. "Do whatever you want with the basement. But honestly, you should move closer to the city. That way you'll be near the restaurant, and you won't have to travel so far when you work late. This house is too big anyway."

Her father looked around. "Yeah, I guess you're right. Maybe we can look at a few places while you're here?"

"Sure, if that's what you want."

"What I want," he started slowly, "is for you to tell me how you're doing in New Jersey. You were pretty adamant about leaving Chicago. At first I thought it was a good move and encouraged your mother to give you more time.

Your grades are up, and you're even dating and making friends. But your mother called—"

"I knew it."

"She's still worried that being here will set you back even more than the last few weeks."

"Dad, first of all, leaving Chicago was not about leaving you," Radha said. Even though she couldn't read his expression, she knew she had to make that clear. Especially since she'd burst into tears when she first saw him. "I knew that if I stayed in Chicago, I'd be forced to face the disappointed people that treated me like a screwup after the Kathak Classics. I couldn't get away from the community. My grades plummeted, I didn't do well on my first round of SATs, and I was always on edge. I had a second chance in New Jersey."

Her father nodded. "I'm glad. We talk more, even though we don't live together. But, chutki, when we did live together, I loved you just as much as I love you now." He cleared his throat as if the words were getting stuck in the wrong pipe. "When you were happy, I was happy. I guess what I'm trying to say is … I hope you'll still come to Chicago to visit me, even if you're not a fan of the city."

Radha wiped her fingers before she squeezed her

father's arm. "Try to keep me away."

"Not a chance. Well, unless you bring your mother."

"*Dad.*"

"Kidding." He chuckled for a second, then grew solemn again. "I'm happy for you. But that's not all. Your mother also said something about 'stress cooking,' and how it's my fault?"

"She says a lot of things that are wrong, but in this case she's not. Let's just say that I really, really want to thank you for Dada's notebook."

He laughed, then lifted his soda can and tapped it against hers. "My father knew how to make cooking an experience. I hoped that you'd find the same escape in food."

"I did. I think I found more than escape. I found a new passion."

Her father gave her a contemplative glance before he took another drink. "A new passion is good. But you still don't look happy, chutki. I saw you downstairs just now. Maybe you're so sad because you've embraced a new passion, but you're worried that you have said goodbye to the other?"

How did parents *do* that? she wondered. Half the time

she felt like she didn't even need to go to a therapist, because her folks could read her so well. But, then again, she'd been more honest with her therapists than with her parents.

Radha looked down at her dal and rice. "There are probably some things you need to know before I tell you why I'm so confused."

"I have all night, Radha."

And because that meant the world to her, Radha told him everything. About the director, the school, Jai, and her mother. She even talked about her deal with Sujata, and how she was hoping to secure her parents' support for college. He raised an eyebrow at that but remained quiet until she finished.

"Now I'm here," Radha said. She pushed her empty plate forward.

"Radha, I know your mother is … driven. But in the long run, it doesn't matter if you perform or not. You're our bacha. Nothing will change that."

"That's not true, though. Performing is what caused me to lose Mom. She changed when I started winning competitions. Performing is what caused me to lose –" she cleared her throat – "to lose you, because I was so busy."

"You can't take the blame for that, Radha," he said quietly. "I spent so much time working too. I'm just as much at fault."

Hearing her father admit that he'd been absent was bittersweet. Radha hated that there was any blame between them at all, but it was a relief they were finally acknowledging it. More importantly, she felt like she'd been blaming herself for so long, but shifting some of that responsibility off her shoulders helped. "When I stopped performing, that's when I discovered that we had this whole food culture. I missed out on things like visiting the dhaba every time I went to India. And Dad? Performing, or in this case not performing, is what's causing me to lose Jai."

"Well, I can't speak for your mom. All you and I did was lose time, but we can make up for it now. We have been making up for it, right? And as for your half-Punjabi boyfriend … have you really lost him too?"

"What do you mean?"

He picked up her plate and his to take to the sink. "I mean," he called over his shoulder, "is there no chance you can get back together? I don't know how you American kids date, but he kept something from you, and you had a fight, so the next step is for you to talk, right? You know, when we were growing up in Punjab, your thaiji used to see this girl in the next sector over, and he was always saying something stupid. Then the girl would throw her jutti at him, he'd apologize, and they'd be fine."

"Throw her jutti … yeah, no one is throwing a shoe here, Dad."

Her father shrugged. "It worked for my brother's girlfriend. Now that I think about it, when I went to college here in the US, your mother threw her heels at me quite a few times. Those heels hurt, too. Probably a warning, now that I think about it. What are you going to do instead?"

Radha was at a complete loss as to how to respond. Yes, she was mad at Jai. His reasons were inexcusable. He was hurting himself. But could she forgive him? More important, could she perform again, this one last time, for him and the team?

"Dad?"

"Yes, Radha?"

"I think we're going to have to do a lot more stress cooking for me to figure this out."

"I can always talk to your desi boy. You might want

to prepare him by telling him I have the sharpest knives in Chicago."

"Dad," she said, even though the thought made her smile. She closed her eyes and dropped her forehead to the table. Hopefully all the food she was about to make would help her decide what she needed to do.

It was pretty clear, though, that since she loved Jai, the idiot, and she wanted to support her team, she'd have to dance again. He'd been right about how much she was running away from her issues. Her father nudged her upright as he sat up in his chair. He put both Dada's recipe notebook and hers between them. "I'm glad you brought these."

Radha picked up Dada's and ran her fingers over the worn leather cover, the leather string wrapped around the body, and the aged, food-splattered page edges. Some of those food splatters had probably come from her. She held the notebook to her chest for a moment. It had been her safety blanket, but now it was time for her to let it go.

She slid it across the table.

"I'm giving this to you," Radha said. "It was important to me, but I've translated all the recipes, and I think you should have it with you. He was your dad, after all."

Surprise flashed across his face. "I gave it as a gift, though."

"I know. I'm giving it back to you as a gift. I'll borrow the book again from time to time, but for now I think Dada should keep you company."

Her father held the notebook like a priceless artifact. He then touched it to his forehead in reverence. "Are we still going to use it for stress cooking?"

"Nope." Radha opened her own recipe log. "We're going to use mine." She showed him the note cards and sticky notes she'd tucked in the back. "I have some ideas, but I didn't want to write them in the book without trying them. What do you say?"

"I say let the stress cooking begin!"

Chapter Twenty-One

CHRISTMAS

Jai

MASI: I'm sorry you're upset. Your mother said you're trying to visit Nana but don't want to run into me at the stroke unit. Why don't you bring your father to visit him on Christmas? The three of you can have a few hours.

MASI: I miss you, sweet boy. Merry Christmas.

Jai sat between the hospital bed and his father's motorized chair. Nana Veeru was sleeping while his father was watching *Sholay*, which Jai had brought with them. It had taken nearly an hour to set up, since the hospital had serious accessibility issues, but luckily, Nana was in his own room now that he'd been transferred out of the ICU, so there was more space.

Jai had his laptop open and was researching some of the notes he'd taken when he'd talked to the last attending physician who'd come by on rounds.

Hemiplegia: paralysis on one side of the body.

Memory loss. Decreased speech function.
Partial face paralysis.

If a stroke victim has had a stroke before, they'll most likely have it again. Chances of survival after a stroke are less than 25% after seven years.

Nana Veeru had made it longer than that, probably because Masi had worked hard over the years to make sure he had regular checkups, medications, healthy food and exercise, and psychiatric care.

There was also a bit of luck associated with it too. Sometimes, though, strokes were unexplainable.

And now Nana would require extensive speech therapy, physical therapy, and psychiatric care based on the severity of his second stroke. If Jai was being honest with himself, he knew that his adopted grandfather had a clock that was ticking down faster and faster.

Jai opened another blank document and started making treatment notes and jotting down information on mobility and rehabilitation for maintaining quality of life. He wanted to look it all up later. He'd have to check the cost, too. Dad's treatment had been so expensive that they still hadn't recovered from it. Hopefully, Nana was in a better situation.

If Jai's dance team had still been talking to him, if Radha had still been talking to him, Jai would have leaned on them for some support. But now he was on his own.

"You are sad," Jai's father said quietly.

Jai looked up from his research and saw the questioning look on his father's face. He set his laptop on the small side table and put his socked feet up on the edge of Nana's bed.

"I'm not sad. I'm tired."

"From dancing?"

"No, from reading. I want to help Nana Veeru when he wakes up."

"Your mom," he said, forming each word by first making the shape with his mouth, "says you are an idiot because you don't go to college."

"Well, Mom says a lot of things," Jai said.

Jai's father huffed a laugh.

They sat in silence for a moment while *Sholay* continued to play.

Sholay, time with his father, and hours at the store had been his constant over the last week. Radha had gone to Chicago, and as much as he missed her, he knew she was definitely going to ignore his texts if he bothered reaching out first.

Jai adjusted his father's drinking tube for easier access. "Dad?"

"Yes, beta?"

"Did you ever think that all three of your sons would run the convenience store?"

Jai could tell it was taking a moment for his father to process the words, so he repeated himself, more slowly. When his father understood, he gave an almost imperceptible movement with his head.

"The store was my dream. Was Gopal's dream. You were too young to dream yet," he said in Gujarati.

His brother had told him the same thing. "But now that I am older. Wouldn't you want me to work with the family? Wouldn't you want me to be here instead of off at school?"

His father's mouth moved before the words could form.

"No. That makes my Jai sad."

"It doesn't! I want to help Gopal and Neil. I want to help the family. I didn't do anything when the accident happened because I was too young. It's my turn to help everyone. We need the money."

"Deekra," he said after a few minutes. "You can only help if you be Jai. Not Dad. I can still dream. I don't need you to dream for me."

"Dad—"

"No!" he said, loud and sharp. "No. I dream for me. Gopal dreams for Gopal. Neil dreams for Neil. We are lucky we all dream together. Their dreams happened early, that is all."

"I didn't help after your accident, Dad," Jai said quietly.

"You were a kid, Jai."

"Let me help now. Neil and Gopal helped. Let me be there now. For them, for Mom, and for you."

"I don't need it," his father said. "I don't need help. We did this for all of us, not just for you. I need maro deekro to know that. I need Jai. Jai has to dream for himself. Dream for yourself, Jai. You do what you want. We are not holding you back. You are the only one holding you back."

His father was essentially calling him a coward and

telling him that he was making excuses. Radha had called him a coward too. Maybe both of them were right.

Jai rubbed his hands over his face. He remembered when he was a kid and he'd overhear conversations about how all the money had gone to pay for Dad's treatments. How his brothers had dropped out of school to take over the new store.

How much more could he help his father and his nana if he became a doctor? If he succeeded?

Maybe he'd have to risk being different and taking a chance. He had his family's support, and, honestly, that was the most important part.

Jai looked over to his father. "Hey, old man," he said in as bright a voice as he could manage. "Let's say you're right, and I go after my dream. Will I still be your favorite if I don't make it?"

Jai's father smiled, his mouth spreading in a toothy grin. He chuckled. "Yes," he said. "But only if you try."

"Only if I try. Got it."

Jai turned to Nana Veeru. He still had a tube up his nose, an IV plugged in. His chest rose and fell in slow, soft breaths. One side of his face still drooped. Jai touched the dark, wrinkled fingers of one hand.

He wished so badly he could ask Nana what he thought about sending out his applications. "I would've really liked it if you were here in this moment with me, Nana," Jai said quietly.

His father mumbled something, then coughed.

"What was that, Dad?"

"Your nana," he said slowly, "would be proud, Jai. When he wakes up, he'll tell you himself. Show him that you are trying to follow your dream."

"Show him?"

Jai's father nodded, adjusting his head against the padding of the back of his chair. "A gift. If you follow your dream, that will be a good gift."

"Show him that I am following my dream … oh." He checked his phone. In an hour his mother was going to come and pick them up with the van. Would that be enough time?

He opened a new browser on his laptop, and after making sure he had the right documents ready – an essay from Dr. O'Hare's class, his information for the Common App – he checked the portal for Columbia University first-year applicants.

With his feet still propped up on the bed, he started a

new profile and began drafting Columbia's specific essay questions.

*

It was late when they got home. The nurse arrived shortly after to help with the bath and personal-care routine. Mom then tucked Dad into bed, and once he'd fallen asleep, she sat with Jai and his brothers at the old kitchen table. They ate takeout chole bhature and drank huge mugs of masala chai. There was also dhokla, his father's favorite, but Neil had gotten into it earlier, so Jai didn't want to touch it until his dad had had his share.

"How is Nana doing?" Gopal asked.

"He slept most of the time," Jai said. "I spoke to him for less than five minutes before we left. He's still not verbal, and he's frustrated because of the facial drooping and the new paralysis. His attending physician was really nice, because I asked a bunch of questions and the guy stayed around and answered them for me."

"What kind of questions?" Jai's mother asked.

"About treatment plan, length of treatment, medication, quality of life. I know that Masi is going to be a little overwhelmed with everything once Nana comes home, so I figured I'd try to get a head start and help her with it all. I have a couple quizzes coming up based on winter break reading, the Winter Showcase, work, and all that, but I can probably have something put together in a few weeks."

"You need to sleep, too, my bacha."

"It has to be done, right? And this is my way of helping now."

"You know," Neil said as he motioned with a piece of bhature, "I don't think this will make Masi feel better. She's really upset that you're mad at her. She was just trying to do her job."

Jai pushed his plate aside and took a long drink from his mug. He was not going to argue with his brothers about Masi. He'd talk to her directly if he had to. Besides, he'd pretty much apologized for giving her the cold shoulder with the note he'd left in Nana's room.

"Jai, puttar, you should talk to her. She only has your best interest at heart."

Nope, Jai thought. He was not going to take the bait.

Gopal had opened his mouth to say something when the doorbell rang.

"Who is here this late?" Jai's mom said. "I'll get it."

"Who do you think it is?" Neil asked. "One of your friends?"

"Not me," Jai and Gopal said simultaneously.

A few minutes later, Jai's mother returned, with Masi following close behind.

Jai's stomach twisted. Why wasn't she with Nana Veeru?

As if reading his mind, Masi said, "Everything is fine. They're letting me spend the night with him in his room, so I decided to drive home and get a change of clothes. I wanted to stop on my way – to see Jai."

She looked at him with fierceness in her eyes as she produced the folded piece of paper from her coat pocket. "I got your Christmas present."

"Christmas present?" Neil asked. "Dude, we don't do presents."

"We don't," Jai said. He hadn't done presents with his family in years. Mostly because they didn't have the money to do it. Besides, they didn't really celebrate Christmas. Some of his desi friends had the whole tree-and-presents thing, but for the Patels, Christmas was mostly an excuse to eat really good food with family.

"What changed your mind?" Masi asked.

As his brothers and mother looked on, Jai stood and

shoved his hands in his back pockets. "First, I thought you would tell me when you were going to go to the team with your recommendations. You didn't have to, I get that, but it felt like you didn't give me a chance. You're always pushing me to be better, to do better, but this wasn't fair, Masi."

"Jai!" his mother said. "You don't speak to Masi like—"

"No, no, it's okay," Masi said, interjecting. The woman's face, clear of makeup, looked tired and worn. She'd tied a scarf around her head today instead of one of her colorful dhukus, and she wore a sweat suit. Everything about her screamed burnout.

"I never meant for you to feel that way," she said. "But I'm a teacher, too, Jai, and I had a responsibility to those students. I also gave you plenty of time to act on your own. And the only reason I push you harder than anyone else is because I know you have the potential to give more."

"I know that. But you have to let me figure things out on my own sometimes. You can't box me into corners, okay?"

"I never meant to—"

"But you did. With my recommendation letters, with my essay, with everything. Then with telling Radha she needs to dance. Really? You didn't give me another alternative.

And I'm not saying I'm not grateful for what you do, but I need to make my own decisions."

She pressed her lips together until they formed a thin line and nodded.

"You're right about something, though," he continued. "I can't help Nana if I can't help myself. So, uh, I talked to Dad today." Jai looked at his brothers, his mother. "He gave me some advice, which basically was about making sure I do what I want to do in life, and to give you a gift to thank you for helping me along the way. So, there you go. The paper I left was your gift. I still have some supplemental essay questions to answer before it's done and submitted, but I asked one of the nurses if she could print the screenshot for me."

"What?" Gopal burst out. "What gift? What screenshot?"

Masi unfolded the paper. She passed it to Jai's mother first, who pressed a hand against her chest when she read the words at the top, and then to Gopal and Neil.

"You're applying to Columbia?" Neil said. He broke out into a grin. "Finally! You're pulling a *Good Will Hunting*!"

"Okay, I have no idea what that means, but yes. I'm applying."

"And your father was the one who changed your mind?" Masi asked.

"He just put things into perspective. He also called me a few choice names in Gujarati. You deserve most of the credit, though. Thanks, Masi. For always being there for me."

She opened her arms and pulled him into a warm hug. He buried his face in her neck. She'd been his rock. The dancing, the long hours of quiet conversation, and the constant lectures to be stronger and better.

When he pulled back, Masi held his face, and with tears in her eyes she said, "You are going to be a brilliant doctor. Just like your nana Veeru."

"We'll be okay, right?" he said to Masi, his mother, and his brothers. "Not like before. Not like when we didn't have … when we were struggling to pay for food, and the house—" He was horrified when his voice broke, but thankfully Masi just held him close. Then his mother came over and hugged him.

He couldn't respond, so he just held on. Then his brothers jumped him in a group hug.

"Columbia!" Gopal and Neil started chanting.

"Don't let your fool brothers get to your head," Jai's

mother said. "You are just sending in your application. It's not like you have gotten in yet."

"Thanks, Mom," Jai replied. "I can always count on you to keep things real."

"It's my job, puttar. Jammie, why don't you sit and have a cup of chai? It's still hot. I'll pack some food for you too. Take a few minutes before you go get your things. It's Christmas, and you could use a little break, no?"

They all crowded around the old, scarred table, with refilled cups and Jai's application screenshot in the center of the table. He hadn't realized until this Christmas dinner that his family wanted this for him as much as he wanted it for himself.

"So, what are you going to do now?" Gopal asked.

"What do you mean, what is he going to do now?" Neil replied. "He's the brown version of Will from *Good Will Hunting*. He's gonna see about a girl!"

Chapter Twenty-Two

Radha

From the Recipe Book of Radha Chopra

Dada's Signature Chole

To make Dada's signature chole recipe, you must have:

Chickpeas
Cumin
Fennel seeds
Cardamom
Cloves
Bay leaves
Dried gooseberry powder
Dried mango powder

Onion

Tomatoes

Garlic

Turmeric

Red chilies

Pomegranate seeds

Salt

Pepper

Ginger

Dhania

Grind ginger and garlic into a paste using a mortar and pestle (or a blender with a little water). Cook the chickpeas in the pressure cooker. Sautee sliced onions, ginger, and garlic until they turn brown in color. Then add tomatoes. Cook until soft. Add all the spices to create our gravy. Add cooked chickpeas and water as needed. Simmer for three hours on low. Garnish with dhania.

Note: It's almost impossible to find gooseberry powder outside an Indian grocery store.

To make the bhature, the yeasted fried bread to eat with the chole, a cheat is to buy biscuit dough in a can, roll it into thin, four-inch flat disks, and drop them in hot oil. Same taste, a fraction of the work.

SHAKTI: Happy New YEAR!!!

RADHA: Happy New Year! I just got back. My mom picked me up from Philly airport bright and early, loaded me up with Starbucks, and I am ready to get started.

SHAKTI: Started? Today? On New Year's? Have you talked to Jai yet?

RADHA: Not yet. I have no idea how I'm going to, either. This is a huge change in the choreography.

SHAKTI: Well, you have to soon, since he's the one getting a new dance partner. And by new partner I mean you.

RADHA: Yeah, let's figure that out later. Any chance we can get in one of the school studios today? Does someone have a key?

SHAKTI: The drama club is rehearsing today. We can ask them to let us in.

RADHA: Okay. Can you gather the seniors? We'll start with them, like we started the first time. Then we'll bring in Jai.

SHAKTI: You got it, boss babe.

Radha packed her dance bag, opting to include her ghungroos just in case. She stripped out of her travel gear and into the comfiest pair of workout clothes she owned, complete with bright green leg warmers and a bandana.

She was halfway down the stairs when her mother called out to her.

"Are you going somewhere?" she asked. She stood in her office doorway, wearing leather pants and a cashmere sweater.

"I'm meeting with the dance team," Radha said. "We're making some adjustments to the choreography."

"Oh." Her face fell, and she picked up a card on her desk. "I was hoping that we could spend the day together. I still haven't given you your gift for Christmas."

"Oh? What is it?"

She handed the card to Radha. "Something I hope you like. It's because I know you like cooking so much now. And your newfound love for choreography of course.

Consider it a peace offering."

Inside were three folded pieces of paper. The first was a flyer for an intensive summer class at the local cooking academy. The second was an entry into the New Jersey Food and Wine Festival as an amateur competitor in her age bracket. And the third was an entry for a dance competition in the choreography category.

Radha's stomach bottomed out. Besides a few comments here and there, her mother had been so hands-off since her panic attack that Radha had hoped she was turning over a new leaf and listening to what Radha wanted to do. In fact, she'd planned on telling Sujata about her decision to dance in the showcase after all. Thankfully, she'd waited just long enough to find out that her mother hadn't changed at all.

She folded the papers up, put them back inside the card, and tried to smile. "Thanks, Mom. I appreciate it."

Sujata's grin faded. "What, you don't like them?"

"No, that's not it. Thank you. Really."

"Then what? The classes were really expensive, Radha. You've been learning how to cook with your father and cousin. Imagine what a class could do for you!"

Radha sighed. "It's not ... I'm not learning to be a

professional. I'm learning my family history. Food is a cultural gateway. I know your family history, which is kathak and all about your background as a dancer. This was about Dad."

"I don't understand," Sujata said. Her arms crossed over her chest.

"Mom. I don't want to compete. It takes the fun out of cooking."

"Oh, don't be ridiculous," Sujata said, waving a hand like she was brushing away a fly. "The competition would be a slam dunk. I looked at last year's winner and you're already way better than them. Same with the choreography. If you insist on doing that as part of your course curriculum, then I can't stop you—"

"Mom, did you even hear a word I just said?" Radha asked. "I don't intend on *ever* competing. I love cooking. I love dancing. It's okay to be good at something without competing. Please don't take this joy away from me too."

"I'm not taking anything away from you! I'm trying to *help* you. Why are you always making me the bad guy? It's my job to make sure you're the best you can be, and this is how you can be the best."

"You don't have to try and make me the best. You just

have to support me so I can figure it out on my own. Cooking is something I share with Dad—"

"Your father!" her mother raged, her words as pointed as daggers, her finger jabbing in her direction. "He's the reason you've given up, isn't it? You know what? I think it's time to call it. You haven't given a bit of effort to your dance career here—"

"What? How do you even know that?"

"—and if you love your father so much, if you love cooking with him and being with him more than me, you should probably move back to Chicago."

"One minute I have to go back because I'm not doing what you want, and then, when I agree to visit Dad, you change your mind. I'm tired of you threatening me with Chicago," Radha said, trying to keep her voice even.

"*Threatening* you? I may be more liberal than some of the other Indian parents here, Radha, but don't you forget that in this house, you do not talk to me like that." Sujata's accent was as hard as the words spewing out of her now.

"I don't know how else I can get you to listen to me. You still blame me for Kathak Classics and refusing to perform. You think that I screwed up, when actually I made a choice. I think you're the one who screwed up, all on your own. You can't use me to rewrite your own history anymore."

Her mother slapped her across the face.

The sting was sharp and quick. Stunned into silence, Radha pressed a hand to her burning cheek.

"How dare you?" Sujata shouted, her voice trembling. "How dare you, when I've given up everything for you!"

"That's what I'm saying! Who asked you to, Mom? Who asked you to do any of it when all I wanted was to dance or, I don't know, cook a freaking meal?"

"Then you could do that in Chicago," Sujata replied.

"Fine. But before you buy my ticket, you should probably talk to Dad, because I'm pretty sure that you can't just send me wherever when you have full custody."

Radha tossed the card on the desk, spun on her heels, and grabbed her dance bag. She was racing out the door in her UGGs moments later. She couldn't deal with her mother right now. She had bigger fish to fry. Like making sure her boyfriend and her Bollywood dance team won regionals.

*

"Are you sure you're okay?" Shakti asked.

"Yeah." Radha stretched her legs in front of her and bent so that her forehead touched her knees. "I'm used to fighting with my mother."

"I don't understand why you didn't tell her you were going to perform after all. Wouldn't that have made things better between you two?"

Honestly, Radha wasn't sure. She wanted to do this on her own, and Sujata would try to take over. The cooking classes were a reminder of that. Radha's mom had a primary goal, and that was for Radha to be the best – competing, performing, and pushing for success. The truth made her heart hurt, because it was the reason why they'd never get along. Not completely.

Radha switched positions and leaned into another stretch. If she focused on what she had to do, as opposed to what her mother thought she had to do, hopefully she'd find happiness.

Never in a million years had she thought the stage would be a part of that equation.

"Wow," she said after a moment. "I'm getting onstage again."

"You are!" Shakti cheered.

"I have to remember my breathing exercises and all that; otherwise I'm going to pass out before the show even begins."

"We won't let that happen," Shakti said. She jumped to her feet and pulled Radha to hers. "Anita and Hari are coming later, by the way. Hari just woke up. Is it okay to start without them? I have a lot to do before we get to the showcase."

"Sounds good to me." Radha walked over to the speaker unit in the corner and plugged in her phone. "I was thinking about your role in the choreography, and how the whole routine is about a wedding. I was going to ask if you'd be interested in a sister-of-the-bride or the best friend role, because then you can get two solos. But I also hate that idea because you've told me how much you don't like the 'gay best friend' stereotype. So I'm asking you what you want to do."

Shakti shrugged. "I want solos. I want recruiters to see me, and I want to dance in my style. I am not a stereotype, and I sure as hell plan on being the leading lady in my own romance. But this romance is yours. I'm okay with it. Just make me look good."

Radha wrapped her arms around Shakti and hugged

her. "Thanks," she whispered.

"Don't mention it." She pulled back. "Don't you have to ask Jai first before you start making changes, though?"

The thought had crossed her mind, but she had no idea how she was going to start that talk. *Hey, I know we fought, but I decided to perform and need you to okay a change in the routine.*

"I don't know, Shakti. We didn't exactly leave things in an okay place."

"So what?" Shakti said. "Just tell him how you feel, how he made you feel, and then he'll apologize. You're done."

"Hey, aren't you mad at him too?"

Shakti shrugged, and her oversized sweater – the Death Star wrapped in Christmas lights – glittered. "He texted over break. He said he was sorry. I believe him. You should too."

"I'm thinking about it. After all, this is really for Jai."

"What's for me?"

Radha jerked at the sound of his voice. He stood in the doorway, in thick boots and a sweatshirt. He looked slightly disheveled and out of breath. And tired. He looked really tired, and Radha wanted to hug him.

She glanced at Shakti, who shrugged.

"Traitor," Radha murmured.

"You'll thank me later," she replied. "Happy New Year, Captain. I'm going to run to the vending machine to grab myself some water; then I'll go up front to see if anyone else is here. That gives you two plenty of time to talk. Fix this, please. Your drama is bad for my skin. I don't look good with stress breakouts."

She closed the door behind her with a resounding snick.

It was the same place they'd left off on the last day of school before break. She remembered their fight so clearly that it still stung, like her mother's slap. Radha got to her feet.

"Uh, Shakti called me," Jai said.

"I figured."

"It took me some time to get here, because I was working."

"I'm sorry, I know you're a person short—"

"No, it's okay." He stepped forward, his boots squeaking on the wood floor. "I didn't – uh, I didn't hear from you at all over break. How was Chicago?"

"It was good. It was great. I spent it with my dad. Jai, you could've texted me."

"Well, I didn't know if you wanted to hear from me."

"Well, same," she burst out. "You know what has kept me up at night over the last two weeks? Why did you keep the director's feedback to yourself? I mean, especially from me. I may not be a relationship expert, but we were dating."

"I didn't intentionally keep it from you," he said, waving his hands at her like she should've realized it. "Well, maybe intentionally, but just long enough for me to figure out how to tell you without hurting you and making you worry. I didn't want you to feel like I was guilting you into getting back on the stage!"

"I wouldn't have felt that way." She took a step toward him, her hands linked tightly behind her back. "Part of why I wanted to choreograph was because I wanted to help you. This would've helped you even more."

"No, not at the high price you'd have to pay."

His fierceness was always so surprising for her, and it made her palms sweaty as she faced him down. "You don't make those choices, Jai. I do."

He rubbed the back of his neck. "You're right. You can make the choice of whether to dance or not on your own. But I wasn't thinking of it like that, Radha. Yes, some of my reasoning was selfish, but I was thinking of you, too."

They were going to keep running in circles unless one of

them made the first step, Radha realized. "Well, Captain, you really need to talk to me next time. I can take care of myself. I know what I'm capable of."

"And that's why I really love you," he said quietly. "Because you're badass."

"W-what?" Her heart started pounding in a rapid staccato.

Jai's quick grin kept her off-kilter. "I'm sorry we fought," he said, walking toward her slowly in small steps, his boots squeaking on the floor. "I'm sorry that I ever let you think you were not as amazing as you are. I know I'm asking for a lot. After so many screwups, you have every right to be mad."

"Same. I mean, I'm sorry that we fought too," she said, and took a step back to keep the distance between them. Her pulse began to race. "And you deserve the right to make your own choices for school."

"But you never really pushed me. You just sort of told me your opinion and supported me despite everything. I should've done the same for you instead of accusing you of not understanding me."

He was so close now, even as she continued to retreat. "I want to do something else for you. Well, it's for me, too," she said.

Her words were jumbled now as he came closer and closer. "I think it's time that I get back on the stage. I'm going to perform in the showcase, Jai. We're going to get you to regionals and win, because I love you, too—"

He rushed forward and his mouth was on hers. The tension inside her shattered. Radha wrapped her arms around his neck, and when he shifted his hands to the backs of her thighs, she jumped up and wrapped her legs around his waist.

"You're performing in the showcase," he said between kisses.

"I am." Radha held on. "I missed you. I don't care how that makes me sound. It's true."

"I missed you, too." He squeezed her, and she wanted to burrow into him.

When they finally separated, Jai held her close. "Happy New Year, Radha."

"Happy New Year."

He pulled out his phone and unlocked it. "Guess what I did." A Columbia University logo and application status filled the tiny window.

"Oh my God," she gasped. "You applied?"

He nodded and sniffed at her hair. "I did. And now that you're performing, it feels right. That we're doing these really hard things together. By the way, your shampoo is still the same. I like kiwis."

"Jai!" She jumped him again and squealed. "I'm so happy for you!"

"Well, like my mother keeps reminding me, it's an application. We'll see what happens. I also applied to Princeton and Rutgers."

"Well, when we win regionals, that money will go a long way no matter where you decide to go."

"You're serious about that?"

Jai cupped her face in his palms. She felt safe here with him. "I have a few weeks to get myself together, but yes. I'm serious."

"Does your mom know?"

"Nope. That's a story, thanks to events earlier today."

Pulling her close, he nuzzled her neck. "Come on, new girl. Tell me all about it. Then, when you're ready, we'll get to work."

Chapter Twenty-Three

THE WINTER SHOWCASE

Jai

MASI: Please come to the dressing room at intermission. Bring Radha and the other seniors on your team.
JAI: Okay?? Is something wrong?
MASI: We'll see.

TARA: Good luck today! I know you have Winter Showcase. Listen, I wanted to explain myself because I suck at texting as much as I do at first impressions. I know you're busy, but it looks like other people know that Radha is a part of Bollywood Beats now. Other people who are part of the classical dance world. So ... just a heads-up. I want you to know I wasn't the one who told them, but I feel bad about Diwali so I'm reaching out. Peace offering.

TARA: You're a great guy, Jai. I really hope you two are happy.

Radha sat in a corner against the wall, wrapping ghungroos around her ankles. Jai could see that it was the last part of her outfit. She'd finished dressing in the red anarkali that her cousin Simran had sent from India. Her makeup was complete as well, a dramatic look that contrasted the simplicity of her clothes. Her lips were scarlet red, and her eyes were framed in long, thick black lashes. Her hair was tied in a low bun and parted down the middle. A tikka lay along her part and ended in a diamond-shaped gold piece on her forehead.

In the backstage chaos, she looked like a figure of calm as she completed her transition into a dancer. Shakti sat at her side, her polar opposite, and talked to her in what looked like a steady stream of chatter. Shakti's outfit was not for the lead role anymore. Instead she wore a fusion pantsuit for the flips she'd be doing onstage.

Jai wanted to sit next to them and make sure Radha was okay, but he'd learned something vital in the three weeks since New Year's Day.

Radha Chopra did not like hovering.

She had a spine of steel, and if he was worried about her, then he'd just have to worry in silence and be supportive in other ways.

Moments later, Shakti stood, patted Radha on the shoulder, and walked toward him.

"How is she doing?" he asked when Shakti reached his side.

"She said she took vitamin beta-blockers her doctor approved of, so she's sort of calm," Shakti replied. "She's also only drinking protein shakes today, because she's worried that if she eats something, she's going to be sick. I think if we keep checking in on her, though, she's going to rip our heads off."

"You're probably right. Hey, any word on whether her mother is going to show?"

"I think she will," Shakti said. "Radha told me that her mother never misses a performance, even if she thinks that Radha isn't dancing."

"Shakti, she's been quiet all day. Like when she first came to the academy."

Shakti rolled her eyes. "Listen, just because she's not making her adorable quirky sarcastic comments or telling dad jokes doesn't mean she's backsliding. It's a tough day for her. She keeps going through these anxiety exercises. It doesn't help to know that people at Princeton found out about her experience in London."

Jai gaped at her. "What are you talking about?"

"Wait, Tara didn't tell you?"

"Tara? As in my ex, Tara?"

Shakti nodded. "She said she was trying to talk to you about it and give you a heads-up. Radha's past has caught up to us."

"I think she texted but I didn't ... I've been busy."

Jai remembered that she'd been trying to get in touch with him, but he'd never called her back. "Does Radha know?"

"I told her. I don't think anyone has said anything to her yet, but she's always with the team, so I doubt they'd have the guts to approach all of us."

"Okay," he said. "I mean, we can't do anything about it now, and hopefully tonight goes smoothly without anyone bringing it up, right?"

Shakti shrugged. "Yeah, I guess."

They both watched Radha meticulously straightening the bells on her ankles.

"Shakti, what am I going to have to do to make sure my girlfriend is okay?"

"Just be there when she needs you, Jai," Shakti said. She patted his shoulder. "And maybe hold her dance bag while she kicks ass."

"Five minutes!" the stage manager called. "I need performances one and three in the right-wing holding areas, and performances two and four in the left. Just like walk-through during dress rehearsal. Let's go!"

The flurry of activity backstage became even more chaotic and dancers and musicians ran past them. Jai's adrenaline started pumping through his body.

"Let's get everyone together stage left," Jai said. "Have Anita check if our props are ready to go too."

"On it, Captain," Shakti replied before hurrying away.

"Are you done talking about me?"

Jai turned to see Radha standing with her hands on her hips. Her cheeks glittered under the hanging lights.

"We weren't talking about you," Jai said, gently skimming his thumb over the sharp curve of her jaw. Did it look more … defined somehow? He probably shouldn't have touched her because she was makeup-ready but she didn't seem to mind. "We were talking about the routine.

You just happened to be a part of that routine."

Radha's eyebrow winged in a perfect arch.

"Okay, whatever," he said. "Let's go get married."

She gasped, and her mouth made a perfect O. Jai couldn't help but laugh at her expression.

"Relax, it's not like we're getting married for real," he said, mocking her and the way she'd first teased him about the routine.

She smacked him on the arm but then tangled her fingers with his.

"Thirty seconds!" the stage manager shouted.

Radha's breath hitched, and he pulled her close as they moved to the wings.

Everything happens so fast on performance day, Jai thought. The auditorium went dark, and cheers echoed past the curtain.

Then the music began, the curtains parted, and Principal Miller stepped up to the podium to deliver his introduction.

"Good evening and welcome to the Princeton Academy for the Arts and Sciences Winter Showcase!" The audience applauded. Principal Miller began talking about the importance of STEAM education, and the success of past students who'd gone on to illustrious careers after the academy.

Radha's breathing grew faster as they waited in the wings, and Jai pressed her hands against the beadwork of the sherwani he was wearing for the performance. He inhaled and exhaled, watching her do the same.

Their foreheads touched, their eyes closed, and the audience clapped again, before Masi's voice echoed from the microphone.

"Thank you, Principal Miller. Tonight we celebrate the passion, dedication, and hard work that our performers have poured into their routines. We're excited to welcome four esteemed judges with expertise in dance, theater, and music. Our judges come from around the world, and their areas of expertise cover every performance you'll see tonight.

"Once the judges rank each routine, the highest-scored performances will go on to represent the school in regional competitions. Details about that are included in your program guide, and we'll be announcing the winners at the end of the showcase. Now, to get this evening started..."

Jai could hear Radha's breathing even out. Their performance was fourth. They had to get through at least thirty-five minutes, including introductions and stage changes.

"Hey," he whispered. "Radha?"

"I thought I was fine," she whispered. "I thought I would be fine. I'm looking forward to doing this again, actually, but then, well, here we are."

"You are fine. You're *great*."

Her shoulders continued to rise and fall. Her ghungroos chimed as she shifted.

The first routine finished, and Radha relaxed a fraction after the room applauded. She then stood shoulder to shoulder with him for the second performance. Their hands were slick with sweat, but he wasn't letting go. By the third number, she began to loosen up.

"You know," he whispered, "I don't mean to rock the boat, so to speak, but people usually get more and more nervous the closer they get to their performance. You're … relaxing."

"Shut. Up. Jai, I already have to pee. I don't need your commentary."

"Yes, ma'am," he said, grinning.

The third routine ended in a flurry of applause, and the curtains closed. Thirty-five minutes had flown by.

The crew rushed across the polished floorboards, setting up the mandap, pulling down the backdrop, and placing the props at the far edges of the stage.

"Let's go, guys!" Jai called in his team. His nerves were rock steady. This was what they'd been working toward for so long.

Everyone huddled in close. Jai scanned the expectant and excited faces, then nodded to Radha. "Care to do the honors?"

"*Me?* What, give a pep talk?"

"This is your show. You've made something incredible. We're happy to be a part of it."

There were several nods and cheers.

"Well," she said. Radha stepped into the middle of the group circle. "I've never given a pep talk, but I'll tell you something that blew my mind this morning. I realized that one year ago today, I was on my way to London. I was going to the International Kathak Classics competition, where I eventually made it to the final round.

"I dropped out. I didn't dance because I was freaked. It's a long, boring story that I'm sick of telling frankly, but I learned about regret. I regret not dancing, which is seriously a loaded statement for me, since my mom felt the same way about her career. But I also learned about choices. I don't want any of you to walk away from tonight with regrets, only memories of the choice you made to be a part of the team. As long as you go out there and love every moment of it, then ... well, you've succeeded. Thank you for making me a part of your group. This is ... mushy and totally pathetic, but you're all the best."

There was a round of "awwww."

"Bollywood Beats!" the stage manager called. "Places! Thirty seconds."

Jai winked at Radha and put his hand in the center. "One, two, three – let's go!" The team scattered. He didn't have time for nerves anymore as he rushed to his first position. He was ready. His team was ready. Radha ... well, she'd always been ready to perform, whether she knew it or not.

Masi's voice came through the speakers and introduced their performance.

Finally.

He looked across the stage to where Radha stood. She leaned down, touched the floor with three fingers, and then touched her chest. When she looked back up at him, he formed a heart with his hands and held it up.

She did the same.

There was determination on her face, and he could see it from where he stood.

The curtain rose, their dialogue voice-over began, and Jai counted down in his head.

Five. Six. Seven. Eight.

He moved toward Radha, and she matched his steps. The song reached a crescendo, and excitement rushed through him.

Shakti burst through the dance line and nailed her cue. The crowd cheered.

Yes, he chanted in his head. He was hitting every beat, just like he'd practiced. Radha met him in the center of the stage, and he picked her up and twirled her, completing part one of the performance. The other dancers rushed forward, and they moved together. Their bare feet slapped against the hardwood in a rhythm of eight and sixteen counts.

Elbows up, shoulders back. He could hear his girlfriend's voice in his head and grinned at the faceless crowd.

After the second transition, the guys exited stage right. Jai hid offstage behind the black partition curtain and watched in awe as Radha shone. He'd seen her in practice, but under the bright lights and at center stage, she was incredible. It made complete sense that Masi said she was one of the best kathak dancers of her generation.

He was so entranced that he almost missed his cue. The ceremony scene was the hardest, and when the music transitioned, he could see the concentration on his team's faces as they moved to the square markers on the stage floor.

One, two, three, four; one, two, three, four, he counted the footwork off.

They jumped into the marked square and turned in unison.

He wanted to fist-pump when they completed the last turn. The music changed again, and Jai and Radha twirled past each other to start the climax.

The reception scene. Every Bollywood Beats member was onstage. They just had to keep pushing, keep the energy up, even though exhaustion was starting to hit hard.

He shut down and let muscle memory take over to get him through the last twenty seconds.

Then he made it.

Eleven minutes. The routine was eleven minutes and nineteen seconds, and he was breathless, sweating, and holding Radha in a dip at the very last note.

The room erupted in applause, and the audience surged to their feet. Jai grinned, struggling to hold the pose until the curtains closed.

The minute they were hidden behind the velvet drapes, he pulled Radha up so that their chests were pressed together, their arms wrapped around each other, and he was kissing her like his life depended on it. His team cheered behind him, almost as loud as the audience.

When he heard the curtains begin to open again, and his team ran forward to form a line, he pulled Radha up to a standing position and spun her out.

They bowed in unison to an audience shadowed because of the bright stage lights, and then they exited stage left.

"Nice lipstick," Shakti said. She tackled him in a hug. "God, we did *so good*. Like better than when we were in practice!"

Jai rubbed a hand over his mouth. "Totally. Now we'll just have to wait to see what the judges come up with."

His team hugged and pounded each other on the back as they moved toward the open space behind the stage. Jai grabbed his phone from the bag that he'd left in the corner. He wanted to text his family, to ask them what they thought. If anyone around them had said anything.

When he saw Masi's text message, he sobered. Fast.

Something was wrong. Very wrong.

He texted Masi back and waited for the response to come in. It was almost immediate.

"What happened?" Radha asked as she came to stand next to him.

Some of the other team members came over to hear. He looked at the faces that had trusted him to lead the team this year.

"I'm not sure. The director wants to see me and Radha and the other seniors at intermission. There seems to be a problem. I don't have a clue what it could be."

He looked at Radha, who'd paled slightly under the thick layer of makeup she wore. He knew what she was thinking. But no. There was no way her mother could've intervened … right?

Chapter Twenty-Four

Radha

From the Recipe Book of Radha Chopra

Chicken Makhani

As much as I love Dada's recipe for chicken makhani, I made a few tweaks that work better for me. It's perfect after competitions. To make my recipe for butter chicken, you'll need:

Boneless, skinless chicken thighs cut in cubes
Fresh lemon juice
Red chili powder
Plain full-fat yogurt (Greek is better)
Turmeric, garam masala, red chilies, sea salt, crushed

dried fenugreek, cumin, coriander, fresh cilantro

Melted butter, and softened butter

Black cardamom, crushed

Garlic cloves

Minced ginger

Tomato paste

Crushed tomatoes

Chicken stock

Heavy cream

Dry-roast the seasoning, then crush with mortar and pestle before using.

Combine yogurt, turmeric, garam masala, garlic, ginger, lemon juice, and salt. Stir well. Massage mixture into cubed chicken, and marinate three to six hours.

On medium heat, panfry chicken cubes until cooked through. In a Dutch oven, melt softened butter, then add garlic, cardamom, and fenugreek, and cook until fragrant. Stir in ginger, chilies, and tomato paste. Then add crushed tomatoes and chili powder. Add chicken stock and keep stirring to prevent contents from sticking

to the bottom of the pot. Blend with immersion blender.
Turn heat to medium until sauce begins to thicken and
boil. Add chicken, and cook covered. Stir in cream and
garam masala. Simmer for the final twenty minutes.

Radha knew that if something was wrong, there was
a very good chance it had to do with her. Scenes from
London flashed in her brain like a horror movie on
repeat. She didn't have to use her inhaler once, but there
was a chance that after this meeting, she was going to be
sucking on it.

She followed Jai and the other senior dancers into the
dressing rooms that were reserved as a meeting place for
faculty. The director and Principal Miller were already
inside. Principal Miller, a slender man with a shock of
white hair, stood with his arms clasped in front of him.
Radha had only seen him at assemblies, but people seemed
to like him.

"Can you all please file in?" Principal Miller asked. "Yes,
thank you. Please close the door, Anita. Great, thanks."

The director spoke first. "You all did a wonderful job.
I asked Jai to bring you here, because this particularly
affects your future as performers more than your junior

team members. A group of parents formally submitted a complaint at the start of the show about your place in the showcase. They would like for us to disqualify your team from being judged as part of the competition."

"What?"

"Why would they do that?"

"Is it because we're a Bollywood dance team?"

Principal Miller held up his hand for attention. "I'm so sorry that your performance is shadowed by this, but we have to ask a few questions."

Radha waited, holding her breath.

"Director Muza has given me her answer, but I have to hear it directly from you. Did some of you go to the Bollywood Blowout at New York University?" Principal Miller asked.

Every single person in the room nodded.

"And, while there, did you talk to one of the judges? Guru Nandani Modi?"

"Guru Nandani is a judge?" Radha burst out. "Of the showcase? She's outside right now?"

The director nodded. "Guru Nandani was highly recommended to us. We invited her months ago to participate. We haven't gotten a chance to speak with her yet regarding this … situation, because we wanted to come to you all first."

Radha wasn't exactly a straight-A student like Jai, but she was a freaking kathak master. She could read expression and body language better than anyone in the room. "The parents think I'm cheating. Someone found out that we were at Bollywood Blowout, made a connection between me and Guru Nandani, and now is trying to use my history against the team."

Shakti squeezed through the small crowd until she stood shoulder to shoulder with Radha, and gripped her hand. Jai gripped the other.

"I'm not sure how the connection was made—"

"I can guess," Anita said. "We have a few people on the team who are dating other dancers. I bet you someone said something about Bollywood Blowout."

"And the showcase program does list Guru— uh, this judge as an NYU professor and a kathak dance teacher," Principal Miller said.

Radha hadn't seen the program. She'd been too busy trying not to freak about performing again. But she did have a relationship with Guru Nandani, and she was not going through another year of questioning whether or not she was good enough. Her team had done an amazing job, and screw anyone for trying to tear her down.

"Guru Nandani used to be my teacher," Radha said.

The dressing room quieted, and Radha stepped in front of the principal and the director.

"I learned from her when I studied at her school in India. I had like a three-minute conversation with her when we ran into each other in the lobby at NYU. I didn't even know she was going to be here tonight. If anyone is accusing me of cheating, they can talk to me, because I didn't do it, and the team definitely didn't cheat."

Her supporters, her friends, all nodded in approval around her.

The director looked down at her hands and then smiled. "I believe you. But your personal connection with a judge creates a conflict of interest. It's in the rules for the showcase."

"So, what does that mean? We're disqualified?" Hari asked.

"That's for us to decide," Principal Miller said.

Radha's team roared in protest around her. She held up a hand and stepped in front of the director. "Fine. Exclude Guru Nandani's scores."

"Excuse me?"

"If the parents are so concerned that I cheated because I talked to an old teacher once, then exclude her score. There are three other judges, right? That's more than enough to make a fair assessment in the group-performance category."

The director and Principal Miller looked at each other and then at Radha.

"The other judges don't have the background to judge a Bollywood dance routine," the principal said.

"But they can judge a dance performance," Radha said. "If they're experts, they can see that we're the best. You don't need to be a Bollywood expert to see talent, just like you don't have to be Indian to like Indian food. I bet you that we will still have an incredibly competitive score even if the other judges don't know a paran from a toda. People think it's unfair that Guru Nandani knows me? Then this is how we can stay in the competition while making the haters happy at the same time."

Radha felt Jai's hand on her shoulder. "She's right," he said. "We're good enough that we don't need her score. I'm all for it."

"Captain and choreographer have spoken," Shakti said.

"All in favor?"

The team chorused, "Aye!"

The director and the principal shared another look.

"We'll have to discuss with the other teams," Principal Miller said, "and let the parents know our decision. But your ... transparency is appreciated. You all really did a fantastic job, from what we were able to see in the wings. We hope we can resolve this quickly and quietly so we can enjoy the rest of the showcase."

The principal led the way by exiting the room first, and Radha felt a sense of relief when she saw the director mouth *It's okay* to Jai as she passed him.

When Radha was one of the last ones left, she shook out the tremors in her hands and rolled her shoulders back.

"You ready to go sit in the audience?" Jai asked.

She looked over at the exit. If she rejoined the team, she was going to be bombarded with questions. It was all a bit overwhelming, and truthfully, she'd had enough for the moment.

"I'm going to run to the bathroom," she said to Jai. "I also want to take my ghungroos off. I'm a bit noisy with them."

"Okay. Want me to wait here?"

Radha shook her head. "I'll see you up in the balcony with the rest of the team."

"I'll save you a seat, then," he said. "And if the director makes the decision before you come back, I'll let you know." He kissed her temple and headed off in the opposite direction.

Radha tiptoed through the backstage corridors to the dressing area where the team had gotten ready. Her bag was still sitting against the wall. She sat down and began untying her ghungroos. The faint sound of the MC asking people to take their seats was barely audible through all the backstage sound-proofing.

Before she could finish, she heard heels clicking against the floorboards.

"What are you doing here?" she asked as her mother appeared from the entrance.

Sujata surveyed the space and then strolled over to Radha. She dug into her tote bag and produced a familiar glass bottle. "I brought you juice. Have you gone to the bathroom yet? You always have to pee after performances."

"I'm putting these away and then I'll go."

Sujata nodded and tucked the bottle in her bag. When she made no move to leave, Radha resumed unwrapping her ghungroos.

Damn it, Radha thought. "What are you doing here, Mom? Did you call Guru Nandani?"

"Guru Nandani? What? No, I'm here because you said you choreographed a group dance and I wanted to come see for myself. Radha, why didn't you tell me that you were performing?"

Radha looked up at her mother after she put away the first set of ghungroos. "Really? You're asking me that?"

"Yes! I could've helped."

"I didn't want you to help, Mom. I don't want your help unless I ask for it. I'm almost eighteen, and you still make everything about what *you* want me to do, and I lose my dance joy. Being a part of Bollywood Beats brought it back for me, and I really think that it was because you weren't involved."

There was hurt on her mother's face, but Radha couldn't help it. She put her second set of ghungroos in her bag and stood. "I have to go sit with my team."

She was halfway to the exit door when her mother called out. "I'm happy you didn't tell me. About what you were doing, about the performance."

Radha whirled. "What?"

"I'm happy," Sujata said. She gripped her shoulder bag with both hands. "I wish you'd trusted me with it, but I can understand why you didn't. As your mother, I have to work harder on making sure my expectations for you are the same as what you want for yourself."

"Wait … that sounds like … are you seeing Dr. Werner?"

"One of the other doctors at her practice, yes. You're not the only one who can go to therapy, Radha." She angled her chin. "I want to be as close as we once were, and you have to trust me for that. So I'll back up, but I'm here if you want me to help."

"Oh. Uh … okay."

"And, Radha?"

"Yeah, Mom?"

Her mother's eyes glistened. "You looked stunning with your dance joy."

They reached for a hug at the same time. The smell of expensive French perfume and hair product always made her think of her boss-babe mom, and she'd missed that.

"You worked so hard, Radha," her mother whispered against her temple. "I see that. I see you trying all by yourself because *you* love it. I really think you're going to win the competition. Your effort that I asked for is paying off."

She wanted to ask if that meant her mother was going to pay for college, wherever college was going to be, but now probably wasn't the right time. She gave her mother the most dazzling smile she could. "We'll win, all right. Even with these stupid parents fighting us."

"Parents? What parents?" Whatever sappiness Sujata had been displaying immediately dried up.

"Nothing," Radha said. "I'll handle it."

"I don't see why you can't just—"

"*Mom.*"

She let out a deep breath. "Are you sure?"

"Yes. I'm sure."

"Okay. Tell me if you need me. Because I can crush them if you want."

"Mom!" Radha burst into laughter.

Some things never changed, and that was totally okay, she thought.

"Hey, Radha?" Jai stood in the doorway. He'd stopped when he saw Sujata.

Well, now was as good a time as any, she thought.

"Jai, come meet my mother."

"Oh. Hi." He came closer and extended a hand. "Nice to

meet you."

"Mom," Radha said. "This is Jai. He's my boyfriend."

Sujata took Jai's hand and shook it. "Ah. Nice to finally meet you, too. Maybe now you can drop my daughter off by pulling into the driveway instead of leaving her at the curb."

Jai flushed. "Uh, yeah. That would make things a lot simpler."

*

It had been one year.

One year since her last performance.

Since her parents had decided to get divorced.

Since she'd stopped dancing.

Since she'd been so full of questions and had zero answers to any of them.

Radha stood on the stage next to her team and looked out at her mother's calm and confident expression in the audience. The drumroll sounded over the stereo. "And the winner for the group performance is ... Bollywood Beats!"

The audience roared, and Radha was swept off her feet.

Epilogue

Radha

THREE MISSED MESSAGES

SIMRAN: Can't wait to see you! Two months and counting!

TARA: Hey there. It was fun hanging with you guys at the Bollywood Funk workshop. We should do it again soon. If it's not weird or anything.

DAD: Chutki! I need that recipe for mango pie you saw in the Times??

Radha was prying the lid off her pink tiffin when Shakti slid across the cafeteria's tiled floor and collapsed on the bench next to her.

"Look what came in the mail!" she shouted. "I picked mine up from the administration office. You'll have to go get yours." She placed a crystal leaf-shaped statue on the table next to Radha's lunch bag. "It'll match my first-place trophy from the Winter Showcase."

"Is that—" Radha started.

"It is."

"It's here already?"

"Yeah, they were quick."

Radha touched the inscription on the base of the statue. Under Shakti's name and above the italicized date, it read:

FIRST PLACE
Group Performance
Northeast Regional Varsity US Dance
Association

"I still can't believe we won," Radha said softly. "I mean, the competition was tough."

"But we were better. We have to celebrate!" Shakti reached over and took a forkful of Radha's butter chicken. "Oh my God. This is so good."

Radha pushed her dish forward to share. "Didn't we already celebrate after regionals?"

"But now we can celebrate our trophies. And Jai's Columbia admission and your NYU admission starting in the spring semester too. Which by the way, *oh my God.* I can't believe that I'll be a few subway stops away at my dance academy."

"It would never have happened if Jai hadn't helped me study for the SATs and ace my exams and portfolio, and if Guru Nandani hadn't vouched for me."

"Well, it's exciting. You'll go to India for six months, come back, and start an amazing life in New York City with your bestie and your boyfriend."

Radha's phone buzzed.

JAI: Meet me in the arboretum?

RADHA: Weren't you supposed to come and meet me here? I just started eating.

JAI: Woman, pack it up, and come upstairs!

RADHA: Text me "woman" like that again, and I'll give you a thappar so hard that your mother would be proud.

JAI: 😊 Please? LOVE OF MY LIFE, ARBORETUM

Radha sighed. "He wants me to go to the arboretum now."

"Oh, you go ahead," Shakti said. "I can put your food away, and meet you in the arboretum later to drop it off. I want to eat some more chicken first."

"You sure?"

She nodded with her mouth full and gave a thumbs-up.

Radha picked up her backpack and cut through the cafeteria.

It took her less than five minutes to reach the top of the stairs and open the arboretum entrance door. She expected to see Jai sitting at the picnic table where they'd eaten before, but it was empty except for a tent card with an arrow on it.

"What are you up to, Jai Patel?" she said as she dropped her backpack.

Radha pocketed the card and walked down the gravel path toward the center of the arboretum. She smiled when she remembered the first time she'd been there with Jai, in the early fall. She'd wanted to practice her contemporary routine, but she hadn't known if a studio would be open to the new girl.

Radha was halfway down the path when she heard music. The familiar song had her grinning. Only Jai would play Bollywood music to … wait, what was he doing?

She almost screamed when three familiar faces jumped from behind bushes into her path. "Oh my God, you guys … are you wearing tuxes?"

Instead of answering, they circled her, and then broke out into a coordinated dance.

Radha laughed. "What is going on? Oh my God!" She was off her feet and being tossed in the air like a sack of freaking potatoes.

Her Bollywood Beats friends put her down and spun her in a circle before leading her to a bench farther up the path.

Then they danced for her and, in a wave, got to their knees and pointed ahead.

"Oh, I go now? Okay."

She got up and skipped forward, not nearly as surprised when three more dancers jumped out. The song continued to play, and they moved in unison together, urging her forward.

When she finally got to the clearing, she was laughing. This was where she'd danced with Jai. She spun as the entire team danced around her, Shakti included, that sneak.

Then the crowd parted like the ocean, and Jai stepped

through. He wore a tux, and his swagger reminded her of the first time she'd seen him. He extended a hand to her.

She didn't hesitate to grab hold. He spun her out, and then back so she was pressed against his chest, leaving her dizzy with love.

The song ended before she wanted it to, and she jumped up to wrap her legs around his waist in a full-body bear hug like she always did when she was this happy.

"What the heck is happening?" she said with a laugh.

"Radha…" Jai said slowly.

"Yes?"

"I have something to ask you." He swallowed and looked at their team members, who encircled them.

"Radha," he said again.

The team exploded. *"Will you go to prom with him?"*

"Yes!"

An Apology
and an Author's Note

Over a decade ago, I lost both my grandfathers to complications caused by their diseases: Parkinson's and amyotrophic lateral sclerosis (ALS). They were incredible men, and it was imperative for my family and me to always remember their personhood before the disability caused by their diseases. I thought about them a lot when I researched this novel. Although *Radha & Jai's Recipe for Romance* is about … well, Radha and Jai, Nana Veeru and Jai's dad play critical roles in their story. I am an able-bodied person who has tried to address any biases, but I still come from a place of privilege. I am deeply apologetic about any and all errors, which are completely my responsibility.

In all honesty, when working on the concept for *Radha and Jai's Recipe for Romance*, I hoped to tell a story as fun and quirky and fluffy as *My So-Called Bollywood Life*, but dance has never really been fun and quirky and fluffy for me. In addition to losing my grandfathers during the eleven years I studied kathak, I experienced insecurity and manipulation from people I trusted. That led to a rejection of the art form for years before I had the guts to sit down and write about it.

Thank you for reading and cheering me on as I worked on Radha. I learned a lot about myself while writing this book, just like Jai and Radha learn about themselves and their passion. In the end, I hope you discovered what I have, too: that you don't have to have a recipe for happiness. You can figure things out along the way.

Xoxo

Nisha

Acknowledgments

Writing acknowledgments has always been one of the most difficult parts of completing a novel for me. I get choked up and super emotional to the point where people think that I've watched the ending of *Kal Ho Naa Ho* on repeat or something. With this book, I'm even more sappy because it was one of the most difficult novels I've ever written.

First, you should know that my novels start the same exact way: with an email to Joy Tutela at the David Black Literary Agency. Joy, you've seen all the ugly that I've gone through to finish this book, and I want you to know that I wouldn't have made it if it wasn't for your support, guidance, and faith. Thank you for being the best advocate, friend, and agent a girl could have. Thank you also to Susan Raihofer and my UK agent, Caspian Dennis, for advocating for me. I also have the calm, easygoing support of my film agent, Jon Cassir of CAA. Jon, I didn't get to thank you enough for your work with *Bollywood Life*, so I hope this suffices to show my appreciation.

To my publishers, Crown Books for Young Readers and Stripes Publishing in the UK: Without the support of the marketing departments, phenomenal cover art departments, publicity departments, and literary assistants, this book wouldn't be possible. Special shout-out to Elizabeth Stranahan, Charlie Morris, and Lauren Ace.

To my editors: Phoebe Yeh and Sarah Shaffi. Phoebe, we've been together since 2014, and despite our ups and downs, you've made me a better writer. I will always appreciate and love you for changing my life. Sarah, we haven't known each other quite as long, but I knew you were the right one for my books from the moment we met. Thank you for believing in me and my stories.

Thank you to my beta readers and my sensitivity readers, who have requested anonymity. Speaking about stroke experiences and paralysis with you has been humbling, and any and all mistakes I've made in telling this story are my own.

Thank you to Sabeen Aslam for your excellent advice on Bollywood and school dance teams. I appreciated the time you made for me even though you have a full plate being an amazing person.

To my mom, Neeta Sharma, who was never a dance mom, thank God, but who showed up to every performance with safety pins, hairpins, and a backup copy of my music. Thank you for the countless hours of driving to performances and dealing with all the kathak drama for years. Love you, Mom.

To Smita Kurrumchand. What can you say about a best friend who is more like a sister? Thank you for sitting with me late into the night after long days at work, talking through plot until our eyes were gritty with exhaustion. Thank you for picking up the phone early in the morning to help me work through the kinks in my story. And thank you for listening to me complain about the hurt this book revealed. I would've never finished Radha's novel without your support. Love you, girl.

Thank you also to Ali Magnotti-Nagel, Monica Liming-Hu, Adriana Herrera, Meg Cabot, and Dee Ernst for giving me invaluable guidance and support. To Jordan Reiser and the Strott family for all the love and support that always seems to come at the exact time I need it most.

To Sona Charaipotra, Falguni Kothari, Sonali Dev, Suleika Snyder, Preeti Chhibber, and my other desi writer friends who support me, advocate for me, and set the bar high as the most amazing, authentic, vibrant women. Thank you for helping me strive to be a better writer every day.

To Rita's writers' room for rolling with my outbursts while I was working on the draft and revisions for this novel. Sarah Maclean, Alexis Daria, Sierra Simone, Andie Christopher, Adriana Herrera (again!), LaQuette and Joanna Shupe, I'm so glad I get to call you friends.

To the friends I've met at my day jobs who have had the unfortunate luck of listening to me talk about writing all day. Marc Diamondstein, Tracey Sumler, and Tiffany Williams, you are all gems and I'm infinitely richer with you in my life.

Last but not least, thanks to my uncle, Rohit Punj, who took me to get my first library card at the New York Public Library. It may be standard to thank the dance teacher, but I'm giving you the kudos. Thanks, Mamu. This book is as much for you as it is for me.

About the Author

NISHA SHARMA is the award-winning author of
the YA rom-com *My So-Called Bollywood Life* and
the contemporary romance drama The Singh Family
Trilogy. She grew up immersed in Bollywood movies,
'80s pop culture, and romance novels, so it is no surprise
that her work features all three. Her writing has been
praised by *Entertainment Weekly*, NPR, *Cosmopolitan*,
Teen Vogue, BuzzFeed, Hypable, and more. She lives
in New Jersey with her Alaskan-born husband; her cat,
Lizzie Bennett; and her dog, Nancey Drew. You can find
her online at nisha-sharma.com or on Twitter
and Instagram at @nishawrites.